WALKING AMONG THE TREES

By Frank Oliva

2021 Sage's Tower Publishing

Published in the United States by Sage's Tower Publishing.

Sage's Tower Publishing is a registered trademark.

Hardback ISBN 978-1-63706-020-9
Paperback ISBN 978-1-63706-021-6
eBook ISBN 978-1-63706-022-3

Printed in the United States of America

www.sagestowerpublishing.com

To Mom and Dad

CHAPTER 1

As Father Nathaniel Kerrigan sat on the half-rotten wooden bench overlooking the natural pond in front of him, a smoldering Marlboro cigarette he'd forgotten about burnt the tips of his fingers and fell to the ground. Kerrigan, a sixty-five-year-old Catholic priest and Vietnam War veteran, quickly stomped out the cigarette with his foot. He removed a white handkerchief from the inside pocket of his dark overcoat and used it to pick up the cigarette butt, depositing it carefully into the wire trash receptacle next to the bench he was sitting on. He went back to staring out into the sky, past the ducks floating on the pond and the children chasing them with their radio-controlled model boats, his thoughts lost in the dark gray clouds, which were hovering in the distance like harbingers.

Though at sixty-five Kerrigan was beginning to feel his age, a life of discipline and restraint kept him strong and healthy. He made every effort to eat well, he trained with weights and ran for miles, and he seldom consumed alcohol. Kerrigan's discipline, a practice he learned from the Marine Corp and honed through the priesthood, influenced all aspects of his busy life. It showed in his physical appearance—his short and silvering goatee always well-kept and immaculate, for example—and in his judicious use of time. An early riser, Kerrigan's mornings and afternoons were spent tending to mass, confessions, and other pastoral duties. The hours in between were for volunteer work at local VAs and children's hospitals. An hour each night was reserved for exercise, another for prayer. If there was any time left before Kerrigan retired for the evening, he might watch that night's episode of Jeopardy on playback. That program had grown on him years earlier when he spent his evenings tending to his cancer-stricken father, who would hurl insults at Mr. Trebek from his sofa-chair when he got the answers wrong.

If Kerrigan had one vice, it was the cigarettes. He picked them up again only weeks earlier, after a twenty-year hiatus. He mulled lighting another, but the minute-hand on his wristwatch showed five-to-eight, which meant the man he was there to meet would soon arrive. That he was smoking again was a fact he wished to keep to himself, so he double-checked that his pack of Marlboro Reds was tucked safely inside his overcoat, and spritzed himself with aftershave. Then he went back to thinking, and waiting.

Kerrigan had been sitting on the bench for over an hour, at times rehearsing in his mind the conversation he was about to have, and others staring thoughtlessly into the cool autumn sky. Though he was there to meet his trusted mentor, a man he'd known since he joined the seminary nearly forty years earlier and with whom he'd confided many things, Kerrigan was terribly nervous. Somehow, he'd become so wrapped up in his own affairs he hadn't called or written to his old friend in over two years. And now here Kerrigan was, out of the blue, about to ask favors.

That thought continued to swirl in Kerrigan's mind as a

gust of wind rustled the leaves hanging from the towering trees above his head. A black bird fluttered down from one of the trees and landed next to Kerrigan on the bench, startling him so badly he jumped in his seat. As the bird took to the sky, Kerrigan noticed a dark figure approaching from one of the dirt trails converging on the pond. He stood up and squinted through his reading glasses— at first, he wasn't sure he was looking at the right man. But when it was clear he was, Kerrigan felt awash with concern. The man, hunched inside a dark overcoat similar to Kerrigan's, had aged significantly since Kerrigan saw him last. Though the man was nearing seventy-seven, after all, he'd always been strong and healthy. A seasoned boxer, the old man could be found in Catholic school gymnasiums jumping rope with students just two years ago. Yet now he approached with the assistance of a cane and an obvious limp, and he looked several shades grayer. As the distance between the two priests narrowed, Kerrigan made a conscious effort not to let the worry show in his face.

"Monsignor Carmichael!"

"Father Kerrigan." The Monsignor bore a wide smile that stretched the many more lines showing on his weathered face. "It's good to see you."

"It's good to see you too, Monsignor."

Kerrigan leaned in and hugged Carmichael, mindful not to interfere with his cane. From up close it was even more apparent Carmichael lost serious ground—his thin, silver hair had receded even further, and Kerrigan could feel through Carmichael's bulky overcoat that he'd lost a good deal of weight. Kerrigan also noticed a small patch of razor stubble sprouting from Carmichael's pointed chin, which was uncharacteristic. Carmichael was always dutiful about keeping a clean shave. The two priests embraced each other for several moments before separating.

"Shall we walk and talk?" Carmichael asked.

"Are you sure?" Kerrigan didn't realize it, but his gaze was trained squarely on Carmichael's cane.

"What, this?" Carmichael raised his cane off of the ground for Kerrigan to examine.

"Since when did you start using a—"

"Don't worry." Carmichael thumped the cane back into the soft earth beneath their feet. "I've had it a couple of months now. The doctors keep telling me I need hip surgery, and I keep telling them I do not."

Kerrigan smiled a hesitant smile. While Carmichael's aversion to doctors and medical advice didn't surprise him, he knew there was more going on than a bum hip. He also recalled hearing through the grapevine that Carmichael recently cancelled a trip to Spain, one he discussed making for years.

"Come on," Carmichael insisted. "Let's walk. I have a feeling it will do us both good."

"Where?" Kerrigan looked at the pond just in front of them and into the surrounding trees. Another gust of wind ruffled the trees, sprinkling golden-brown leaves into the pond. Kerrigan eyed the various trails. They seemed to burrow infinitely into the woods. Kerrigan had never visited that particular nature preserve and had no idea where they led. He'd had a hard enough time finding the pond. It was Carmichael who had chosen the preserve for the meeting.

"Let's do one of the trails." Carmichael nodded toward a trail just behind Kerrigan. "How about that one? Looks as good as any."

Kerrigan twisted around. The trail stretched further into the woods than he could see. "You know the way?"

"No. Not really. Haven't been here in years, actually."

"What if we get lost? These trails probably go on for miles and end up who knows where."

Carmichael leaned into his cane with one hand and waved dismissively with the other. "Don't worry. We can always turn back. Besides, I'm told there are beautiful live oaks for us to see. I've always liked live oaks."

Kerrigan only nodded. Though he felt compelled to yield to Carmichael's wishes since he was the one taking the elder priest's time, the prospect of losing hours in the woods made him nervous. He didn't have hours to lose. Kerrigan hesitantly followed Carmichael's lead.

"I'm sorry to trouble you on such short notice, Monsignor."

"There's no trouble here, Nathan. None at all."

Leaves crunched beneath Kerrigan's feet. Though it was barely September, the dirt trail was covered by a layer of brittle leaves. It seemed the trees inside the nature preserve were further along in their shedding than elsewhere. Kerrigan could feel the cooler air.

"Listen, Monsignor, I know I haven't called in a while . . . I just—"

Carmichael grabbed Kerrigan's forearm and stopped him in place. "Never mind all that. Something troubles you. Something serious. What is it?"

Kerrigan paused. "Is it that obvious?"

Carmichael chuckled. "Well, aside from the fact that you reek of cigarettes, I knew something was off the moment you called and asked to meet in private, away from both our parishes."

Kerrigan blushed, then sniffed his overcoat. He really thought the aftershave would do the trick. Carmichael tugged on his arm and eased him forward again.

"Ah, Nathan. You should know by now that all the perfume in the world can't cover up that stench. Besides, how long have we known each other now, thirty years?"

"Almost forty, believe it or not. That's how long ago I was in the seminary. You know, even after all this time, sometimes it's still hard to believe I'm a priest at all. I just—"

"Nathan—" Carmichael tugged once more on Kerrigan's arm. "What's really on your mind, hmm? What's got you all twisted inside? That's why we're here, isn't it?" Carmichael looked up toward the sky. "Among the trees?"

Kerrigan stood silent a few moments while Carmichael waited with watchful eyes. "I need to ask you a favor. I hate to ask, I really do, but I don't, I just—"

"What is it?"

Kerrigan hesitated again. He looked once more into Carmichael's greenish-blue eyes and was overwhelmed with shame. Two whole years, and he hadn't once thought to call. Not even a lousy text message. He took in a breath and sighed.

"The bishop—he wants me to do something. Something I cannot do."

"Bishop Gailey?"

Kerrigan nodded.

"Believe it or not, I've known him longer than I've known you. We spent time in the seminary together."

"I know."

"Which is why I know once he's made up his mind there's nearly nothing anyone can do to change it. Myron Gailey is a stubborn man."

"I know he is, Monsignor. But if there's anyone he might listen to, it's you."

Carmichael leaned into his cane, one hand on top of the other, and stared out into the trail, contemplating. Even his hands looked older, arthritic even. "What is it he wants you to do?"

Kerrigan opened his mouth to speak but quickly closed it. Though he'd gone over this many times during the hour he'd spent on the bench, it seemed no easier. He retreated toward an edge of the trail and gazed for a moment into the trees. Birds cawed in the distance. When he returned to Carmichael, he leaned in close so strangers wouldn't overhear. The two priests were far enough along the trail that the pond was no longer in sight, but they could still hear children giggling in the distance.

"He wants me to perform an exorcism." Kerrigan shuddered. He shook his head in disbelief. Despite everything, it was still difficult to accept this was happening to him.

Thunder suddenly cracked, startling Kerrigan nearly off his feet. The roaring sound reminded him of the bombs he heard in the jungles of Vietnam. It sounded like the sky was splitting open. Yet, even as rain began to fall, Carmichael remained stoic, unfazed.

"I'm sorry, Monsignor. I didn't think to bring an umbrella. It wasn't supposed to rain today. I checked."

Carmichael reached into his overcoat. "Here, hold my cane."

Kerrigan took the cane and immediately noticed it was far heavier than it appeared. He watched anxiously as Carmichael removed a small extendable umbrella, held it up, and fidgeted with the button. "Now, if I could only get the blessed thing open."

The umbrella blew open with a whooshing sound that startled Kerrigan a second time. After what he'd seen and experienced these past few weeks, he was particularly jumpy.

Carmichael held up the umbrella, but his arm buckled under the weight.

"Here, let me," Kerrigan said. He took the umbrella from Carmichael and held it over both of their heads.

"Over there," Carmichael said, his eyes focused toward another wooden bench a few yards up the trail, just beneath one of the live oak trees he'd spoken of only moments earlier. Kerrigan held the umbrella as the two priests shuffled their way over to the bench.

"Wait!" Kerrigan shouted. Before Carmichael sat down, Kerrigan took out his white handkerchief and wiped the bench dry. When he was finished, the two priests sat next to each other under the cover of the umbrella, the raindrops pattering above their heads.

"An exorcism?" Carmichael asked. "Myron Gailey wants you to perform an exorcism?"

Kerrigan nodded. He was staring into a puddle just in front of his feet. The splashes from the raindrops were so large it looked as if small pebbles were falling into the water.

Carmichael sighed. "Oh my, Nathan. Oh my. I didn't quite know what to expect, but it certainly wasn't this."

"Well, he wants me to assist, anyway. Whatever that means. Someone else will lead the ritual."

"Who?"

"I don't know yet, the bishop's still looking for an experienced exorcist who's available as far as I—"

"No," Carmichael interrupted. "Who needs the exorcism?"

"Oh. She's just a kid, Monsignor. Barely fourteen years old. Armenian. Lives with her mother and brother in one of those old section eight buildings downtown."

"What's her name?"

"Her name is Marianna. Marianna Petrosian."

Kerrigan felt a twinge of doubt. Just mentioning the girl's name stirred up painful memories.

"You know her?"

"Actually, I haven't spoken a word to her. She's a . . . she's gravely ill. She's been confined to her bed since the beginning. Since before I got involved, anyway."

"I see. And that's why the bishop wants you to assist? Because you're involved? Familiar with the case?"

"I suppose. I really don't know what he's thinking."

"I see. So why can't you?"

Kerrigan's eyes widened. He knew the question would come, but he hadn't expected it so quickly. "Why can't I?"

"That's right. Why can't you?"

Kerrigan hesitated, his tongue twisted. "I'm . . . I'm just not right for it."

"What makes one right or wrong for an exorcism? The question isn't rhetorical, Nathan. I ask because I don't know."

"Well, that's just it. I don't know any more than you do. I don't know the first thing about performing an exorcism. I have no experience with the supernatural, whatsoever. Before all this, I hadn't crossed paths with a black cat let alone a demon. I've never even met a priest who's been anywhere near an exorcism. Have you?"

Carmichael's brow wrinkled. "Me? Hell no. I've managed to steer clear of such things. But I've heard stories, stories that make my skin crawl when I'm reminded of them. Like now. Didn't you say Bishop Gailey only wants you to assist? That someone experienced will lead the ritual?"

Kerrigan shook his head. He was frustrated—not with the Monsignor but with the situation. "Yes, but . . . these priests, these exorcists . . . it's like they are born for it. Hand-picked by God himself. Many of them attest to having a strong intuition that they were being called upon to do it. They don't just get pulled in as a matter of happenstance."

"Is that what happened, Nathan? You were pulled in as a matter of happenstance?"

"Yes . . . I suppose." Kerrigan shifted in his seat. "I don't know."

"You don't sound so sure. Maybe God is calling you."

"No."

"How do you know?"

"Because . . . it would be a mistake. God doesn't make mistakes."

Carmichael leaned back slowly into the bench, a pensive look on his face. "I'm not following you."

Kerrigan mumbled. "I know. I know."

Carmichael chuckled. "Well, it's good that you know. But if I'm going to help you, to guide you, if that's why you called me here—"

"I'm not asking for guidance. Not this time."

Carmichael, his arms crossed, leaned forward again. "Oh. I see. Just the favor, then?"

Kerrigan, feeling even more ashamed now, stared back down at the ground. Water was pooling beneath his feet now, too.

"I'm sorry, Monsignor. I mean no disrespect. I'm just in a bind and I don't know any other way out."

"Do you realize what you're asking of me?"

"I know you and Bishop Gailey aren't on good terms. If this wasn't serious, I wouldn't—"

Carmichael shook his head. "Oh, I don't give a damn about any of that. Sure, we have disagreements from time to time, but it's been that way since the beginning. He's a good man, but also an asshole. Suppose I do go talk to him. What do you think his first question will be, the one after he asks me how this is any of my fucking business?"

"He'll ask why."

Carmichael nodded. "Bingo. And what will I tell him?"

"That I'm unfit. That I don't have—"

"And you think that's going to cut it? Hasn't so far, has it?"

Kerrigan turned away, before looking up into the sky. The raindrops were still falling, but they were lighter now.

"Come on. Let's walk," Carmichael said. He pressed his cane into the ground and stood back up. Kerrigan could see that it took some effort. "The rain's letting up."

Kerrigan remained seated a while. The clouds seemed to be growing darker. He thought about how far his car was from where they were standing. It was parked in a small lot a ways from the pond. And now Carmichael wanted to burrow deeper into the woods. "Maybe we should go back. It doesn't look so good out here."

"Ah, we'll be alright. Come on."

Reluctantly, Kerrigan stood up and took his place alongside Carmichael. As the two priests walked, Carmichael placed his free hand against the small of Kerrigan's back.

"You understand that if I were to talk to Myron, you'll have to give me more to work with, hmm? Talk to me, Nathan. It's just you, me, and the trees."

Kerrigan stopped in place. His hands trembled. His heart pounded against his breastbone. His breaths shortened. He felt dizzy and unsteady on his feet. He spotted a tall cypress tree along the side of the path and headed toward it. His legs shaking, he leaned against the cypress for support.

"Are you alright?" Carmichael asked. The alarm was evident in his voice. As he approached from behind, Kerrigan raised his hand as a signal for Carmichael to give him some space.

"I'm okay . . . I just need . . . I just need a cigarette."

Leaning against the tree with one arm, Kerrigan fumbled inside his jacket pocket with the other. He dug out his pack of Marlboro Reds and a book of matches from a fancy steakhouse a parishioner had taken him to. He backed off the tree just enough to free both hands and tried to light a cigarette. He tried several times, but his hands were too shaky, and the rain kept on extinguishing the flame.

"Here," Carmichael said. He took the matchbook from Kerrigan and huddled up against him to block the wind. He lit a match and lifted it toward the fresh cigarette hanging from Kerrigan's lips. When it was lit, Kerrigan immediately took in several deep drags and breathed thick plumes of smoke out into the trees. After seven or eight repetitions, his hands and legs settled.

"She's dying."

"The girl?"

Kerrigan nodded. He took another drag from his cigarette. Tears pooled beneath his eyes. "If she doesn't have the exorcism, or if it's not successful, she will die."

"But she will have the exorcism?"

"Yes. I was able to see to that much. Now it's just a matter of who does it."

Carmichael approached Kerrigan and put his arm around him, slowly easing him forward. "Come on, Nathan. Tell me about the girl, at least."

"I don't even know where to begin."

"Why don't you start with how you got involved? That's as good a place as any, isn't it?"

Kerrigan quietly nodded. He took one last drag from his cigarette and put it out on the bottom of his shoe.

* * *

By the time Kerrigan first saw Marianna Petrosian in the flesh, he was already feeling uneasy. Even though everything in his life was proceeding as usual, he couldn't shake the feeling there was a dark cloud forming just over the horizon. A bad dream the night before had kept him up, and his stomach was out of sorts. Despite not feeling well, he agreed to cover the evening mass for his colleague. Now that the mass was finished, he was anxious to tidy up and get back to the rectory.

Like everything Kerrigan did, he reset the vestments with a level of precision and care far above his peers. He took care to leave no creases, to make each fold neat and crisp, and he paid close attention to symmetry and cleanliness. His efforts were such that the three other priests serving the Roman Catholic Church of Saint Michael's always knew when he said the last mass. Kerrigan was in the middle of this ritual when he first thought he heard a voice behind him, but he dismissed the distant sound as a figment of his imagination and went back to concentrating on his prayers.

But the voice called out a second time.

"Excuse me," it said.

Kerrigan set down the cincture he was about to lay out and turned toward the voice. A boy, no older than seventeen or eighteen, was standing in the doorway of the sacristy. The boy looked European or even Middle Eastern. He was tall and slender, with fair skin and dark hair. His eyes were obscured beneath a pair of reflective wire-framed glasses.

"Hi there," Kerrigan said.

"I'm . . . I'm sorry. I'm sorry I bother—" The boy turned around as if to scurry off.

Kerrigan took a step forward. "Whoa, whoa. Hold on a second. You're not bothering me. Not in the slightest."

The boy slowly turned back around. He stood there silent several moments before speaking. "Are you priest?" he asked, through a heavy Mediterranean accent. Turkish, Kerrigan thought to himself. He was thrown at first by the fact that the boy didn't know he was a priest, but he realized he didn't have his robes on.

"I am. I'm Father Kerrigan. Some people like to call me Father K, for short."

The boy nodded. He continued to stand silent, staring down at his feet, which were wrapped in a pair of badly worn converse sneakers. Parts of his white socks showed through.

"What's your name, young man?"

The boy flinched, like he was startled by a loud noise. "My name?"

Kerrigan took another step forward. "Yeah, why not?"

"My name is Harout. Harout Petrosian."

Kerrigan wanted to kick himself. Harout was an Armenian name, not a Turkish one. It was clear from Harout's broken English he was born there.

"Harout? That's a wonderful name. You know what it means, don't you?"

Harout nodded. With a long, slender finger, he adjusted his reading glasses.

"So, what's up?"

Harout's gaze shifted nervously toward the door frame just in front of him. Despite the dim lighting inside the sacristy, Kerrigan could see Harout was incredibly stiff, like he was standing in cement. His feet were planted close together, and he barely moved a muscle.

"Harout?"

"My sister—she needs priest."

"Pardon me?" As Kerrigan took another step forward, he saw Harout flinch again. He immediately stopped in place and spoke more gently. "Did you say your sister needs a priest?"

Harout nodded.

"Why does she need a priest?"

Harout just stood there, twirling his long fingers.

"Harout—"

"I'm sorry. I make mistake. I go now."

"No, no. Wait a second. I'll tell you what—if you give me just a minute, I'll finish tidying up here and we can take a walk over to the rectory. There's a nice quiet office there we can—"

"No!" Harout blurted. His voice was so loud it echoed through the church. Kerrigan saw his eyes widen, even behind the glasses. "I'm sorry," Harout said more softly. "Is okay if we stay here? Please?"

Kerrigan just stood there a moment and looked at Harout. He had never seen a boy so distressed in his life. Not once. It was terribly disturbing. "Is someone looking for you outside, Harout?"

Harout shook his head.

"Are you sure? Is everything alright?"

Harout said nothing. He only bowed his head.

"Alright, I'll tell you what. The church should be empty now. How about you wait for me outside? We'll sit in a pew right up front and we'll talk a little. How's that sound?"

Harout raised his head, but kept it just low enough so that their eyes didn't quite meet. "Okay."

Kerrigan watched Harout turn away and disappear into the corridor leading back to the church's seating area. A knot formed in his stomach. Whatever brought Harout to Saint Michael's, it was serious. Kerrigan quickly removed his alb and dropped it hastily onto the table besides the other vestments. For the first time in nearly forty years, he wouldn't remember to return and lay it out properly.

Kerrigan stepped back into the church and found Harout seated in a pew just in front of the altar. Harout was waiting patiently, staring down at his hands, which were folded neatly between his thighs. Kerrigan approached slowly and slid into the pew next to him. Under the warm glow of the byzantine lamps above their heads, Kerrigan noticed Harout's fair skin was peppered with adolescent acne. His short hair and eyebrows were dark and wispy. He could now see Harout's eyes, which were hazel-colored and striking. They had an honest, genuine quality to them.

"You don't belong to this parish, do you, kid?"

"No. We belong to Saint Matthew's."

"Who's we?"

"My family."

"Saint Matthew's? Where do you live, down in Lawlry Heights?"

Harout nodded.

"That's a long way, kid. How did you get here?"

"I take bus."

"Why?"

"No license. No car."

Kerrigan shook his head. "No, I mean why did you come here? To Saint Michael's? To my church? If you belong to Saint Matthew's, then you must know the priests there. Father Peck, Father Timmons?"

Harout nodded.

"Yeah, nice guys. Good priests. Very easy to talk to. But instead of talking to one of them you came all this way to speak with a priest you've never met. I can't imagine that makes it easier, no?"

Harout looked at Kerrigan momentarily, but then bowed his head again. He was picking at his fingernails, which looked like they had been chewed down too far.

"My mother—she volunteer for church."

"Ah, I see. You don't want her to know?"

"No."

Kerrigan still wasn't satisfied. Harout's desire to keep the visit from his mother explained why he visited another parish, one he didn't belong to, but it didn't explain why he made the trip all the way to Kerrigan's particular parish. There were many churches in between, many that wouldn't have involved such a long ride on the city bus. No, Kerrigan suspected Harout chose his parish for a reason. What it was, he would never really know. He would only surmise.

"What's on your mind, kid?"

Harout was about to speak, but stopped. It took Kerrigan a moment to notice, but Harout was fighting back tears. Kerrigan removed a crisp, white handkerchief from his shirt pocket and offered it to the boy.

18

"It's clean," Kerrigan said, smiling briefly. "Just out of the laundry as a matter of fact."

Harout gazed at the handkerchief a few moments before he took it. It seemed he wasn't sure what to do with it. Then he took it, lifted up his glasses, and dabbed his eyes dry. Neither he nor Kerrigan would realize it, but Harout would leave the church with the handkerchief in his pocket and never return it.

"Tell me what's going on, kid. It's just the two of us."

Harout crossed his arms and leaned forward. He was still sniffling. "I am scared, Father."

"What are you scared of?"

Harout went silent again. Instead of answering he rocked slowly back and forth, like he was nursing a bellyache. Kerrigan went to place a hand on Harout's shoulder. "Hey, what's the matter—"

Kerrigan pulled his hand right back, as if he'd just touched a hot iron. Harout was trembling. Kerrigan felt a shiver run down his own spine, and he suddenly felt cold and uneasy, like someone with ill intentions was watching from a distance. He resisted the urge to look over his shoulder. He didn't want to worry Harout any more than he was.

"What's going on, kid?"

Harout kept rocking.

"You're afraid to tell me, aren't you?"

Harout nodded. A tear fell from his face and landed on his pant leg. Kerrigan was beginning to suspect Harout was a victim of domestic abuse. He genuinely hoped that wasn't the case—he was involved in a handful of abuse cases during his tenure as a priest, and he never felt good about how they turned out. Having been a priest for nearly forty years, he learned, as most priests do, that a large part of the job involves witnessing all manner of human suffering. Still, it was always that much harder when kids were involved.

"Okay. I understand," Kerrigan said. "Well, you don't have to tell me anything at all if you're not up to it. You can leave whenever you'd like. I'll go back to tidying up back there, and we'll both forget this happened, and that will be the end of it. But since you rode the bus all this way, I think you should at least ask yourself one question before you go."

Harout stopped rocking for a second and looked at Kerrigan. "What question?"

"What are you more afraid of? Hmm? What happens if you do tell me what you came all this way to tell me, or what happens if you don't? It's up to you, kid."

Harout looked directly into Kerrigan's eyes for the first time that night. He used the handkerchief to wipe his nose and eyes. A tear he'd missed rolled down his face.

"My sister . . . she is dying."

Kerrigan leaned in closer. "She's very sick?"

"Yes. Doctor say there is nothing left to do. They say is only matter of time."

Harout sunk his head down into his lap and wept into the handkerchief.

Kerrigan could sense his sadness and despair was profound—the boy wore the emotions like the thick, heavy robes Kerrigan just removed. Kerrigan felt terrible. He patted Harout's back.

"I'm sorry, kid. I'm so sorry. What's wrong with her, if you don't mind me asking?"

Harout lifted up his face and used the handkerchief to wipe more tears and snot from his face. "Nobody know. Nobody see. They give her all these treatment, all these medicine. But it does not get better. It get worse."

Kerrigan looked up momentarily into the lights above and sighed. While a part of him felt relieved this didn't appear to be a case of child abuse, he felt awful just the same. By now, he'd already lost count of all the children he'd watched parents bury, whether it was because of car wrecks, overdoses, cancer, or other senseless tragedies. As awful as it was, watching parents bury their children was just another part of the job. The truly difficult part was trying to explain to those parents why God might allow such things to happen. Or even worse, trying to explain it to kids.

"What's your sister's name, Harout?"

"Marianna."

"Marianna. Marianna and Harout. Those names go together very nicely. You said your sister needs a priest. Are you looking for a priest to be with her when it is her time?"

Harout rocked back and forth again, harder this time. "No."

"To pray for her?"

"No."

"What then, kid? Tell me how I can help."

Harout said nothing. He just rocked back and forth.

Kerrigan looked over his shoulders. He wanted to make sure they were alone. "Does anyone know you're here?"

"No. Just you, Father."

"Well, then it's just the two of us. Nothing you tell me has to leave this church if you don't want it to. Anyway, it's up to you what you wanna do, kid."

Harout flashed Kerrigan a momentary glance but continued to rock in his seat. Kerrigan could tell Harout wanted to tell him whatever it was he had come there to tell him, that it was right there on the tip of his tongue, burning a hole in it. Yet for some reason, he was holding back.

Kerrigan put his hand on Harout's shoulder. "Hey kid, it's alright—"

Harout snapped toward Kerrigan with wide, bulging eyes. "It is the devil," he finally said.

Another cold shiver flowed through Kerrigan, passing this time through the small of his back and up into the base of his neck. The small hairs on his arms stood on end.

"Pardon me?"

"Satana," Harout said. His eyes glared right into Kerrigan's. "He is with her. He is responsible."

The lamps flickered. Just as Kerrigan looked up at the lights, a door slammed somewhere nearby, the piercing sound amplified by the volume of empty space inside the church. Kerrigan shot up onto his feet like he'd been hit with a cattle prod. When he turned toward the sound, he saw an old man enter the church through the main entrance. The old man had allowed the door to slam behind him.

The old man, who walked with the assistance of a walker, waved an apology and shuffled his way over to a nearby pew so he could kneel and pray. While Kerrigan didn't know the man on a personal basis, he'd seen him praying there many times before. He wasn't sure why, but he felt a strange need to reassure himself the timing was only a coincidence.

Kerrigan looked back over to Harout, who was still seated, and sat back down next to him. Kerrigan looked up toward the ceiling, into the lamps that flickered only moments earlier, and thought carefully about what he was going to say next. For the first time in as long as he could remember, he was at a loss for words. In nearly forty years as a priest, he'd never once seen or experienced anything remotely supernatural. He'd never seen or heard of any hauntings, near-death experiences, white lights, or deathbed visitations, and he'd certainly never been anywhere near a case of demonic possession. Nor did he know anyone who had. He did hear, however, from credible sources within the church, that demonic activity was on the rise, and the Vatican was training more exorcists to combat the recent surge. As a man of God, Kerrigan knew he was in no place to deny the existence of the devil; he just preferred to ignore it.

"Harout, I—"

"I know. You do not believe."

"No, it's not that I don't believe you. It's just—" Kerrigan nervously scratched his head. "I don't know. What about your mother? If what you say is true, then why would she be upset if she found out you brought this to a priest?"

Harout shook his head. His expression changed from sadness to frustration and anger. "He is very smart, Father."

Kerrigan's brow wrinkled. "What do you mean? Who's very smart?"

"My mother is very holy. She say God will not let this happen. She say God love us. God give us protection. He knows this. So he does not show himself."

"Who doesn't show himself? The devil?"

Harout nodded.

"Well, then I have to ask, Harout, if the devil doesn't show himself, how do you know he's there?"

"I pray. I pray and God give me vision. So I can help Marianna. This is why I am here."

Kerrigan looked deeply into Harout's eyes and saw conviction. He knew then Harout believed what he was saying. That or Harout was the most talented liar he'd ever met, and he'd met his share.

"Father?"

Kerrigan was staring out into empty space, lost for a moment in his thoughts. He blinked his eyes and shook his head, as if to shake himself from a daydream. "Sorry, kid."

"You think I lie."

"No, no. It's not that. It's just . . . I'm not sure I'm the right priest for this. We have priests who handle these kinds of things, who have experience, training. They know what to look for. Me . . . I have no idea."

"Oh," Harout muttered.

"It's not that I don't want to help. I do. I just don't know anything about this. I don't have any experience."

Harout wiped his nose with the handkerchief. Tears were still rolling down his face. "I understand."

"You have to understand, kid. Things aren't how they were in the old days. It's very, very easy to confuse these things with mental illness. You need someone who knows how to make sure your sister's not just very sick. Otherwise you can do more harm than good. Do you understand?"

"She is not sick. He's there. I know he's—"

"It's just—even if you are right, I still don't know what to look for. Now you said yourself that your own mother can't see what's going on, right?"

Harout slowly nodded. He was staring down at his hands again, which continued to fidget. Kerrigan could sense he was losing hope.

"What makes you think I'll be able to?"

Harout said nothing. He just sat there, quiet.

"That's why we need someone trained," Kerrigan went on, "somebody who knows the signs. Someone who knows what to look for. I can make some calls."

Harout looked at Kerrigan and nodded. He continued to pick at his raw fingers.

Kerrigan leaned back into the pew. While he was surprised Harout let him off the hook so easily, he couldn't shake the nagging feeling he was leaving the kid out in the rain without an umbrella. He looked up for a moment toward the altar, toward the large wooden crucifix suspended from the ceiling. He asked himself why this was happening to him, of all people. He was the last priest in the world anyone should look to for help with a case of demonic possession. Then he looked back at Harout, and pushed those thoughts aside. He told himself Harout was more than likely mistaken, that if he went to see Marianna he might be able to convince Harout this was all in his mind. He didn't want to say the words he said next, but they found their way out of his mouth anyway.

"Look, kid, if you think it will help, I'll come see your sister. I'll take a look at her."

Harout's head twisted toward Kerrigan, his eyes wide with hope. "Please! Please."

"I'll come see her tomorrow."

"Thank you, Father! Thank you."

"But you have to tell your mother, and she has to be there. I want to talk to her."

The hope suddenly left Harout's eyes.

"That's the deal, kid. You can't ask me to do this behind her back."

Harout looked out toward the altar. It took him a few moments, but he eventually nodded in agreement.

CHAPTER 2

"I wasn't even supposed to be there," Kerrigan grumbled.

He and Carmichael traveled several yards deeper into the woods, surrounded now by hundreds of tall cypress trees. The rain had ceased entirely for the time being, and some of the clouds had thinned enough to allow pockets of the blue sky to show through like small glimmers of hope. Still, dark gray clouds loomed in the distance.

"What do you mean?" Carmichael asked. Carmichael had been walking the trail at a relatively slow and deliberate pace, slow enough that Kerrigan needed to make a conscious effort not to get ahead of him. While Kerrigan still felt the pressure of time upon his shoulders, it seemed Carmichael was biding his.

"That night. I wasn't supposed to be there. Jonathan does the evening mass on Tuesday nights. He called me up an hour before, said he'd come down with strep throat. Asked me to cover for him. Strep throat. Do you believe that? It was the beginning of summer. I shouldn't have been there. I should have been at the rectory, watching Jeopardy."

"Is that what you meant when you said you were pulled in as a matter of happenstance? Hmm?"

"That's right. He wasn't looking for a particular priest, Monsignor. Not as far as I know. He wasn't looking for me, that's for sure. He didn't even know I was a priest. I just happened to be in the wrong place, at the wrong time, and now I'm stuck."

"Did you ever find out why the boy chose your parish?"

"He never told me. I never asked."

"Could it be he chose it because it is named after Saint Michael, the Archangel?"

Saint Michael the Archangel, Kerrigan thought to himself. Commander of God's army against Lucifer, charged with rescuing the souls of the faithful from the devil. Somehow the thought had never crossed his mind. "I know where you're going with this."

"I wasn't going anywhere—"

"I already told you God didn't send him to me."

"I didn't say—"

"No, but you were thinking it. Maybe God sent him out for a priest, I'll give you that much. I believe it myself. But somehow . . . somehow he chose the wrong priest."

Carmichael shrugged. "Okay."

Kerrigan felt his nerves act up again. He took out another cigarette and lit it himself.

"It's ironic, isn't it?" Kerrigan asked.

"What is?"

Kerrigan blew out a thick fog of smoke up into the air. "This smoke . . . this poison. It's the only thing that helps me breathe easier these days."

Carmichael flashed Kerrigan an understanding smile.

Both priests were heavy smokers in a past life. They'd smoked together on countless occasions. They'd even quit together.

"Nathan?"

"Yes?"

"Why won't you help this girl?"

Kerrigan stopped in place. The question hit him like a punch in his gut, which was already tender and uneasy. He took in another heavy drag from his cigarette. Carmichael realized Kerrigan was no longer by his side and turned around.

"I am helping her."

"I'm talking about the exorcism. Why won't you just do it?"

"I told you."

"Nathan, I've known you almost forty years, am I right? Forty years. And in all that time, not once have I known you to turn down an opportunity to help someone in need. To help a child. Not once. That's how I know this is about more than you say it is. So, what is it about? Really?"

Kerrigan shook his head and stormed off toward an edge of the trail. He turned his back on the monsignor and looked out into the trees, the empty spaces between them. He smoked his cigarette until it was spent.

"Maybe you don't know me as well as you think you do."

"Well, then talk to me. Tell me what I'm missing. Tell me what's really got you all twisted up. Did something happen to you? During the war?"

Kerrigan stood silent several moments before he responded. He spotted some dark-colored birds in the distance, darting from one tree to another. "You know, I never wanted to go.

I wouldn't have gone. I'd just graduated medical school, I was lucky enough not to have been drafted. I wanted to finish my residency. I'm sorry . . . I didn't come here to talk about this, Monsignor. I don't want to talk about this."

"I'm trying to help you."

"If you want to help me, then talk to the bishop. Please."

"I told you. If I'm going to do that, I'll need more."

Kerrigan shot back around and faced Carmichael directly. "Goddamnit, haven't I said enough? I'm just not right for it. What else do you need to know? For Lord's sake, I got her this far, why do I need to be in the fucking room?"

"I can see you are frustrated, Nathan. But I still don't understand. I'm sorry."

"Ah Christ," Kerrigan grunted. He reached into his overcoat and replaced his spent Marlboro Red with another. He lit it hastily and pulled on it deeply. Carmichael let him be for a while. It was the first time he'd heard Kerrigan take the Lord's name in vain.

"What are you afraid of, Nathan?"

Kerrigan scoffed. "Do I really have to explain it?"

"It's not so obvious to me."

"Not so obvious? I'm staring directly into the abyss, and you need to know why I'm afraid?"

Carmichael took a step toward Kerrigan. "But you've stared into the abyss before, haven't you? Risked life and limb for others? During the war?"

Kerrigan waved his hand, dismissively. "I don't know about any of that. This is completely different, anyway. Completely different. This is the devil we're talking about. If not Satan himself, one of his minions. And I never signed up for this."

Kerrigan turned back toward the trees. He fought back tears he didn't want Carmichael to see.

"You know," Kerrigan said. "Lately . . . lately I wonder why we even need him at all."

"Who?"

Kerrigan dabbed his eyes dry with his handkerchief and turned back around. "The devil." He took another drag from his fresh cigarette. "Aren't we ugly enough to each other? Do we really need encouragement?"

Carmichael approached Kerrigan and took his arm. He pulled Kerrigan closer, placed his hand against the small of Kerrigan's back, and gently eased him forward again. After walking a few more yards, the two priests came upon a fork in the trail.

"There's no marker," Kerrigan said. "We should go back, before we get lost."

"Not yet."

Kerrigan looked at Carmichael, into his green-blue eyes, and saw that he was focused straight ahead, that he had no intention of going back any time soon.

"Which way?" the monsignor asked.

"I don't know where these lead. Do you?"

"I say we go left."

Kerrigan nodded. Although his patience was running short, he resigned himself to following Carmichael's lead. The truth was he had nowhere else to go. Nowhere else at all. "Okay."

The left fork carved through long rows of towering birch trees. The trees seemed alive, looking down at the priests and watching from above.

"It is an interesting point you make about the devil," Carmichael said. "I suppose if anyone might be entitled to such a dim view of humanity, it'd be you. You've seen the very worst of it, haven't you? Those years you spent in Vietnam? Yet I can't help but feel it's a bit pessimistic, even coming from you. Especially coming from you."

"It's not just the war."

"What else then?"

"I don't know what I'm saying, Monsignor. I'm wasting your time."

"No," Carmichael insisted. "Go on."

"It's just . . . I find myself wondering what God was thinking."

"What about?"

"He must have known that when he created man, gave him free will, that we would end up being so terrible to each other. I mean, just look at us. Look at what we do to each other. We're violent, we're selfish, we kill for sport, we take pleasure in watching each other suffer. We're destroying this beautiful planet. We're . . . we're cruel. We're just wired that way. I mean just a few months ago, I saw these kids . . . ."

"What kids?"

"Never mind. I'm rambling."

"No, go on, Nathan."

Kerrigan looked at Carmichael's legs before he went on. Despite his frail appearance, Carmichael seemed to be getting along just fine. "Alright, fine. It was at the beginning of summer, not long before Harout came to see me at Saint Michael's. I was walking home from town. I'd met a friend there for dinner. Anyway, it was a gorgeous day. Warm, not very humid. So rather than drive, I walked. I was on Levy Street, making my way toward Geise Park, I think you know the one. It's about three blocks from Saint Michael's."

"Yes, there is a soccer field there if I remember correctly. And a very rusty playground. The church hosted some picnics there."

Kerrigan took one last drag from his latest cigarette. "Yeah that's the one. Only they replaced that rusty playground with a plastic one a few years back. Anyway, it's starting to get dark and I'm coming up on the park, and I hear this . . . this shrieking sound. It was an animal. I knew that right away. Sounded like cats fighting. As I'm getting closer to the park I hear it again. And again. Then I hear the giggling."

"Boys?"

"Boys, teenagers. I'm not sure. I didn't get a good enough look at them. It was too dark. Either way, they were certainly old enough to know what they were doing. When I reached the chain fence, I saw five or six of them huddled around in a circle. They were laughing. And that terrible shrieking, it was coming from somewhere inside the circle. At that point, I knew they were torturing the animal so I approached, hollered at them. In response they cursed at me and took off running, left the animal there on the grass. When I got close enough I saw that it was a kitten, a few weeks old maybe. Just a tiny little thing. Innocent. You know what they were doing, those kids? Those children of God?"

"What were they doing?"

"They were burning that poor kitten's—" Kerrigan choked up. "They were burning the kitten's ear with a butane lighter. I found that out later, from the veterinarian. The poor animal was so stunned it didn't even have sense enough to run away when the kids ran off. Instead it just lay there on the grass, its spirit broken I suppose. But you see, even at that young age, we're capable of such ugliness. It's how we're wired. It's in our DNA."

Kerrigan side-stepped to avoid a large puddle. Carmichael just walked right through it, surely wetting his feet, and yet he did not flinch. He just kept on walking as if nothing happened.

"May I ask what happened to the kitten?"

Kerrigan failed to respond, lost for a moment inside his head.

"Nathan?"

"Oh, yes, sorry. I brought it over to the shelter in town. Last I heard, she was adopted by a nice family. A family with children. The kids, I never found out who they were. They ran off before I could get a good look and that was that."

"Well, your story doesn't have such a terrible ending, does it?"

The trail began to slope upwards now. Kerrigan noticed a light fog rolling in toward the crest of the hill.

"No, I suppose not," Kerrigan said. "But for weeks I couldn't stop thinking about those kids, what they did to that poor kitten. Still it makes me feel so angry, so . . . I don't know why it bothers me so much. I . . . I don't know what I'm saying."

"It bothers you, Nathan, because you are a good man. I don't believe it's any more complicated than that."

Kerrigan looked up and into the trees, the spaces between the thousands of leaves rustling above his head. He didn't feel like a good man. Hadn't for a long, long time.

"Will you tell me more about the girl?" Carmichael asked. "You went to see her?"

"Yeah, I went to see her. I went to see her that very night."

"I thought you agreed to see her the next day, after the boy spoke to his mother?"

"That was the plan. But that's not how it happened."

* * *

After Kerrigan agreed to see Harout's sister, he brought Harout back into the sacristy so he could take down his telephone number and home address. According to Harout, neither him nor his mother had a cellular phone; only a home phone. When Kerrigan finished taking the information down, he folded the sticky note he wrote it on and slid it into his wallet. Harout only watched quietly, his arms crossed as if to keep warm, his eyes heavy with burden. Harout looked exhausted, like he'd been carrying a heavy cross for a long time.

"I'll call tomorrow," Kerrigan said. He extended his hand. Harout took it, and they shook. Harout's grip was limp and unassuming.

"Thank you, Father. I have to go now. My Aunt, she leave for work soon. Marianna will be alone."

"Your Aunt?"

Harrout nodded. "She help us."

"Okay, Harout. I'll walk you out."

Kerrigan followed Harout as he walked out of the sacristy and back into the church. Even then, thoughts were swirling around in his head so quickly they were making him dizzy. While he wasn't convinced Marianna Petrosian was possessed—he wouldn't be until the demon lurking inside her tried to ward him off—he knew that if she was, he needed to stay as far away from her as possible. He would visit Marianna as he promised—Kerrigan was not one to go back on his word. But the moment he had the slightest inkling she was in fact possessed, he would recuse himself and refer the matter to one of the experts. That's what was best for Marianna, Kerrigan told himself. It's what was best for everybody.

Kerrigan continued to watch Harout as he made his way down the aisle splitting Saint Michael's rows of pews down the middle. He couldn't help but notice the way Harout walked, hunched over, his shoulders slumping forward. This was not the average teenager, one with no care in the world. This was a young man carrying the weight of the world. Whether Marianna Petrosian was possessed or not, her brother was suffering. Kerrigan had little doubt of that.

As Harout approached the door the old man allowed to slam earlier, Kerrigan looked down at his watch and saw it was already after nine. The city bus was no place for someone Harout's age at that hour, not without an adult to accompany him, and certainly not as far south as Lawlry Heights. Once it was dark, the bus stops tended to attract vagrants and teenagers looking to make trouble.

"Harout! Harout! Wait a minute."

Harout turned around and looked at Kerrigan.

"You're not taking the bus home, are you?"

"Yes. It is too far for walk."

Kerrigan shook his head. "No, no. Come with me. I'll drive you."

"It's okay, Father. No problem. I always take bus."

"No, it's not okay. You are too young, and it is too late, and now you are my responsibility. I'm driving you. I'm not asking. I'm telling."

Harout stared blankly at Kerrigan until he responded. He seemed hesitant, unsure of himself. "Okay."

Harout waited patiently as Kerrigan gathered his things and pulled his '72 Impala around the front of the church. The Chevrolet was a homecoming gift from Kerrigan's father, who had surprised him with it when he'd returned from the war. Like Kerrigan's other possessions, the Impala was immaculate and mostly original. One of the perks of serving at Saint Michael's was that he could use the rectory's garage, which he did religiously. Though he had been told many times by friends and parishioners that the vehicle would fetch a high price, Kerrigan never considered selling it. He was a nostalgic man.

Kerrigan leaned over from the driver's seat and unlocked the passenger door. Harout looked both ways as he walked down the staircase connecting Saint Michael's to the curb, then climbed inside. The heavy passenger door shut with a solid thump.

Other than to direct Kerrigan, Harout barely said a word during the ride. Initially, Kerrigan chalked it up to the loud and overbearing Turbo Fire V8 under the hood, which Harout would have had to talk over. But then it occurred to him that if Harout really believed his sister was possessed, he might be worried the demon inside her was well aware of his pilgrimage to Saint

37

Michael's and his desperate bid for assistance. That would explain why Harout was so hesitant to tell Kerrigan his sister was possessed. Kerrigan felt the knot in his stomach tighten. One doesn't need to be an exorcist or demonologist to know that Satan and his minions can read minds, see one's deepest, darkest secrets.

"You can stop here," Harout said. He pointed to a stretch of sidewalk adjacent to an abandoned basketball court. Even the dim glow from the moon was bright enough for Kerrigan to see that the court was in shambles, reclaimed by nature. Large chunks of the asphalt protruded from the surface, displaced by roots and vegetation. Empty burger wrappers and soft drink containers danced across the court with the light breeze and spilled into the street. Kerrigan hadn't been all the way down to Lawlry Heights in some time, and he had forgotten how run down it was.

Kerrigan gazed toward the large, multi-story apartment complex further down the block. "Isn't that your building, up there?"

"Yes, Father. But . . . ."

"You don't want to be seen in a strange car."

Harout nodded.

Kerrigan brought the Impala to a stop next to the curb in front of the basketball court and killed the engine. With both of his hands still gripped firmly around the large, thin steering wheel, he sat for a moment in silence, staring out into the night through the windshield. The neighborhood was eerily dark. Street lamps on both sides of the road were out.

"So, you'll talk to your mother? Tell her we spoke?"

"Yes."

"When? Tonight?"

Harout shook his head. "No. Not tonight. Tonight she work. Maybe she get home three, four in the morning."

Kerrigan's eyebrows lifted. "Three, four in the morning? What does she do?"

"She has three job. She work in restaurant, she is seamstress. She make uniform for policeman. Treatment for my sister very expensive. We still pay."

Kerrigan looked back out through the windshield. He wondered where Harout's father was in all this. Harout had yet to mention him.

"So tomorrow then?" Kerrigan asked.

Kerrigan extended his hand again. Harout took it, and they shook. Harout's grip was a little firmer this time. He got out of the car and walked up the block toward his apartment complex. For a brief moment, he looked back at Kerrigan.

As Kerrigan watched Harout walk home, he felt the knot in his stomach tighten again. He reminded himself he had yet to see or hear a shred of evidence that Harout's story was anything more than a fiction of his imagination. He told himself that most cases of demonic possession turn out to be undiagnosed mental illness. Still, he wished he'd never agreed to cover that evening's mass for his colleague, that he'd stayed back at the rectory with his feet up, a glass of seltzer next to him on the TV stand, and the television tuned to that night's episode of Jeopardy. God only knew it would have been easy enough for him to say no.

When he could no longer see Harout, Kerrigan restarted the car and pulled away from the curb. Rather than turn back home, Kerrigan headed toward the apartment complex and passed by. Despite his unease, he felt oddly curious. The complex itself looked vaguely familiar, and he wondered whether he'd been there before, perhaps to anoint someone on their deathbed or bless a new apartment. He wasn't sure.

He rolled by slowly in case Harout was still outside. He had to squint through the passenger window because the building's facade was poorly lit. From up close, the building looked even more familiar, and Kerrigan was certain he'd been there before. He just couldn't remember why.

Once the building was behind him, he turned around and headed toward home. As he passed the complex a second time, he saw a woman dressed in nursing scrubs exit through the main entrance. Harout exited a moment later and chased her. Kerrigan, acting more on impulse than deliberation, quickly pulled over and parked the car on the opposite side of the road. He killed the engine and watched. Harout caught up to the woman and handed her something small. She took the item and stuffed it inside a large handbag she carried over her shoulder. Then she hugged Harout tightly and kissed his forehead. Harout ran back inside, and the woman headed toward the street.

Kerrigan didn't notice right away, but the woman was headed right toward the Impala. He panicked and slouched into his seat. He heard the chirp of a car alarm just in front of him. A car door clicked open and then thudded closed. Kerrigan slowly raised his head and squinted through the spokes in his steering wheel. The woman was inside a small, white Toyota parked just in front of him. She started the engine. Though he could barely hear it over the exhaust pipe rattling beneath her car, the woman was sobbing. She cried for three or four minutes while Kerrigan watched through the windshield. When she finally gathered herself and pulled away, Kerrigan sat back up and watched her tail lights fade into the night.

The night was quiet now. Kerrigan checked that there was no one else around. He restarted the car, activated the turn signal, and put his hands on the wheel. The Turbo Jet V8 growling into the warm summer night, Kerrigan stared at the empty patch of asphalt the Toyota had occupied just a moment ago. He heard two voices inside his head now, both speaking at once. One shouted at him to get as far away as he could and never come back. He could still get a run in before dinner. He could even catch Jeopardy before bed. But the other voice, speaking more softly, reminded him of a promise he made long ago.

Kerrigan reached into his wallet and pulled out the sticky note with Harout's address and telephone number. He held it under a shaft of moonlight shining through the windshield. Apartment 241B, it said.

* * *

Those two voices continued to wrangle with each other as Kerrigan approached the apartment complex, yet he forged ahead anyway. Though he wasn't sure exactly what he planned to do or what he would even say to Harout (or anyone else in the apartment, for that matter), he decided to take things as they came.

As he approached the small awning hanging over the main entrance to the building, a middle-aged woman emerged from the shadows. Her clothes were old and tattered, her hair thin and greasy. A fresh, unlit cigarette hung from her lips. She rifled through the pockets of her light jeans, which were torn at the knees and several inches too short. Kerrigan smiled politely as he made his way past her.

"Say, Father," the woman said.

Kerrigan stopped and turned back toward her. She caught him off guard—he was surprised she could make out his clerical collar under the dim lighting beneath the awning. She took the cigarette out of her mouth and held it up.

"You got a light?" she asked.

"No, sorry. I don't smoke."

"How 'bout a dollar?" The woman smiled at Kerrigan. Her smile was short a few teeth but charming nonetheless. "That way maybe I can buy one."

Kerrigan smirked. Classic bait and switch, he thought. Still, he was a priest, after all. He reached into his pants pocket and took out his wallet. From there, he pulled out a crisp five dollar bill and handed it over to the woman. She took it eagerly. "Here. Maybe you can buy yourself five."

The woman's eyes lit up like Christmas. "Whoa, must be my lucky day!" She lit her cigarette and blew out a cloud of smoke toward Kerrigan. The cloud slowly enveloped him.

"What's the matter, honey?" the woman asked. Kerrigan didn't realize it, but he was staring at her cigarette, its glowing tip. She held the cigarette up. "Oh, this? You want one?"

Kerrigan shook his head. "Uh, no. No. Thank you."

"Come on, Father. Take a break. I can see you want one."

"Pardon me?"

The woman chuckled. She shook her finger at him. "You got that look. I know that look. Here, have a drag." She held her cigarette out toward Kerrigan and smiled. The gaps in her teeth seemed even wider.

Kerrigan backed away. "I quit those a long time ago. You probably should too."

The woman laughed again. "Thanks for the advice, Father."

"Have yourself a good night." Kerrigan slid his wallet back into his pants pocket and turned back toward the building's entrance.

"Bless you, Father."

Kerrigan entered the building through a set of glass doors and left the woman outside with her cigarette and his five dollar bill. "I hope so," he mumbled to himself.

Just behind the entrance was a short staircase that led to the second floor. Kerrigan climbed up and followed signs until he was in a narrow corridor that led to apartment 241D. Once he was inside, he remembered being there on parish business, and the building's condition had worsened considerably. The industrial carpet lining the hallways was thin from years of foot traffic, worn in some places all the way to the concrete floor beneath it. The air was thick and heavy and smelled vaguely of mildew and stale cigarette smoke. Faded gray paint hung from the walls in sheets large enough to wrap small Christmas gifts. Even though it was subsidized housing, Kerrigan found it hard to believe the budget didn't allow for a few rolls of carpet and some paint. He could only imagine what other problems the management was neglecting, and he thought what an awful place this was for a young man like Harout to grow up.

When Kerrigan spotted apartment 241B, he stopped just short of it. He was having second thoughts. It was late, after all, and Harout wasn't expecting him. For all he knew, Harout might have even retired for the night. Kerrigan looked down at his watch and saw that it was just after ten-thirty. He looked left and right. Other than himself, the corridor was empty. He could slip out as easily as he slipped in and just call Harout tomorrow. It's just a sick girl, he reminded himself. Just a sick girl and nothing more. He took in a breath and knocked on the door.

There was only silence at first, but Kerrigan eventually heard the sound of slippers shuffling over a wooden floor. The slippers stopped just behind the door. Kerrigan noticed there was a peephole and looked into it. A moment later, the deadbolt slid open with a thud and the door slowly opened. Harout stuck his head out through the gap. When he saw it was Kerrigan, Harout pulled the door closed to unfasten the chain lock and then opened it all the way. Harout and Kerrigan just looked at each other. Then Harout stood aside so Kerrigan could enter. Kerrigan found himself inside a small foyer separated from the rest of the apartment by a beaded curtain. To his right, a small white statue of the Virgin Mary sat atop a wooden cupboard, a set of rosary beads wrapped around her hands. The statue was surrounded by a half-dozen unlit candles, some red, others white, and a half-opened matchbox.

Kerrigan stepped through the beaded curtain and into the living room. He waited for Harout. Inside, he immediately noticed this was a religious household. The space was decorated with holy items of all sorts. Crucifixes and pendants hung from the walls. Figurines sat on top of cabinets and dressers.

Embroidered cloths draped over the furniture. Kerrigan could smell freshly burnt incense.

"Something to drink?" Harout asked. He had just stepped through the curtain.

"No. No, thank you. I'm alright." Kerrigan's voice wavered slightly. He felt the knot in his stomach tighten another notch, and he wondered again whether this was a mistake, whether he should have just gone home.

Harout made his way past Kerrigan and headed toward the kitchen. "This way."

Kerrigan followed Harout through the small kitchen and into a narrow hallway that led past a small bathroom and toward a closed door. Harout rested his slender hand on the door handle and glanced back at Kerrigan. He flashed Kerrigan a serious, somber look, as if to warn Kerrigan he should ready himself. Then Harout opened the door and walked inside. Kerrigan followed.

The first thing Kerrigan noticed was the smell; unlike the sweet smell of incense just outside, the bedroom reeked vaguely of feces and urine, like a public restroom. Then he laid eyes on Marianna Petrosian and was shocked by what he saw. Only a passing glance was necessary for him to see that her condition was as bad as Harout made it out to be, if not worse. With the exception of one of her arms, which was raised strangely into the air as if she were at school, Marianna lay there completely still, lifeless. Even though most of her body was hidden beneath a fresh set of white bedsheets, it was obvious she was dangerously thin. Her eyes, the same mixture of colors as her brother's, were open widely and fixated. Her pupils were dilated. Her skin, pale and devoid of color, looked as thin as tissue paper, stretched too tightly around fragile bones. Had he not known better, Kerrigan might have assumed he was looking at an old woman on her deathbed, not a budding teenager barely fourteen years old.

He tracked a set of tubes and wires from Marianna's flaccid arm to intravenous drips and monitors at her bedside. She was clearly under someone's care. Kerrigan thought back to the woman from the Toyota and remembered that Harout mentioned his aunt was at the apartment and had to leave for work. She was dressed in nursing scrubs. Even if she was a nurse, Kerrigan couldn't help but wonder whether Marianna belonged in a hospital, under constant supervision.

Kerrigan heard sniffling. He turned and saw Harout was weeping. He walked over and put his hand on Harout's shoulder.

"It is not fair, Father. She hurt nobody. Never."

"I know, kid. I know."

Kerrigan noticed a folding chair next to Marianna's beside and sat down next to her. He made a sign of the cross and began a silent prayer. Harout approached his sister and gently lowered her arm down to her side. He lowered it carefully and methodically, like he was molding a clay statue. Kerrigan presumed Marianna was suffering from a form of catatonia. Though he'd never seen a real case in person, he'd read about the condition in medical school, before he had joined the Marine Corps and flew off to Vietnam.

Harout headed over to a bookshelf in the corner of the bedroom and removed something from one of the shelves. He approached Kerrigan and held out a framed photograph of Marianna. She was posing in front of a Christmas tree with a tuxedo cat in her arms. Her smile was wide and bright. It looked like the photograph was taken somewhere outside the apartment. "This was Marianna before. Two years ago now."

Kerrigan took the picture frame from Harout and gazed at it for a while. He struggled to reconcile the photograph inside with the image in front of him. The young lady in the photograph stood tall, confident, and proud. She looked far more confident than Harout. Thick, healthy brown hair stretched all the way to her slender shoulders. Her skin glowed with color. Her eyes, just as striking as Harout's, were warm, focused, and communicative. The contrast between the past and present was as stark as life and death.

Kerrigan handed the picture frame back to Harout. While Harout returned it to the bookshelf, Kerrigan glanced around the bedroom. Other than the presence of the hospital bed and medical equipment, it seemed the bedroom was preserved as it was before Marianna fell ill. The walls were covered with posters of what Kerrigan presumed were boy bands. The ceiling was littered with dozens of glow-in-the-dark stars and comets. A vanity table with three mirrors, a half-opened jewelry box, and a scattered assortment of lipstick and eyeshadow lay abandoned. Against another wall there was a towering armoire, decorated with dozens of stickers and postcards. A half-opened door revealed it was full of dresses and blouses. Kerrigan felt as though he was sitting inside a time-capsule, a snapshot of a life just as it was beginning to blossom. Though decades had passed since he was a teenager, he still remembered with fondness that period of his life, how frightening and wonderful it was all at once. No matter the cause of Marianna's condition, it was just a terrible, terrible shame.

Kerrigan saw from the corner of his eye that Harout was approaching the bedroom door. "Where are you going?"

"I have dishes. I wash for my mother."

Kerrigan nodded. "Okay, go ahead. I'll be right there." Harout left the bedroom and closed the door behind him. Kerrigan wondered again what the hell he was doing there, alone now in a teenager's bedroom while her mother was out. He looked down at his watch and saw it was approaching eleven. He took one last look at Marianna. He looked hard, but all he saw was a sick girl. A very, very sick girl.

* * *

When Kerrigan left Marianna's bedroom and closed the door behind him, the pit in his stomach blossomed into a full-blown bellyache. Even though he saw no evidence she was possessed, questions he could not answer burrowed their way into his mind. If Marianna really wasn't possessed, why did Harout believe she was? Was he so consumed with despair and denial he resorted to blaming an imaginary demon for his sister's deteriorating condition? While he felt it was possible, he couldn't convince himself it was likely. Kerrigan liked to think he was a good judge of character, and aside from Harout's fantastic claims, he seemed perfectly grounded. Kerrigan wondered whether someone or something had planted the idea in Harout's mind, a superstitious relative perhaps, or something he'd watched on television. Kerrigan knew from experience that people tend to latch on to all kinds of possibilities when a loved one is sick, no matter how improbable or incredible they might be.

Kerrigan stepped out into the kitchen. Harout was washing dishes, just as he'd said. He heard Kerrigan approach from behind and turned off the faucet.

"Can we talk for a minute?" Kerrigan asked.

"Yes." Harout's eyes shifted to the small pile of dirty dishes next to the sink. There were only three or four left.

"Finish up, finish up," Kerrigan said. "I'll wait for you in the living room."

As Kerrigan left the kitchen, Harout got back to work on a dirty frying pan. He scrubbed at it fastidiously with a small lump of steel wool.

Kerrigan took the time to look around. He found several photographs of Marianna, some on top of the entertainment center, others above a faux fireplace. Many were taken with a woman Kerrigan presumed to be her mother, others with Harout. In a corner of the living room, Kerrigan noticed a photograph of a man in uniform atop a wooden bureau. The man stood in front of an American flag. He was a fellow Marine. Like Harout, the man in the photograph had dark, wispy hair and fair skin. A small unlit candle lay just in front of it.

Kerrigan heard Harout turn off the faucet. He quickly stepped away from the photograph and waited for Harout in the middle of the room. Harout walked in a moment later, his shirt blotched with water.

"You mind if we sit?" Kerrigan asked.

Harout nodded. He sat down on a small reclining chair and swiveled it toward Kerrigan. Kerrigan sat down on a loveseat opposite the recliner and folded his hands. He rested his elbows on his thighs and leaned forward.

"You weren't born here, were you?"

Harout reset his glasses with the tip of his index finger. "No. In Armenia."

"What about your sister? What about Marianna?"

Harout shook his head. "No. She was born here, in United State. After we come to America."

"You came over with your mom and dad?"

"Yes. When I was young boy. We come from Turkey."

"Turkey? Not Armenia?"

"Yes, Turkey. We live first in Armenia, but my grandfather have business in Turkey. One day he have heart attack, and after that he need help to run business. We go to Turkey so we can help."

"So why come to America? Why leave turkey?"

"We are Christian, Father. In Turkey, Christianity not very popular. People throw stone at us, ruin our church. They destroy my grandfather business. Because we are Christian. When my grandfather die, my father say this is enough. No more. He take us to America for better life."

Kerrigan nodded. He knew little about it, but he heard Christians were being persecuted in Turkey, and that the situation had grown worse in recent years. He looked over to the photograph of the Marine. "Is that your father? In that picture?"

Harout nodded. The expression on his face confirmed what Kerrigan already surmised. Harout began to weep.

"I'm sorry, kid. I'm so sorry. What . . . what happened?"

"He love this country. After the planes fly into tower, he say he must fight. He believe it was duty because America bring us freedom, opportunity. He die in Iraq. They tell us it was I.E.D. Bomb."

"When?"

"Next month, seven years."

Kerrigan let out an audible sigh. Even as a priest, he sometimes couldn't help but wonder what God was thinking. Sometimes the same old answers just weren't good enough. He also felt guilty. He regretted his initial suspicion that Harout was a victim of domestic abuse. While he had known of cases where the mother was the abuser, the truth was Harout's father came to mind first. He imagined the moment the family received word of his passing. Although Kerrigan wasn't born until after the war, his mother often recounted the long days and nights she suffered through while his father was in Germany. Kerrigan imagined Harout's mother suffered similarly, except that for her the dreaded news actually came one day. It came and probably changed everything. And now Marianna. It was just too much.

"It sounds like your father was a very brave man."

Harout wiped his nose and eyes with one of his sleeves. "Now I worry for my sister."

Kerrigan took in a breath before he spoke. "Yeah. I . . . I can see she's not doing so well."

"She will die."

Kerrigan opened his mouth to speak but then closed it. His instincts told him to reassure the boy, to tell him it would be alright, but he knew he couldn't do it with a straight face. Not with what he saw in the other room. He generally didn't care to encourage false hope. He saw no use in it. "Can I ask who's caring for Marianna?"

"Us. My family."

"Who's your family?"

"Me. Mother. My Aunt Yeva—she is nurse for hospital. When she is not working, she is here. We take care of rest."

"And your mother works . . . works a lot, I take it?"

Harout nodded. "She have no choice. We have no insurance. We owe doctors and hospital lot of money. For treatment."

Kerrigan crossed his arms and leaned back into the loveseat. He felt terribly sorry for Harout. He should be out with his friends, drinking beers. Playing video games. Not tending to his dying sister. "Is Marianna seeing a doctor now? I mean, is a doctor watching her now?"

The expression on Harout's face changed from sadness to frustration again. It was the same look Harout had worn when he'd told Kerrigan his mother couldn't see the devil. "Doctor give up on her. They say we can do nothing, only put her in facility. Mother refuse."

"I see. Well, I understand why you wouldn't want to put her in a facility. But what I'm wondering is, is there a doctor watching over her now, making sure she's getting what she needs, that she's comfortable? Or is it just your Aunt?"

Harout hesitated before he spoke. "She needs priest, Father. Not doctor. Doctor cannot help her."

Kerrigan took in another breath and leaned forward. "Look, Harout, from what I can see, your sister is very sick. That's all. That's why I'm asking if a doctor is looking after her. It worries me that she's home. If it's a question of money, I might be able to—"

"Doctor cannot help her." Harout's voice swelled. "Only priest."

"What if you're wrong, kid? Huh? It can't hurt to get another opinion. Like I said, if it's about money—"

"Please, Father. You are not listen to me."

"I am, kid, but . . . . Look, I saw you move your sister's arm, alright? Now as far as I know that's a form of catatonia. It's a disease. A known disease. It has nothing to do with the devil. I know a really good psychiatrist who knows all about this stuff. He's a good friend of mine. I can ask him to come see Marianna and tell us what he thinks. It can't hurt."

Harout shook his head incessantly. He didn't want to hear it. "We waste time. She already see many doctor. Ten different doctor. They try everything already. Many treatment. And she is same. Like this."

"Harout, I'm just not—"

"Please, Father. She needs priest. Not medicine. Please, no more medicine."

"I . . . it . . . it's not that simple, kid."

"Please."

Kerrigan leaned back into the loveseat again. He realized there was no reasoning with the kid. He took a moment and thought carefully about what to say next. "Alright, alright. Now listen to me for a second, okay? You listening?"

Harout was staring down at his hands, but he looked up at Kerrigan.

"Okay, now listen. Even if you're right, the church will never authorize an exorcism without having a doctor look at her first."

"But, she—"

"It won't happen, kid. The church . . . it's on its toes now. They're not gonna take any chances, not with all the stuff that's been going on. You understand? Either way, a doctor's going to have to look at her."

Harout stood silent a moment, contemplating. "Then what?"

"Then we'll take it from there. But we won't be wasting any time. You understand?"

Harout shook his head again. "You do not believe. Nobody believe. This is my problem."

"Harout, I'll be honest with you. I was just in there. I looked at her, just like you asked. With my own eyes. And I'm sorry, kid, but all I see is a terribly sick girl. A sick girl who needs help."

"That's because he hide."

"How do you know? Tell me how you know. Did you see something? Hmm?"

Harout sat there silent, twirling his fingers.

"Talk to me, kid. Help me understand this."

Harout's fingers moved more quickly, but he said nothing. It seemed he was holding back. Why, Kerrigan didn't understand.

"Alright, look," Kerrigan went on. "Let me get a doctor here to see her. At least we'll know what's what. It's the only way, kid."

Harout mulled it over a few moments and then nodded reluctantly in agreement. Kerrigan could sense the resignation in him, but this was the only way.

"Alright, good," Kerrigan said. "Now I know you said you were going to talk to your mother tomorrow, but it's very important you have her call me as soon as she can, okay? I need to speak with her. It's very important that I speak with her. Do you understand?"

Harout nodded.

"Okay."

Kerrigan stood up and headed for the door. Harout walked him out.

"I'll pray for you and Marianna."

"Thank you, Father. Thank you for coming."

Harout shut the apartment door. Kerrigan stood there for several moments, frozen. That other voice in his head was right, he thought. This was a mistake. A big mistake.

CHAPTER 3

Kerrigan pulled deeply on another cigarette and blew a plume of smoke out above his head, where a gentle breeze carried it behind the priests. The further he and Carmichael walked into the woods, the cooler it got. The cigarettes helped keep Kerrigan warm.

"So that's how I got involved," Kerrigan said. "Been involved ever since."

Carmichael was still there next to him, walking steadily by his side. The monsignor walked the trail at the same slow pace he'd kept since they started. Kerrigan had finally adjusted to the pace.

"It doesn't make any sense, does it?" Kerrigan asked.

"What doesn't?"

"This family. Why them? They leave their country so they can escape religious persecution, so they can continue praising God, and this is what they get? They're holy people, Monsignor. The holiest I've met in a long time."

Carmichael shook his head. "I don't imagine there's any sense to be made from it, Nathan. None at all. Perhaps the Armenian girl got herself mixed up in some bad business, dabbled in the occult? It's been known to happen."

"I asked Harout about that."

"And?"

"Well, he didn't know for sure, but he doubted it. He said his sister was very well-behaved. Very loyal. He did mention something about how she started acting a little differently just before she got really sick. And then one day, she just never woke up."

"Different how?"

Kerrigan was distracted momentarily by a small, white rabbit. The tiny creature hopped its way through the shrubbery along the path. Its clean white fur contrasted starkly against the dull brown earth. "Eh, it's hard to say. I wasn't able to pin that down. You know with Harout, I don't think it's intentional but he speaks in very vague terms. Problem is his English still isn't great. But he said something about how Marianna was talking back to their mother all of a sudden, disobeying her. But . . . I don't know. Sounds pretty normal for a teenage girl to me. She's at that age where you would expect her to start pushing boundaries."

"How long ago was it the boy first came to see you?"

Kerrigan thought for a second. He hadn't been keeping good track of time of late. "Two months. A little longer, maybe. When he came to see me, the summer was just beginning. The second or third week in June, I think."

"And the girl . . . her condition is worse now?"

Kerrigan nodded. "Much, much worse, Monsignor. I honestly don't think she has much time left at all. Bishop Gailey, he knows. I made sure. He's moving as quickly as he can to get everything in place. That's why this exorcism . . . it can move forward any time now."

Carmichael flashed Kerrigan a quick glance, then focused back on the trail. "Uh huh. So, you haven't much time to sort this out?"

"That's right. The sooner you talk to him, the better."

"Mmm," Carmichael muttered. Kerrigan hoped he would say something more, but he didn't. He only scratched the pocket of gray razor stubble sprouting from his chin.

"You heard what I—"

"Yes, I heard you."

"Okay, I just thought—"

"Tell me more about the boy. This Harout Petrosian. You didn't believe him at first?"

Kerrigan paused a moment before he responded. He looked at Carmichael and then out into the trail they were walking. It stretched as far as the horizon. He felt that knot in his stomach again. It had come and gone ever since Harout had visited him at Saint Michael's. The thought of wandering even deeper into the woods made him anxious.

"I honestly don't know," Kerrigan said. "I suppose the truth is I didn't want to believe him. I hoped to prove him wrong."

"And now you do believe him?"

"I don't have a choice anymore."

"What changed?"

"At first nothing. Not for a while."

"You brought a doctor to see the girl?"

Kerrigan took a drag from his cigarette and blew out another cloud of smoke into the cool air. "Yes. Yes, I did."

* * *

"Are you going to tell me what this is really about Nathan, or not?"

Kerrigan chose to ignore the man sitting in the passenger seat of his Chevy Impala for the moment, focusing instead on the road ahead and the heavy traffic he was navigating. That man was Doctor Alexander Delaney, a prominent board-certified psychiatrist who headed up the psychiatric department at the Gift of Mercy Medical Center, a Catholic hospital just up the road from Saint Michael's. Doctor Delaney, who had spent many years in private practice treating local celebrities and socialites, was one of Kerrigan's oldest friends. The two men had studied medicine together, and even though Kerrigan never finished his residency, they kept in touch and remained close. Kerrigan had put in a good word when Delaney was up for his position at the hospital, and Delaney had felt indebted to Kerrigan ever since.

"I know I owe you a favor," Delaney said. He adjusted his expensive sunglasses and looked over toward Kerrigan. "Probably more than one as a matter of fact. But this . . . this I don't understand. There's something you aren't telling me."

"I just want you to have a look at the girl." Kerrigan's hands were wrapped around the steering wheel, his grip steadily growing tighter. He was already feeling tense, and the traffic was unusually heavy for that hour of the afternoon.

Delaney shook his head, and then ran his fingers through his slicked-back silver hair. His hair was silver, but it was full. He was aging well. "Yeah, but I told you it won't make a difference. I already pulled all of her records like you asked. Probably violated every goddamned HIPAA law while I was at it. I could go to jail, you know?"

Kerrigan tried to ignore Delaney again. Delaney was the best psychiatrist Kerrigan knew, but he was a whiner and an egomaniac. Kerrigan had felt for some time that success had gone to his head.

"She's already been to ten fucking psychiatrists, for Christ's sake," Delaney went on. "And they all reached the same conclusion."

"Yeah, but none of them are first-rate psychiatrists like you, are they?" Though Kerrigan was intentionally stroking Delaney's ego, there was some truth to the statement; many of the psychiatrists Marianna had seen were far less experienced and successful. Some were just out of school.

Delaney paused a moment, contemplating as he gazed outside through the passenger window. He looked down at the large watch on his wrist. "Eh. They're okay, nothing special. But sometimes there just isn't much . . . look, I'm good at what I do, yes. But I can't work miracles, Nathan."

"I'm not asking you to work miracles, Alex."

"I get what you're doing. I do. But I still don't understand how this is on you. There's a piece missing somewhere."

Kerrigan shook his head with frustration. He was trying to keep his cool, but Delaney was testing his patience. He'd pleaded with Delaney for days before he'd agreed to visit Marianna. "I already told you. Her brother came to me because he's concerned about her condition, and I'm trying to help. I can't just turn him away, Alex. I have a duty to my parishioners, same as you have a duty to your patients."

"Except this kid's not one of your parishioners. He's from the projects."

"You know what I mean."

"I still don't understand it. So, this kid takes the bus all the way uptown to talk to you, because his sister is sick? You are a priest, not a doctor."

Kerrigan bit his tongue again. He said through his teeth: "Yes, I'm aware of that. You don't have to keep reminding me."

"I can see him going to one of his teachers at school, the guidance counselor maybe, or how about a priest from his own parish?"

Kerrigan's grip on the steering wheel tightened a notch. His knuckles were turning white.

Delaney stared at Kerrigan, awaiting a response. "Well?"

Kerrigan shrugged. "I don't know."

"You don't know?"

"I'm still trying to figure it out myself."

Delaney scoffed. "Yeah, sure."

Kerrigan took his eyes off the road and flashed Delaney a scornful look. He was losing his cool. "If you've got something on your mind, why don't you just spill it? Okay? Stop fucking around and just get on with it."

"Yeah?"

"Yeah! Come on. Let's get it over with."

"Yeah? Alright, fine. Did that kid come to see you because he thinks his sister is possessed by some evil spirit or something, a demon or whatever? The devil? Is that why he came all that way to see you?"

Kerrigan's tongue was tied. He was good at many things, but lying was not one of them. Instead he had decided to avoid the topic altogether. "She's not possessed, Alex."

"Is that why the boy came to see you?"

"She's not possessed."

Delaney's face crinkled with resignation. "Jesus Christ. I knew it. Krista said it. She said it, and I didn't wanna listen." Krista was Delaney's wife. Kerrigan had known her as long as he had been a priest. He'd presided over their marriage shortly after he was ordained. She was very superstitious. Even priests made her nervous.

"What did she say?"

"She said the girl's probably possessed or something. Now of course I gave you the benefit of the doubt, told her she was being ridiculous. That if that were the case you would at least have had the decency—do you know I slept on the fucking couch last night? My fucking back is killing me."

"Alex, just relax, okay? Please. I've already seen her. I promise you she's not possessed."

"Goddamnit, Nathan. You should have told me. You can't just pull people into shit like this without telling them what's going on. It's not right."

"If I had said anything, you wouldn't have come. I want you to look at the girl."

"You're goddamn right I wouldn't have come!"

"You shouldn't use the Lord's name in vain. Especially not in front of a priest."

"Fuck you, Nathan. How's that?"

Kerrigan looked over to Delaney, and then back out at the road. The traffic opened up and he was able to pick up speed. "She's not possessed, okay? If I believed she was, I would be trying to convince the bishop we need to do something about it."

"Yeah, well, how do you know?"

"Because, she doesn't show any of the signs. She doesn't move, she doesn't talk, remember?"

"Then why does her brother think she is? Huh? He must have his reasons. He must have seen something."

"What, you don't think I asked him?"

"What did he say?"

Kerrigan shrugged again. "He didn't say anything. I asked him what he had seen, and he couldn't even tell me. He's just confused, that's all. His sister is dying and he doesn't know how to process it. Doctors haven't been able to help her, so now he's looking to the supernatural."

Delaney let out a condescending chuckle, one Kerrigan had heard many times before. It never failed to get under his skin. "Now you sound like the psychiatrist."

Delaney rested his hand on his chin and gazed out through the passenger window. They were rolling past a public playground busy with children. Kerrigan could see Delaney was anxious—he was rubbing his fingers together like he was counting money. Kerrigan first noticed the habit when they were in medical school—Delaney would rub his fingers the same way when they had exams in front of them and were waiting for the proctor to give the green light for them to begin.

"Krista's gonna have a conniption."

"Then don't tell her."

Delaney snapped back toward Kerrigan. He was shouting now. "Did you hear what I said? She already knows. She's got a nose for this shit. She always has. You know how she gets about these things. She won't even let me keep horror movies in the house, Nathan."

"Alex—we're just going to see a sick girl. That's all. If anything, I'm hoping you can help me convince the boy his sister isn't possessed. Because that's really what I'm trying to do."

Delaney shook his head angrily. "You should have told me. I would've come anyway."

"You just said you wouldn't have. Two seconds ago."

"I don't need this right now. Things are going good. I don't need to be caught up in this kind of shit. My God, Nathan—couldn't you just ask for something else?"

Kerrigan groaned. His knuckles were paper white. "Here we go."

"Here we go, what?"

"I knew it."

Delaney flailed his arm. "You knew what?"

"This is exactly why I didn't say anything to you."

"What is?"

"I know how your mind works."

"How does it work, Nathan? Hmm? Tell me."

"You don't give a shit about Krista or her fucking superstitions. You're just worried someone's gonna place a curse on you, ruin your career. I told you already, there's no fucking demon, alright? No one's going to place any hexes on you, no one's casting any spells. You understand? You're not gonna wake up tomorrow and find one of your fucking Mercedes missing from the drive—"

"Jesus Christ, Nathan! You just hate the fact that I'm successful, don't you?" Delaney pulled off his sunglasses, revealing wide, angry eyes. Both men were shouting now.

"It was just a matter of time before you played that card. Just a matter of time. How many times are we going to go round and round—"

"Because it's the fucking truth! You know, as well as I do, that you would've been as successful a trauma surgeon as I am a psychiatrist, if not more successful. And you hate that. Well, I've got news for you, Nathan. Nobody made you give it up. God knows I certainly didn't. You come back from the war and all of a sudden you're quitting medicine for the priesthood, and no one understands why the hell you're doing it because you won't talk to anybody. And you seem to forget I practically begged you to at least finish your fucking residency, so you at least had the option, just in case you changed you mind. But you didn't listen. You knew better. So, don't sit there and hold my success against me."

Kerrigan, infuriated now, took his eyes off the road again and yelled at Delaney directly. "You ungrateful prick! If I didn't want you to be successful—"

"Nathan!"

"—if I didn't want you to be successful—"

"Nathan!"

"—I wouldn't have helped you get the fucking job you have now, you dumb son of a bitch!"

"Nathan, the brakes! Hit the brakes!"

Delaney assumed a brace position. Kerrigan looked out the windshield. They were barreling toward a black car at a dead stop behind a red light.

Kerrigan clenched the steering wheel and jammed on the heavy brake pedal with all his might. The tires screamed but the hulk of the car continued to barrel forward, the tail lights ahead still growing larger. Kerrigan closed his eyes and waited. Hearing only silence, he slowly opened them. The Impala had stopped just in time, with only a few inches to spare. Two young children raised their heads above the rear window of the black car and looked out at him.

"Christ," Kerrigan uttered, his hands still gripped firmly around the steering wheel.

Delaney breathed a sigh of relief and looked at Kerrigan. "So, it's okay for you to use the Lord's name in vain?"

Kerrigan looked back at his old friend, and let out a chuckle. Before he knew it, the chuckle developed into a bout of genuine laughter. Delaney joined him.

"Alex . . . all I'm asking is that you have a quick look at her. She's just fourteen years old. Maybe you can think of something the other doctors haven't."

A solemn look washed over Delaney's face. "We're almost there, aren't we?"

* * *

"You ready?" Kerrigan asked Delaney, who was gazing up at Harout's towering apartment complex as if it were a haunted house. Delaney carried a leather briefcase containing the rudimentary medical instruments he would use to evaluate Marianna's condition.

As they made their way through the corridor leading to Harout's apartment, Kerrigan was struck by the commotion. Though it was early in the afternoon and a workday, he heard laughter, shouting, and music blaring from behind many of the closed doors they passed on their way to unit 241B. He also smelled pot.

"Shit!" Delaney groaned. He dropped his sunglasses onto the worn carpet below. As he knelt down to retrieve them, a door a few yards ahead flew open and slammed against the adjacent wall. A woman dressed only in a t-shirt and a pair of revealing nylon underwear was forced outside. A pair of black shoes flew out after her. A male voice hollered expletives from inside the apartment. She shouted back at the man. The door slammed in her face. Hollering more loudly now, she banged against the door with her fists while Kerrigan and Delaney watched. The two men were frozen in place. The woman gave up banging and noticed them staring at her.

"The fuck y'all lookin' at?" she barked.

Neither Kerrigan nor Delaney responded. Instead they looked away and stood quietly as the woman shuffled past them. She mumbled something under her breath, then disappeared around a corner, shoes in hand.

"The kid sure came a long way to see you, didn't he?" Delaney whispered.

"Yeah, he did."

"You really don't know why he got off at your stop?"

"No. Haven't asked him yet. Here it is."

Kerrigan and Delaney were in front of 241B now. Kerrigan glanced down at his watch, then knocked on the door. Footsteps approached from inside, then the door opened. It was Harout.

"Hello," Kerrigan said.

Harout held the door open and stepped aside. "Please, come in."

Kerrigan looked at Delaney and made his way into the apartment. Delaney followed.

"This is my good friend, Doctor Alexander Delaney. He's a very good psychiatrist, and he was gracious enough to take time out of his busy schedule to come see Marianna."

"Hello, Harout," Delaney said. Delaney extended his hand. Harout shook it.

"Nice to meet you, Doctor. Thank you for coming."

"You too, kid," Delaney said. "Happy to be here."

Kerrigan noticed Harout's voice sounded strained. He also looked paler than usual.

"Is everything alright, Harout?" Kerrigan asked. "You look tired."

Harout shrugged nervously. "Last night was long night."

Kerrigan chose not to press further. Instead he looked back at Delaney, who was already looking at him.

"Something to drink? Water, soda?"

"No," Kerrigan said. "We're okay. Is your mother here?"

Harout bowed his head slightly. "No, Father."

"No? What do you . . . what do you mean?"

"I'm sorry, Father. But she have to work. Her boss make her work overtime today. She have no choice."

Kerrigan stood silent a moment as Delaney looked on. Then he pulled Harout aside and whispered so Delaney wouldn't overhear. "Harout . . . I don't . . . I don't understand. Why isn't she here? We discussed this and you said she would be here. Doesn't she understand how important this is?"

"Yes, but her company, they make uniform for policeman."

"Yeah, you've told me that."

"They have big order. Boss make her work extra so they can finish. She cannot say no."

Kerrigan glanced quickly back over to Delaney, who watched with crossed arms and looked impatient. Kerrigan suspected Harout hadn't kept his end of the bargain. Since they'd met, Kerrigan had yet to meet or speak with Harout's mother, and this was the second time she'd stood him up on account of work.

"Harout, we discussed this. Your mother has to be involved. I can't be doing this without—"

"She have no choice. If she say no, she will lose job. We cannot afford."

"Well, okay, but she hasn't even called me, kid. You gave her my telephone number, right? She hasn't called. And every time I call here you pick up and say she isn't home. Why don't you tell me where she works? I'll go see—"

"What's going on?" Delaney asked. He took a step toward Harout and Kerrigan.

"Nothing," Kerrigan said. "Harout's mother is running late from work."

Delaney rolled his eyes and looked down at his watch. "How long will she be? I have meetings later."

"He's not sure. It could be a bit—"

"Nathan, I got things I need—"

"Why don't we just get started?" Kerrigan asked. "We'll get started, and we'll speak with Harout's mother when she gets here." He didn't like the idea, but he knew he would never get Delaney back there again.

"Go ahead? Are you crazy? Nathan, no. We can't. Not without a parent's supervision."

Kerrigan grabbed Delaney's wrist and pulled him away from Harout. This time he whispered so Harout wouldn't overhear. "Alex, just listen—"

"No, I'm not doing this. Okay? I don't care."

"Will you just relax—"

"Don't tell me to relax!" Delaney barked. He pulled his arm away.

"Will you be quiet! The kid's right there."

"Do you realize how serious this is, Nathan? Huh? God forbid they accuse us of abuse or something. No way. I'm not doing it. This isn't what I agreed to."

"Just listen to me for a second. We're here now, and I know you don't want to come back. Let's just do what we came here to do and then you can be on your way. I'll stay back and talk to the mother when she gets home."

"Nathan—"

"We'll be square, okay? You'll never have to feel like you owe me something ever again."

Delaney looked at Kerrigan, contemplating.

"I'll take the responsibility," Kerrigan said.

Delaney shook his head in disgust. "What the hell did you get me into?"

"Never again. Okay? Now let's do it and get the fuck out of here. Alright?"

Delaney said nothing more. He stood there with his arms crossed, a sour expression on his face.

Kerrigan and Delaney followed Harout into Marianna's bedroom. Kerrigan walked in first and headed over to the foot of Marianna's bed. Delaney followed reluctantly behind him. The expression on Delaney's face changed from anger to dismay. Even for Kerrigan, who had seen Marianna just a few days earlier, the sight was appalling.

Harout headed for the door.

"Wait," Delaney said. "What's the kid's name again? Hey, where are you going?"

"Do you smell that?" Kerrigan asked. He smelled cigarette smoke all of a sudden. Fresh cigarette smoke. "Was someone smoking in here?"

Kerrigan looked at Harout, then Delancy, but neither of them responded. "Cigarettes. Someone's been smoking in here."

Delaney and Harout just stood silent, expressionless. They clearly didn't know what Kerrigan was talking about.

"You don't smell it?"

"No," Harout said. "I smell nothing."

Delaney shrugged his shoulders.

Kerrigan sniffed the air. Sure as rain, he smelled cigarette smoke. Not the foul stench of stale cigarettes, but the fresh smell of burning tobacco, like the kind he used to roll by hand. It was a delightful smell, so crisp it was as if someone was smoking in the room that very moment. "You guys don't smell that?"

"No," Harout said. "Nothing."

"I don't smell anything, Nathan," Delaney said curtly. His patience was running thin again. "Maybe there's a vent or something. Maybe it's coming from another apartment. I dunno."

Kerrigan looked around for vents, but didn't see any. He decided to let it go. He didn't want to hold things up and lose Delaney's attention.

Harout headed for the door again.

"Wait, kid," Delaney said. "Where are you going? Where is he going, Nathan? He should be here."

"Let him go," Kerrigan said.

Delaney flashed Kerrigan an angry look, his lower lip tucked under his front teeth. Harout looked over to Kerrigan for direction. Kerrigan waved him off. Harout left the room and closed the door behind him.

"Jesus Christ, Nathan. Now we are two strange men in a helpless girl's bedroom while her mother is at work. With the door closed. This is unbelievable."

"Will you shut the fuck up and just look at the girl? We're here, so let's just get it over with."

Delaney groaned, but said nothing more. He looked down at Marianna, who was as still and lifeless as she had been the night Kerrigan first laid eyes on her.

"Who's taking care of her?" Delaney asked.

"They do. Her aunt's a nurse. Works at North Shore. She's here when she's not working. She's the one who got the bed and the equipment."

"She belongs in the hospital"

"I know, Alex. They don't have insurance."

"She's worse than I thought."

"How much worse?"

"I don't know yet. Let me take a look at her."

While Delaney removed instruments from his small briefcase, Kerrigan poked around Marianna's bedroom. He noticed a row of marble notebooks on Marianna's bookshelf and pulled one out. He opened it and flipped through the pages. The pages were filled with written school work—math problems solved in longhand, handwritten essays, and original works of short fiction. There were no strange notes, no strange drawings. No obvious references to the occult. If anything, her neat and careful work reminded Kerrigan of himself. Unlike his peers, Kerrigan very much enjoyed school and always took it seriously. With Marianna's notebook in his hand, he recalled experimenting with many courses and disciplines before a class in biology aroused curiosities that would eventually lead him to medical school, and he couldn't help but wonder what path Marianna might have gravitated toward. He felt sorry the answer to that question might remain a mystery, locked away somewhere inside the lifeless body a few feet away. Even if Harout was wrong about her being possessed, he was dead right about one thing—it just wasn't fair. It wasn't fair at all.

Kerrigan returned the notebook to the bookshelf and looked back over to Delaney. Delaney was listening to Marianna's heart and lungs with a stethoscope. Kerrigan approached cautiously from behind and placed his hand on Delaney's shoulder, so as not to startle him. Delaney stood up and let the stethoscope hang from his neck.

"What do you think?" Kerrigan asked.

"She's wasting away. She's very, very weak."

"Harout told me they use a feeding tube."

Delaney nodded. "Yeah, I saw."

"Maybe they need to up the nutrition?"

Delaney pulled the stethoscope off his neck and returned it to his briefcase. "It's not that simple, Nathan."

"Why not?"

"This is what happens when the body doesn't move for a long period of time. You just waste away until . . . our bodies aren't built to lie around like this. Throwing calories at her won't change that."

"Is it definitely catatonia?"

"Oh yeah. That might be the only thing we know for sure."

"How?"

"I'll show you." Delaney gently picked up Marianna's closest arm and raised it above the bed. When he let go, the arm didn't fall back down. Instead it hung there, suspended, fixed in place. Then Delaney gently bent Marianna's elbow and manipulated the arm into a different position. Again, her arm stood there fixed, stiff as the limb of a posable action figure. "This is waxy flexibility. I can literally mold her into any position I want."

Kerrigan nodded toward the erect arm. "How long will she stay like that?"

"It could be hours, days . . . in some cases as long as weeks. Typically, she'll be like that until someone moves her back. Waxy flexibility is a very strange thing. There's still a whole lot we don't understand."

Delaney gently repositioned Marianna's arm down by her side. Kerrigan noticed there was a significant degree of resistance, as if the muscles in Marianna's fragile arm had stiffened from underuse.

"Actually, when I saw her for the first time," Kerrigan said, "her arm was raised all the way up like she was in school. Can she do that on her own?"

Delaney nodded. "Yeah, sometimes they move. Typically, they're immobile most of the time, but they can assume different positions every now and again. It's really at random. We don't know what makes it more likely or not. But you might leave the room and come back to find her with a leg in the air, her arm raised up high like you said. You could find her curled in a fetal position. We see that sometimes, believe it or not. We're not sure why. Any number of positions really, even ones that seem strange or even very uncomfortable. It's usually very upsetting for the family, unfortunately. But again, typically, unless someone repositions her, she'll stay that way for a while."

A light bulb went off in Kerrigan's head. He'd also read that catatonic patients might spontaneously assume positions on occasion, and he wondered if that might explain why Harout believed his sister was possessed. Perhaps Harout, thinking his sister couldn't move on her own, found Marianna in strange positions and concluded something sinister was at work.

"What caused this?" Kerrigan asked.

"It's hard to say." Delaney struck Marianna's kneecaps with a rubber mallet to test for reflexes. Kerrigan watched but couldn't discern a response. "It could be something as simple as an electrolyte imbalance, or a lesion on the brain, maybe. She might have had a bad case of meningitis that nobody diagnosed, a bad reaction to antipsychotics. We just don't know. The problem is she tested negative on pretty much every diagnostic test we have, so we really don't know what the cause is. But if I were to guess, I would say this is probably secondary to schizophrenia."

"Schizophrenia? You're saying she's a schizophrenic?"

"Catatonic schizophrenia—it's a little different than what you're thinking. We don't see it as often as we used to with all the medications we have today, but it's still known to happen."

Delaney took out a small flashlight and shined it into Marianna's eyes.

"You won't see any of this in the medical records, Alex, but the boy mentioned she was acting a bit strange before this happened."

"What do you mean? Strange how?"

"He said she was acting out. Talking back, staying out later than she's supposed to. Testing boundaries. Before that she was extremely well-behaved."

Delaney shrugged. "May have something to do with this. But probably not. She's a fledgling teenager—it would be more remarkable if you said she wasn't doing those things. Look, Nathan, there's really no sense in getting caught up in why this happened."

"Why not?"

"Because the treatments are the treatments. And I'm sorry to say, she just hasn't responded to any of them."

Kerrigan shook his head. "That's got to be something we can try."

"Nathan, I know this isn't what you want to hear, but they really have tried everything."

Kerrigan heard a commotion from over his shoulder. He approached a window just above Marianna's vanity table and peered outside. The window overlooked a small courtyard in the center of the rectangular apartment complex. There was a small child running in circles around a fountain green with algae. A small, faded yellow kite trailed behind her. Even from his vantage point two stories above, Kerrigan could see the young girl was wearing a smile wide enough to light up a room. He looked back at Marianna, and all he saw was darkness.

"There's got to be something," he insisted.

"I've been through the records, Nathan. I wasn't exaggerating when I said she's seen ten different psychiatrists. Ten psychiatrists over the course of the past two and a half years. That's why these people are broke. She's been given every treatment we have. Benzodiazepines, barbiturates, electroconvulsive therapy, antipsychotics. She's been through rounds of anticonvulsants, antidepressants, muscle relaxants. Lithium, Topamax. Even medicine we don't traditionally use to treat catatonia—Zolpidem, NMDAs. She's had it all, Nathan. Different doses, different combinations of drugs. And the results are all the same. No measurable improvement."

"So, we try again."

Delaney let out a dejected sigh. He approached Kerrigan until the two men were at arm's length. "Nathan, look at her."

Kerrigan did as Delaney asked, and the answer was as clear to him as it was to his old friend, only more difficult to accept.

Marianna Petrosian was dying. Her body was far too frail for heavy psychiatric medication. Kerrigan didn't need to be a psychiatrist, or even a doctor, to understand that much.

"Sometimes we can't bring them back," Delaney said. "If you want to know the truth, now we just make sure she's comfortable. I'm sorry, Nathan. I truly am. I know you want to help her. Look, I know they may not have the money for real hospice care, but I can help with that. I can work something out."

Kerrigan crossed his arms and walked back over to the window overlooking the courtyard. The young girl outside was gone. He turned back toward Delaney. "Just tell me this. If she were your daughter, would your answer—"

"Stop it!" Delaney snapped furiously, eyes bulging. He was so angry Kerrigan flinched. "Stop it right there."

"Alex, I—"

"Don't you bring her up."

"Alright, I didn't mean any—"

"Don't talk about my family in here. Alright? Just do me that favor, okay? Don't say their names."

It took Kerrigan a moment to process Delaney's visceral reaction, but he eventually put it together. "You don't still think she might be possessed, do you?"

"How the hell would I know?" Delaney walked over to Marianna's bedside and packed up his things. "I'm no priest. This isn't my area of expertise."

It isn't mine either, Kerrigan thought to himself. "What in the world would a demon want with her? Look at her. She can't move or talk."

Delaney grabbed his briefcase and let it hang by his side. He was ready to leave. "Nathan, I wouldn't presume to know what interests the devil, and I don't want to know. Let's just leave my family out of this, okay?"

Kerrigan looked at Delaney and nodded. There was nothing else to say.

A gurgling sound startled the two men.

"What was that?" Kerrigan asked. "Is she choking?"

Delaney dropped his briefcase and scurried over to Marianna. He lifted her torso up slightly. "No, I don't think so. She's breathing. Help me lift her up."

Kerrigan hurried over to the opposite side of Marianna's bed and helped Delaney prop her up. He felt her fragile bones through the hospital gown she had on. When she was upright, Kerrigan placed his hand on the small of her back to keep her from falling over, but he soon realized he didn't have to. Her torso was locked into position, as stiff as her arm was before.

Delaney went into his briefcase for his stethoscope and lifted up Marianna's gown from behind. He listened to her lungs. "She's got some fluid in her lungs. It's not too bad, but she's gonna have to be suctioned."

"Edema?"

"Yeah. From lying around. It's bound to happen."

"What's that?" Kerrigan pointed to a large dressing on the small of Marianna's back. It was pink and moist. It corresponded to a pink stain on the mattress.

"I don't know." Delaney patted the dressing with the palm of his hand, then pinched one of the corners and slowly peeled it back.

Kerrigan grimaced at the wound beneath it. It was deep, raw, and covered in thick pus. "Christ, that's a bedsore."

"This isn't good, Nathan. It's infected."

The two men were startled by commotion coming from the other side of Marianna's closed bedroom door. There were at least two voices approaching, one of them female.

* * *

"Who's that? Her mother?" Delaney asked. The two voices were still approaching, growing louder.

"I don't know," Kerrigan said.

"Whoever it is, she doesn't sound happy."

"Let's lay her down. Quick. Before they get in."

Delaney hastily reapplied the dressing to Marianna's bedsore. Then he and Kerrigan gently lowered her back down onto the bed. Delaney threw the sheets back over her torso.

The bedroom door burst open. A middle-aged woman entered, dressed in a uniform fitting for a seamstress. She had on a pair of worn carpenter jeans and a matching denim apron. Her long dark hair, peppered with occasional strands of gray, was tied back into a conservative ponytail. Unlike Harout, her eyebrows were full and bushy. Kerrigan presumed this was Harout's mother. The look on her face made it abundantly clear she had no idea what was going on. She gasped at the sight of the strange men hovering over her daughter's bed. Harout hadn't told her. He hadn't told her anything.

The woman stared at Kerrigan and Delaney for several moments with her mouth open. Then she turned toward Harout, who was standing just behind her with his arms crossed tightly and his head bowed, and shouted at him in Armenian.

"Excuse me," Kerrigan said. He tried to flag the woman's attention. "Excuse me."

The woman stopped yelling for a moment and looked at Kerrigan. "Who are you?" Her accent was far heavier than Harout's. "What do you do here?"

Kerrigan rested his hand on his chest. "I'm Father Kerrigan. This is—"

The woman's eyes widened. "Father? Priest? You are priest?"

"Yes ma'am. Catholic." Kerrigan pulled down his overcoat at the neck so she could see his white clerical collar. He pointed at Harout. "He's your son? Harout?"

"Yes, my son. Yes." Harout's mother looked back and screamed at him again, still in Armenian. Harout stood there quietly, his hands folded behind his back. He was looking at the ground. He knew he was in trouble.

"Maybe we should go," Delaney mumbled. Kerrigan ignored him.

"Excuse me, ma'am," Kerrigan said. "If I can just explain— we're here for your daughter. It came to my attention that she is not well. Your son, he's concerned about her. He asked me to come see her."

Harout's mother looked at Kerrigan, but the expression on her face was one of confusion. It seemed she didn't understand.

"We're here to see if we can help," Kerrigan said. "My colleague here . . . he's a doctor."

Her eyes widened again. "Doctor? Doctor?"

"Yes," Kerrigan said. "To help your family. Your daughter. We want to help if we can."

"No!" she blurted. "No doctor. No money for doctor."

"No, no," Kerrigan said. "No. We don't want money." He looked at Delaney and then back to Harout's mother. "No money. No money."

She turned back toward Harout and shouted at him again, louder than before. Kerrigan watched as something in Harout snapped. Suddenly, he began to yell back at her. Moments later, the two were screaming at each other and flailing their arms.

Kerrigan tried to interject. "Harout, explain to her that we don't want money. Tell her—"

As Harout and his mother screamed at each other, Kerrigan felt someone tug on his arm. It was Delaney. "Nathan—"

Harout's mother grabbed him by the wrist and dragged him toward the kitchen. She looked back at Kerrigan. "I'm sorry. My son make big mistake. Please, you go now."

Harout protested as his mother pulled him into the kitchen. She continued to shout at him. He shouted back. Kerrigan followed cautiously. Harout and his mother screamed so loudly the dishes in the cabinets rattled.

Harout's mother leaned toward him and pointed at several religious items inside the kitchen. She pointed to a statue of the Virgin Mary resting on the shelf above the refrigerator, a crucifix hanging above the stove, and then a postcard of Jesus propped up next to a vase on the kitchen table. She leaned in even closer and pulled out from under her apron a thin, silver chain around her neck. It was a necklace with a small, religious pendant. She pulled the pendant out as far from her neck as she could without breaking the chain and held it up for Harout to see. Kerrigan couldn't understand Armenian, but he could see what she was doing. She believed they were protected by God, impenetrable.

Delaney tugged on Kerrigan's arm again. "Nathan, we should go."

Kerrigan shoved Delaney's hand away and watched Harout fight back. He yelled at his mother with everything he had. It seemed the two of them were full of raw emotion that had been bottled up for some time, and now it was all pouring out.

Harout said something that took his mother's breath away, like someone punched her in the gut. She gasped and covered her mouth with both hands. Without warning, she slapped Harout right across his face, so hard he toppled over like a falling tree. The sharp, smacking sound pierced Kerrigan's ears and reminded him of bamboo snapping in two. Shocked by what she had done, Harout's mother slowly backed away with both hands over her mouth.

Kerrigan rushed over to Harout and helped him up. He was dazed. His lip was split open. Harout's mother, her hands still over her mouth, slowly sat down at the kitchen table. She buried her face into her hands and sobbed.

Kerrigan stood there quietly. He didn't know what to do. Harout approached his mother and put his arms around her. She looked at him and placed her hand on his cheek. The two embraced each other.

Harout looked over to Kerrigan. "I'm sorry, Father."

Kerrigan waved his hand. "Don't sweat it, kid."

Delaney placed his hand on Kerrigan's shoulder. This time, Kerrigan didn't shove it away. "We should go, Nathan." Kerrigan nodded.

As Kerrigan exited the kitchen, he took one last look at Harout. Harout looked back at him, but said nothing. For reasons Kerrigan had yet to comprehend, it was more difficult to walk away than he had imagined.

He and Delaney let themselves out of the apartment. As they walked toward the exit, there was a noise behind them. Someone was fidgeting with the lock. Kerrigan turned around, hoping that Harout or his mother would come out and wave them back in, but that didn't happen. Instead someone locked the apartment up tight. Delaney continued toward the exit, but Kerrigan stood still and stared at the apartment. When Delaney noticed Kerrigan wasn't at his side, he turned around.

"Come on, Nathan. Let's go."

Kerrigan looked at Delaney and then caught up.

"Nathan, I—"

"Don't worry, Alex."

"Don't worry about what?"

"I won't ask you for anything ever again."

"That's not what I was going to say. I was—"

"Right now, Alex, I don't care what you were going to say."

CHAPTER 4

"Maybe we should head back now, Monsignor. It's getting worse out here."

Thunder cracked, and the rain began again. Only this time, the rainfall was so heavy it overwhelmed Carmichael's umbrella and flooded the trail.

"It's just a shower," Carmichael said. "It'll pass soon enough. The clouds are moving through quickly, see?"

Carmichael nodded toward a patch of gray sky showing through the trees. The clouds were moving very quickly indeed, more quickly than Kerrigan could ever recall seeing, not even when he'd been in the jungles of Vietnam. It was as if they were being driven by the breath of God.

Kerrigan, who was huddled up against Carmichael under the cover of the umbrella, searched for a way out of the rain. The strong wind blew the droplets sideways and soaked his overcoat. Kerrigan could see the same was happening to Carmichael, and he worried his elder might catch a cold.

"Over there," Kerrigan uttered. He nodded toward a patch of tall aspen trees which had grown very close together. Each of the leaves on the ashen-colored trees trembled with the wind, yet the sheer number of them formed a natural canopy.

Carmichael held on to Kerrigan's overcoat as they shuffled over to the aspen trees. The ground beneath them was wet and soggy, but the bright yellow leaves above their heads diverted enough rain and blocked enough wind that the umbrella was able to hold off the rest. It was a temporary safe haven.

"I'm very sorry about this, Monsignor. It really wasn't supposed to rain today."

"There's no need for you to be sorry. Told you that."

"I watched the news just this morning—the weatherman said it was going to be warm and sunny. He didn't say anything about rain."

Carmichael chuckled. "That's what they said."

"But you brought your umbrella."

"Just in case. The weather around here can be funny sometimes."

"Well if I had known it was going to be this bad, I wouldn't have dragged you out—"

"Nathan, I think you might be confused as to who's dragging who where."

Kerrigan looked at Carmichael and smiled. His smile was genuine, one of the first since he met Harout that Tuesday evening at Saint Michael's all those weeks earlier. Most of his smiles since then were only for show.

"Tell me how you felt after you left the boy's apartment," Carmichael asked.

A confused expression washed over Kerrigan's face. "There was nothing I could do. His mother didn't want me there. She didn't speak English, but she made it clear enough, believe me."

"That's not what I'm asking."

Just like that, the rain slowed to a mist, as if someone up in the sky closed a valve.

"Ah," Carmichael said. "You see?"

Carmichael stepped outside the cover of the umbrella and walked through the sloshy mud until he was back on the trail. Kerrigan folded the umbrella and followed, only he tiptoed so as not to soak his shoes. The two priests continued to walk deeper into the woods.

"Did you try going back?" Carmichael asked.

"Twice."

"What happened?"

"Nobody came to the door."

"Nobody home?"

Kerrigan shook his head. "No. They were home. Somebody was. We could hear them behind the door, looking through the peephole. They just didn't want us inside."

"Who's us?"

"Oh, I brought Sister Regina with me. She speaks Armenian, you know."

"Sister Regina speaks Armenian?"

"Yeah. I didn't know it either, not until a few months ago. I forget how it came up. She's got some family in Turkey."

"Interesting." Carmichael cleared his throat. "So?"

"So, what?"

"How did you feel? After you went back, and they didn't let you in."

"How was I supposed to feel? I didn't take it personally."

"That's not what I mean."

Kerrigan stopped in place. His hands trembling again, he pulled out another cigarette and lit it. He took in yet another deep drag and continued walking. "I know what you're doing, Monsignor. You know, there was a moment just before I left the apartment with Alex, when I was walking out of the kitchen. Harout . . . he looked at me after he asked us to leave and I could see in his eyes, clear as day, this . . . this deep and overwhelming sense of despair. He'd had that same look in his eyes the night he'd come to see me at the church. Even if it wasn't true, I knew right then he believed that as soon as I walked out of that apartment, all hope of saving his sister would be lost. No, I didn't feel relieved if that's what you're asking. Not at all. I felt like I was walking out on him. On her. But what was I to do? Even if there was a way Marianna could be helped, her mother wouldn't allow it. It wasn't my place to intervene behind her back."

Carmichael grabbed Kerrigan's wrist and stopped him again. "I'm not asking if you felt you did enough. And I'm not saying you didn't."

"So, what do you want from me?"

"I want to know what makes you think you'll feel any different this time."

"If I don't go through with the exorcism?"

"That's right."

Kerrigan shook his head. "You don't understand, Monsignor. This is different."

"How? Doesn't sound much different to me. From what you've told me, you weren't comfortable with this from the start, from the moment that boy found you at Saint Michael's. Wanted nothing to do with it. And lo and behold, you are given a way out. Clean. Easy. Exactly what you wanted, wasn't it?"

Kerrigan said nothing in response. He didn't know what to say. Instead he turned away from Carmichael and approached the opposite edge of the trail. There, he rested his foot on a tree stump and stared despairingly into the trees.

"And so, to me the question is simple," Carmichael continued. "What makes you think it will be different if you walk away now?"

"You don't know." Kerrigan pulled on his cigarette again. "You don't know."

"What don't I know?"

"This isn't about me. It's about the girl. What's best for her."

From behind, Carmichael placed his hand on Kerrigan's shoulder. "Is that it, Nathan? You're walking away because that's what's best for her?"

Kerrigan stormed away. He made it a few feet up the trail before he stopped and turned around. "Why, Monsignor? Why can't you just leave it alone?"

Carmichael approached slowly, thumping his cane into the earth with each step. "I'm trying to help you." He shrugged his shoulders. "Except I still don't know how."

"I already told you how."

"Nathan, won't Bishop Gailey ask these very same questions? Even tougher questions?"

Kerrigan thought for a moment and then shook his head. "I don't know. If we focus his attention elsewhere, maybe not."

Carmichael took a couple more steps forward, narrowing the distance even further. "So you want me to lie for you?"

Kerrigan's eyes widened. He felt himself blush. "No. No . . . that's not . . . I don't know. I'm just in a real bind, Monsignor, and I don't know what to do. I need your help. I know you want to help in your own way, and I respect that. I do. But please, just this once, can't you trust that I know what's best? For myself?"

Carmichael continued to approach until the two priests were at arm's length again. "Nathan, I push because I'm afraid there's a lot more riding on what you do next than you are willing to admit. Not to me, but to yourself."

"I don't know what you want me to say."

Carmichael pulled on Kerrigan's arm, turned him around, and eased him forward again. "Nothing. Let's just keep walking. When you get to my age you'll find it's even more important to keep your blood moving."

"Maybe you forget that I'm not very far behind you."

"Ah, you're strong as an ox, Nathan. Always were. Me, I'm just a sheep."

"No, you're a shepherd."

Carmichael looked at Kerrigan with a small smile, but said nothing in response. He only continued to walk straight ahead, the leaves crunching beneath his cane.

"The kid lied to me," Kerrigan said. "Never said a word to his mother about me. Never mentioned I was coming over with a doctor. You believe that?"

"Were you angry with him?"

"No. No. Not at all. He knew his mother wouldn't understand. She couldn't. But Harout, he saw. He saw his sister

90

needed help, and he did whatever it took to get it for her, even if it meant betraying his mother's trust, and mine. That couldn't have been easy for him. I know it wasn't. But that's selflessness, isn't it? That's love. How could I fault him for that?"

"Perhaps then we're not all absolutely hopeless?"

It was Kerrigan who smiled a small smile this time, and this time he, too, remained quiet and continued to walk the trail. Up ahead, he noticed the trail branched off again, this time into three directions.

"Which way, Nathan?"

Kerrigan pulled out his cellular phone and opened his navigation app. He held up the phone and waved it around.

"Nathan?"

"I don't have any service."

"So?"

"We've been going a while. We're liable to get lost."

Carmichael waved his hand dismissively. "We'll make our way back. Don't worry. Which way?"

Kerrigan let the arm holding the phone fall to his side, and let out a sigh. Reluctantly, he chose the branch of the trail furthest right. His gut told him that since they turned left the last time, going right might more or less keep them pointed in the same direction. He knew the logic was flimsy, but it was the best he could drum up at the moment.

"The boy," Carmichael said, "what was it you think he said to his mother, just before she struck him?"

"I think he told her Marianna is dying. I don't know for sure, but the look on her face when he said it . . . it was like someone punched her right in the stomach. She was waiting for a miracle, praying for one. She couldn't accept that God would allow this demon to . . . I dunno. But I think he told her Marianna is dying and my guess is this was the first time someone finally had the courage to say it to her out loud."

"I see."

"It took a while, but I'm confident she understands now. She okayed the exorcism, you know. She's on board with it."

"Have you spoken to the boy about who's doing it?"

Kerrigan looked at the ground, at the golden-brown leaves crunching beneath his feet. "No. Not yet. He's still under the impression that I'll be there."

Thunder cracked, but it sounded more distant now. A moment later, Kerrigan heard footsteps from up ahead. A young boy dressed in a yellow raincoat emerged from around a bend in the trail. A model boat was tucked safely beneath his arm. The boy was walking under the cover of an umbrella held by an older gentleman Kerrigan presumed to be his grandfather. Kerrigan took it as a sign they weren't as deep in the woods as he'd thought. He and Carmichael smiled at the passersby and kept on their way.

"Talk to me, Nathan."

"What about?"

"Why are we here? You were off the hook, nothing more to be done on your end, am I right? So, what happened? Did the boy reach out? His mother?"

Kerrigan shook his head. "No. Opposite."

"You went back?"

"After all that, I went back."

"Why?"

Kerrigan paused a moment. His hands were shaking again. He took in several more drags from his cigarette, in rapid succession. The smoke he exhaled hung low and heavy, like a low-altitude cloud. "Something happened. Something I can't explain."

"You saw something?"

"Not exactly."

* * *

"Bless me, Father, for I have sinned," said a man from the other side of the screen inside the confessional box at Saint Michael's. "I don't know how long it's been since my last confession, Father, but it's been years. Twenty years, probably. Maybe even longer than that."

Kerrigan, who had nearly dozed off on his side of the screen, took a moment to remove his reading glasses and rub his eyes. He'd been sitting in that box since his shift started. For some time now, he had been bringing reading material into the confessional to help pass the time, and it often put him to sleep. That dim and claustrophobic box had become a lonelier and lonelier place in recent years. Confession, it seemed, had gone out of fashion.

"Father?"

"Yes . . . yes, I'm here. Sorry, I was just cleaning my glasses. But please, go ahead."

"I don't even know where to start. This isn't easy for me. Tell you the truth, I didn't even want to come."

Kerrigan finished polishing his reading glasses with his sleeve and sat up straight. "Why did you?"

"I don't know, really. I guess the truth is I have no one else to talk to. Not about this. But I'll be honest with you, Father. I'm not really a religious man. I was when I was a kid, but now . . . now I find this whole idea kind of . . . you know—"

"Strange?"

"Well, yeah. Kind of. I don't mean any disrespect."

Kerrigan smiled. Though he was a priest, a devoted one, he tried not to lose perspective. Catholicism certainly had its quirks. "Well, it is sort of strange, isn't it? Talking to a stranger about your personal business, things you're not proud of. I get it. But that's kind of what makes this work. With anonymity, there's no judgment. Only forgiveness. All I'm here to do is listen and help you get there."

The man on the other side of the screen sat silent for a while. Kerrigan imagined he was deciding whether to keep going or leave. It wouldn't be the first time someone walked out in the middle of the ritual.

"I don't know, Father. I messed up. I messed up pretty good this time."

"Tell me about it, son."

The man let out a heavy, defeated sigh. Kerrigan heard him shift in his seat. "It's complicated."

"Yeah, these things usually are." Kerrigan looked down at his watch to see how close it was to the end of his shift. He still had about an hour left. "I've got time if you have."

"I'm . . . I'm a lawyer."

"That's a fine profession. I know many lawyers." The truth was Kerrigan tended to believe the opposite. He found most of the lawyers he knew to be arrogant and selfish, especially the ones who volunteered at Saint Michael's in their spare time. They had a way of butting their noses where they didn't belong and presuming they knew better about what was best for the church than the priests. Kerrigan certainly felt doctors could be that way too, but the lawyers bothered him more.

"I used to think it was, Father."

Kerrigan's ears perked. He found the man's response refreshing. "But not anymore?"

"No, not anymore. Not for a long time."

"Why not?"

The man sighed again. "I don't know. It's just . . . it's all about the almighty dollar. It's not about justice, not about what's right. It's about money. That's all it's about. We're paid to fight over money. We fight over this and we fight over that, meanwhile nobody's paying attention to the truth. The truth gets lost. Then one day you realize it was never about the truth at all."

Kerrigan paid attention to the man's voice and thought of the parishioners he knew that were lawyers. He knew he wasn't supposed to figure out who the person on the other side was, but sometimes he couldn't help it. The voice sounded vaguely familiar, but he couldn't place it.

"I see," Kerrigan said. "I imagine that when you decided to go to law school, you had something different in mind?"

"Oh yeah, absolutely. As a matter of fact, I wanted to be an assistant district attorney. I wanted to put criminals away."

"So why didn't you?"

"Money. I chose the almighty dollar, like everybody else. You see, I'm no better than the rest of 'em."

Kerrigan shifted in his seat and reorganized his legs. He noticed more and more that it was becoming increasingly difficult to remain stationary for long periods of time. His joints ached. Age was creeping up on him. "What kind of lawyer are you now, son?"

The man chuckled. "Speaking of money. I'm a tax attorney. Money's my job. I make sure people don't pay more than they have to, and I make sure they get as much back as they can. That's the long and short of it."

"So, what brings you here now?"

The man paused again, although for less time than before. "You know how attorneys at firms are paid, Father?"

"Well, I'm by no means an expert, but I imagine you're paid a salary and a bonus that fluctuates based on the hours you put in. The more money you make the firm, the more they pay you, am I right?"

"That's right. As for myself, I get a hefty bonus if I bill twenty-two hundred hours for the year. Around twenty-five percent of my salary, actually. You also get something if you hit nineteen fifty, but the percentage is smaller. I forget exactly how much smaller, but maybe it's ten or fifteen percent. Something like that."

Kerrigan looked up at the ceiling above his head. The small, dim light bulb inside the booth flickered. "Got it."

"So, every year since I started at this firm, I've always made twenty-two hundred."

"How many years has it been, son?"

"This will be my seventh year. I've always hit twenty-two. No matter what. Didn't matter if my department was slow, if I was sick, if I had a death in the family. If I fell behind for some reason, I always busted my ass at the end of the year and hit the number. Every single year."

"Except for this one?"

The man let out an uncomfortable, frustrated groan. "This year I was short. Just a couple of hours."

"How many hours are we talking?"

"My wife and I—we just had twins, Father. My wife, she didn't want to put it off anymore so we were trying for our first, and surprise! Doctor does the ultrasound and we see not just one, but two. I still can't believe it."

"Sounds like maybe you weren't too thrilled with the news, son. I imagine it must have been overwhelming at first." Kerrigan took note of the fact that the man glossed over his question about the number of hours. He learned long ago that what people don't say in the confessional box is often as important as what they do say.

"No, no. It's not that. I love them to death. I really do. I'm just . . . I'm frustrated."

"How old are your children now?"

"Ten months."

"Is that why you were a little short on your hours? Had your hands full with the kids?"

"Yes, exactly. My wife's been home, but as you can imagine she needs help. She can't do it alone. What was I supposed to do?"

"Well, I know taking care of one child is difficult enough. I imagine two's a whole different ball game. It seems perfectly understandable to me that you might be taking some personal time. More than usual."

The man scoffed. "You would think so, Father. But the partners I work for, they're bloodsucking vampires. You'd think they would cut me some slack since I had two newborns to worry about, right? Yeah, well, forget it. If anything, they worked me harder. Especially those first couple of months after the kids finally came home from the NICU—they knew my wife and I were barely keeping our heads above water, they knew we weren't getting any sleep. And instead of easing off a little they just kept the pressure on. It was constant, too. Emailing me at all hours of the night about bullshit they could have easily given to a first-year attorney. You know why? Because they figured I was up anyway. You believe that? You know they even gave me briefs to write from home, when I was officially on paternity leave? By law, they're not supposed to bother me. But they didn't care. They knew I wouldn't say no. It's like they were punishing me for having kids. Meanwhile they all have kids of their own, always bragging about who's going to NYU or Yale or whatever the fuck." The man gasped, realizing he swore in front of a priest. "Sorry, Father."

"That's alright."

"Bunch of vampires, the whole lot of 'em."

"I'm sorry to hear that, son."

"Me too, Father. Me too."

"So those hours you missed. Did you lie about them so you could still get the maximum bonus? Is that why you're here?"

The man shifted in his seat again. Then he cleared his throat. "I don't know if 'lie' is the right word."

"What's the right word?"

"It's more that I borrowed them."

"What do you mean?"

"Well, I marked them down for last year anyway and I'm making them up now, this year. But I'm not counting the hours twice, Father. I'm making them up now and then I'll bill another twenty-two hundred on top of that, so everything will be square. If you think about it, no one's really getting hurt. I'm still making the firm the same money."

Kerrigan leaned in closer to the screen. "Well, who's paying for those extra hours you charged? Don't they get billed to the client?"

"Well, yeah, that's true. But I'm giving back those hours to the client now. They won't even know the difference. That's what I'm sayin' Father. It will all be square. I'm making sure."

"I understand, son, but I think you know that doesn't make it okay. Otherwise you wouldn't be here, right? Let me ask you this—what happens if for some reason the work dries up and you can't give those hours back to the firm, or even worse, the client? Hmm? What then?"

"That's not gonna happen, Father. Believe me, there's still plenty of work to do."

"Son, that's not the point."

The man sighed again. "I know. You're right."

"You were trusted to be honest with your hours, and you betrayed that trust."

"I know, Father. I know."

"Maybe what you should have done was talk to your superiors or your partners before the year ended. Explain what was going on. Maybe they would have surprised you."

The man scoffed. "You don't know how these people think. I'm expected to keep my hours up no matter what. Doesn't matter if I have twins, doesn't matter if my mother dies, doesn't matter if I have cancer. If I went to them, sure they would smile and tell me it's okay, just kill it next year. But they would hold it against me. And come time for me to make partner, they would go back and use it as an excuse to pass me over."

Kerrigan looked up at the ceiling again. The light was steady, but he thought he heard a buzzing sound coming from the bulb. "Well, maybe this raises a bigger question. If that's the way the partners treat their associates at this firm, then maybe you don't want to be one of their partners? Have you thought about moving to another firm?"

"It's a fair point, Father, and I've thought about it. I've thought about it a lot, actually. But the truth is they're all the same. That's how these places work. It's about the dollar and nothing else. Us—we're all just cogs in the money-making machine, generating dollars one hour at a time, eighty hours a week. That's it."

"Well, I think it's great that you recognize the people you work for don't have your best interests at heart, son. I think that's very important, actually. But I don't want you to lean on their selfishness and greed as a justification for what you did. Not to mention you could get yourself in a heap of trouble. Maybe even ruin your career. Even worse, jail. And what would happen to your family then?"

"You're right, Father. You're absolutely right."

Kerrigan looked down at his watch again. "Alright. This is very good. Now, how many hours are we talking about that you borrowed? I asked before and you changed the subject."

The man said nothing. Kerrigan knew at that point that the number was substantial, more than just a few. "I ask because it will help me assign penance."

"Penance?"

"What you'll have to do after we're done here. You know, ten Our Fathers, twenty Hail Marys—"

"Oh. Yeah, right. I understand. It was about fifty hours, Father. Forty-nine, actually."

"About how much does that amount to in dollars?"

"It's about twenty-five thousand in billables. I know it's a lot, Father, but I wouldn't have done it if we didn't need the money. It's not easy with the kids. We lost my wife's salary because she's home now and we need two of everything—the diapers, the formula, clothes, the wipes . . . it all adds up. It adds up fast."

Kerrigan's brow wrinkled. He understood diapers and baby formula cost money, but something wasn't right. "So, you're having money trouble? That's why you lied about your hours?"

"Well—"

"Let me ask you a question, if you'll indulge me just a little longer. Don't you earn a good salary, even if we take the bonus out of the picture? The bonus is just a bonus, isn't it? I ask because I know a few tax attorneys myself, and they do pretty well for themselves."

"Yeah, but—"

"Now you said you borrowed fifty hours?"

"Forty-nine."

"Forty-nine. Okay. Well, if you borrowed only forty-nine hours to make twenty-two hundred hours, doesn't that mean you already hit the lower bonus number? What was it, nineteen fifty?"

"That's right, Father."

"So, you still earned yourself a bonus? Even if it wasn't the big one."

The man let out the longest and heaviest sigh he had all night. Kerrigan knew he'd struck a nerve. "Truth is I make a lot of money. My base salary is two hundred and fifty thousand, I think. Or maybe two seventy. Honestly, I forget. It goes up every year."

"So, you make so much money you can't even remember the exact amount, and you get a bonus on top of that? And you lied about your hours because you're having trouble paying for diapers and formula? Is that what you're telling me? Because I know many families who raise more kids with a lot less."

The man sat there silent again, long enough this time Kerrigan worried he might have snuck out of the confessional.

"Ah, shit," the man blurted. "God help me."

Kerrigan leaned in even closer to the screen. "Talk to me, son. Remember, I'm not here to judge you, even if that's what it sounds like I'm doing. And neither is God. I'm just trying to help you."

"I . . . uh . . . I've been gambling. Again. But this time I dug myself into a real hole."

"I see."

Kerrigan heard the man sniffle. Kerrigan thought how difficult it must be for the man to air out his demons, even if he had a screen to hide behind.

"And that bonus money," Kerrigan said. "You took it so you could gamble it?"

"I . . . I thought I could hit big. Dig myself out of this damn hole. Soon as I deposited the check, I went straight to Atlantic

City. I was up for a while, but then I lost the whole thing at the craps table. I just got caught up in it, the excitement. Got ahead of myself. It's all gone."

Kerrigan shook his head. He had heard similar stories many times before, but they never ceased to amaze him.

"I'm a shitty father," the man sobbed. "My wife hates me. I wouldn't be surprised if she takes the kids and leaves, before I clean us out completely. I don't know what to do, Father."

"The first thing you're going to do is say the Act of Contrition."

"I don't know it."

"That's alright. Nobody does anymore. If you look to your left, next to the screen, there's a white card. It's hanging by a brown string. You see it?"

Kerrigan heard the man shuffle around.

"I got it."

"Good. Now read the prayer out loud."

"Oh my God . . . ." The man cleared his throat again. "I am heartily sorry for having offended Thee, sorry Thee, offended Thee, and I detest all my sins because of Thy punishments . . . but most of all because they offend Thee, my God, who art good and deserving of my love. I firmly resolve . . . with the help of Thy grace, to sin no more, and to avoid the near occasion of sin."

Kerrigan nodded approvingly. "That's good, son. That's good. Here's what else you are going to do. First, you are going to pray three decades of the rosary a day for the next thirty days."

"Decades?"

"You can look it up when you get home, but pick up a set of rosary beads if you don't already have one. Second, and more importantly, you're going to get yourself some help."

"Help? What do you mean, like a group or something?"

"I mean treatment. Whether it's a group or something else. I can refer you to a program or you can find one yourself. There are plenty out there."

"All due respect, Father, I don't think that's necessary. I'll get it under control. I've stopped before. It just got away from me a little this time."

Kerrigan shook his head. He'd heard this all before, many times.

"Son, how long have you been gambling?"

"I dunno. A long time. Since I was a kid, I guess. Bet on everything, checkers, monopoly, rummy. It makes the games more interesting. But I always had it under control. These past few years, the stress, the job, my wife. It got away from me a little bit, but I got it. I'm done."

"How long have you been married?"

"We make six years next month, if she doesn't divorce me before then."

"Well if you don't want that to happen, then you're going to get yourself some help. Do you understand me?"

"Father, I appreciate what you're saying, but I'm good. I don't need—"

"Listen to me," Kerrigan insisted. "If you could do it on your own, you would have done it already. You would have done it six years ago when you got married. You would have done it when

104

you found out you were expecting twins. You would have done it when they were born. But you didn't. Because you can't. Not by yourself. It's that simple. Believe me, I've been there."

"What, you gamble too?" The man sounded shocked. Kerrigan got that a lot—despite all the controversy surrounding the Catholic church, some people still seemed to think priests were infallible. But they weren't. Far from it.

"No, not gambling. My vice is cigarettes. Picked up the habit during the war, smoked them for years. For a while I was smoking three, four packs a day, like a chimney. It's a wonder I don't have lung cancer." Kerrigan knocked on one of the wooden panels lining the confessional booth. "Not yet at least, far as I know."

"Which war, Father?"

"Vietnam."

"You served in Vietnam?"

"Sure did, son. As a combat medic. I was there three years. Had my first smoke there. Thought I would leave the habit in Vietnam, but it only got worse when I was home. I tried kicking it on and off again, but I never lasted long. I'd stop for a week, maybe two, maybe even three . . . and then the cravings would come, and before I knew it I was back to burning through three packs. You know why I couldn't quit?"

"You were doing it alone."

Kerrigan nodded. "That's right. Like you, I didn't need help, didn't need those silly support groups or anything else."

"But you kicked it?"

"I wouldn't go that far, but I was able to put them away, at first just for a little while. But then days turned into weeks, weeks turned into months, months turned into years. I had some slip-ups. But you wanna know how I did it? I joined one of those silly groups, went with a dear friend of mine, and we quit together. That was twenty years ago."

"And you haven't had a cigarette since?"

"No. Not one. Oh, I wanted to. Came close more than a couple of times. But God-willing I was able to put them down."

Kerrigan heard the man sniffle, pull out a tissue or a handkerchief, and blow his nose. "I don't know. I don't know if I can do it. I don't know if I'm strong enough."

"Son, now you listen to me. Alright? You've got two small children at home, right? What are their names?"

"Brian and Carla."

"A boy and girl. How wonderful. You're going to do it for Brian and Carla, for your wife, and for your marriage. You're going to do it because your family is counting on you now. And you're going to get this under control now, before your children grow up in a broken home, before you gamble away the house or the college money. And before you go to jail. Because you've already stolen at least once to support this habit, haven't you? What's next? Huh? You hear me, son?"

"Yes . . . I do. I do, Father."

"Well, alright. Is there anything else you'd like to confess?"

"No. That's it."

"Alright, son. Now I will grant you absolution. God, the Father of mercies, through the death and resurrection of his Son has reconciled the world to himself and sent the Holy Spirit among us for the forgiveness of sins. Through the ministry of the Church may God give you pardon and peace, and I absolve you from your sins." Kerrigan made a sign of the cross. "In the name of the Father, and of the Son, and of the Holy Spirit."

"Thank you, Father."

Father Kerrigan waited until the man left the confessional, then let out an exhausted moan. "Yeah right, Kerrigan," he whispered to himself. "Who the hell are you? Who the hell are you?"

* * *

Kerrigan, dozing inside the confessional with his book in his lap, was startled awake by a buzzing sound above his head. The small light fixture inside the confessional booth was flickering again. Kerrigan reached for his reading glasses and put them back on. He looked down at his watch. It was a quarter after seven—his shift in the confessional had ended fifteen minutes earlier. He was anxious to get back to the rectory and try to relax for a change. Maybe even switch on Jeopardy.

The light bulb buzzed even louder. The flicker worsened. Though Kerrigan was in no mood to investigate, he knew he couldn't leave the light the way it was and risk burning the church to the ground. He climbed up on the small bench inside the booth and tried to figure out how to dissemble the fixture so he could access the bulb inside. The ceiling was so low he had to tilt his head.

Kerrigan tried tapping on the fixture first, but that only made matters worse. With each tap the flicker intensified. The flashing light created a strobe effect inside the box, casting slow motion shadows on the walls.

"What the hell?" Kerrigan muttered. He couldn't figure out how to remove the plastic fixture encasing the bulb. He bent his neck even more so he could get a closer look. With half of his face pressed against the ceiling, the buzzing suddenly surged and the bulb lit up so bright it blinded him. At that very moment, something inside the church slammed violently. Kerrigan was startled so badly he banged his head against the low ceiling and nearly fell off the seat. Once he was back on firm ground, the light fixture stopped flickering and went back to normal. Just like that.

Kerrigan groaned. He rubbed the painful lump forming on the top of his head. He stepped through the curtain separating the confessional booth from the rest of Saint Michael's and looked around to see where the noise came from. It sounded like someone dropped a heavy book on the floor or let the door slam again. The handyman still hadn't gotten to it. But the church was empty as far as Kerrigan could see. Tired and irritated, he rubbed the lump on his head again and leaned back into the confessional for his book.

Someone giggled from the other side. The light flickered again.

"Jesus!" Kerrigan cried out. He dropped his book to the floor. His heart in his throat, he stepped back into the booth and took a moment to catch his breath. He picked up his book and looked toward the screen. "Hello?"

There was no response. Kerrigan could just barely make out a rough silhouette through the screen.

"Hello? Is someone there?"

Still no response. Only a barely perceptible giggle, so faint Kerrigan wasn't even sure he heard it. "Look. It's getting late, and I—"

"I'm right here, Father," a young, proud voice proclaimed. It was the voice of a young girl, no older than seven or eight by

Kerrigan's estimation. Kerrigan sat back down and rested his book in his lap.

"Hi there," Kerrigan said. "Are you here to make a confession?" Kerrigan looked down at his watch again. It was a very strange hour for a girl that young to be there in the church, all alone. He wondered if her parents were waiting outside.

The girl said nothing in response. Instead she hummed.

"Hmm, hmm, hmmmmm, hmm, hmm, hmm, hmmm . . . ."

"Excuse me—"

"Hmm, hmm, hmmmmmmmm, hmm, hmm hmm!"

"Excuse me, young lady?"

She continued to hum. Kerrigan was getting annoyed. He was already irritated as it was, and he was certainly in no mood to deal with a misbehaving child. Especially not after his time in the box was done.

"Excuse me!" Kerrigan said more forcefully. The girl finally quieted. "Are you here to make a confession? Because if you aren't—"

"I am."

"You are? Okay then." Kerrigan looked down at his watch again. If only he hadn't dozed off, he thought. He might be back at the rectory already, with his legs propped up on his recliner. "How long has it been since your last confession?"

"I dunno."

"Was it a long time ago?"

"I think so. I . . . I dunno."

Kerrigan didn't appreciate the girl's tone. It seemed playful, aloof. She wasn't taking this seriously. "More than a year?"

"I said I dunno."

Kerrigan shook his head. He wondered now if this was a prank, a young girl acting out on a dare, her friends hiding outside. "What's on your mind, young lady?"

"I dunno."

"Young lady, please. It's late, and I've had—"

"Lots of things."

Kerrigan paused a moment. "Lots of things are on your mind?"

"Uh huh."

"What kinds of things?"

"My mom says my mind wanders sometimes. She says it likes to wander off."

Kerrigan rubbed the lump on his head again. It was beginning to itch. "I see. Well, that's understandable. A young lady like yourself has a lot to think about, especially these days. What about your sins? Have you been thinking about those?"

"Sometimes I don't like where it goes."

"Sometimes you don't like where what goes? Your mind?"

"Mm-hmmmmmmm."

Kerrigan peered into the screen. Still, all he could see was a faint silhouette. "Where does it go?"

"Bad places."

Kerrigan leaned back against the wall behind him and took a moment. Though the exchange was making him uneasy, he felt compelled to see where it went. "Can you give me an example?"

The girl stopped talking again. Kerrigan heard her breathing through the screen. "Are you there, young lady? Young lady?"

"I'm here."

"You seem very distracted. Can you try to focus for a minute? If you stay with me, I promise you we can finish in no time. That's what you want, isn't it?"

"I dunno."

"Come on, now. You came here for a reason, didn't you? Did you want to talk about something? Hmm? Did you do something maybe you knew was wrong and now you feel bad about it? It happens to all of us, you know."

"Hmm," the girl uttered. Her voice trailed off. "No. Not really."

Kerrigan shook his head again. She was testing his patience. "Are your parents out there waiting for you?"

"No."

"Your mom or dad isn't waiting for you outside?"

"I said no."

Kerrigan quietly peeled back the curtain on his side of the booth and peered out into the pews just outside. They were empty. "Alright, okay. Well, if mom and dad aren't here, how did you get here? How are you getting home?"

"I dunno."

"Do you know where your parents are? Do they know where you are? Maybe we should give them a call so they don't worry."

More silence, but the girl was still there. Her breathing seemed heavier than before.

"Young lady?"

"It's okay, Father. They're not worried. Nobody worries about me."

"Well now, are you sure about that? Don't you think mom and dad might be wondering where you are right now if they don't know?"

"No," the girl said, curtly. "Hmm, hmm, hmmmmm, hmmmmm, hmmm, hmmmm . . . ."

Kerrigan felt even more uneasy. Something was off. "Please, young lady, this isn't the place for horsing around. We're in God's house. We need to be respectful."

"Then why are you here?" the girl whispered. Her voice sounded far off, distant. Like the giggling before, Kerrigan wasn't even certain he heard it at all. Still, a cold shiver ran down his spine.

"Excuse me?"

"Hmm, hmm, hmmmmm, hmmmmm, hmm, hmm . . . hmm!"

"Excuse me, young lady . . . did you say something?"

"No."

"Are you sure? I thought I heard you say something."

"I say bad things sometimes. My mom says it's okay because everyone does."

"Well, your mother is absolutely right. We all say and do bad things sometimes, and that's okay as long as we are sorry and try not to do them again. Is that why you came here today, because you are sorry for some of the bad things you said?"

"Nooooooo."

"No, that's not why you came?"

"I'm not sorry."

Another cold shudder ran down Kerrigan's back. This isn't real, he told himself. This was a teenager acting out on a dare. Had to be. "Why aren't you sorry?"

More silence, other than the girl's heavy breaths. They were so heavy now it sounded more like there was a very large man on the other side of the screen.

"Young lady? Stay with me. Why aren't you sorry?"

She whispered into the screen: "Because he won't let me."

The hair on Kerrigan's neck and arms stood on end. "Who won't let you? Your father?"

No response.

"You can tell me. Everything you say in here is a secret. Between you and me."

"Do you like secrets, Father?"

"Me? No. Not really. It's not good to keep too many secrets, even though sometimes we have to."

"Why?"

"Well, sometimes secrets can be a good thing. Sometimes knowing someone will keep a secret makes it easier to talk about things we don't feel comfortable talking about. That's how confession works, you know. Whatever you tell me stays with me. I'm not allowed to tell anybody else. And even if you never tell anyone else what you tell me, God will still forgive you."

"Maybe we should switch sides."

Kerrigan's brow wrinkled. He didn't understand. "Switch sides? Why would we switch sides?"

"So, you can tell me some of your secrets. I hear you have a really big one."

Kerrigan shot up onto his feet like his seat was on fire. He felt queasy and had to swallow hard. "What did you say? Young lady? Who told you that? Huh? Who told you that?"

"I can tell you about some of the bad things I did now."

It was Kerrigan who remained silent this time. He couldn't keep up with the thoughts racing through his mind.

"Hello! Anybody home, Father?"

Kerrigan slowly sat back down. "Yes. Why don't you tell me about the bad things?"

"I hurt people sometimes."

"How do you hurt people?"

"Depends."

"On what?"

"Who I'm tryin' to hurt."

Kerrigan crossed his arms. He suddenly felt cold. "I see. Why don't you give me an example?"

"Hmm, okay."

Kerrigan thought he heard somebody whisper on the other side of the screen again, a voice different from the girl's. It sounded almost as if she was consulting with someone. "Did you say something?"

"No, but I'm ready to tell you a secret now."

"Go ahead."

"Okay . . . so, there's this teacher at my school."

"Okay . . . ."

"She gave me a bad grade on my history project because she doesn't like me."

"Hmm," Kerrigan said. "I see. Well, how do you know she gave you a bad grade because she doesn't like you? Is it possible you didn't do your best work?"

"Cuz—she gave my friend Sissy an A plus, and my poster board was ten times better than hers. And everyone else got at least a B minus, and mine was better than all of theirs, too. I'm the only one who got a C minus. See?"

"I suppose. So, what happened after your teacher gave you the C minus?"

"I got her back."

Kerrigan leaned toward the screen. "Got her back?"

"Oh yeah. I got her good."

"What did you do?"

"I watched her get in her car after school one day."

"Why?"

The girl laughed heartily. "So I could figure out which was hers, silly."

"And then?"

She laughed again. "I stuck a knife in her tires when nobody was looking. I stole the knife from my mom's kitchen. She didn't even, like, notice it was gone."

Kerrigan's eyes bulged. Though what she said shocked him, he couldn't help but believe she was speaking the truth. Somehow, she seemed capable of such an act. "How many tires did you cut?"

"All of them."

"Oh my. Oh my. That's a terrible thing to do, young lady. A very terrible thing. You realize that, don't you?"

The girl sighed noisily. "Why? She started it."

"Well, first of all, your teacher, just like any other teacher, has a job to do. Sometimes that involves giving some students A pluses and others C minuses, because their work isn't as good."

"My poster board was perfect."

"Okay, fine. But even if we assume, for argument's sake, that your teacher really did give you the C minus because she doesn't like you, that still doesn't make it okay for you to do what you did. I can tell you are a smart young lady. I think you know that."

"It's just tires," the girl whined. She sounded annoyed. "She can get new ones."

"Tires are very expensive. I'm sure your teacher works very hard for her money. She has bills to pay, just like everyone else. She may even have kids of her own to take care of, kids who need food and clothes. Just like you. These things cost money. You might not understand this yet, but one day you'll be old enough to go out and get yourself a job, and then you'll see how hard you have to work for money. How did you get it in your mind to do such a thing, hmm?"

The girl clammed up again.

"Young lady?"

"I'm not allowed to say."

"Why aren't you allowed to say? Did someone put you up to it?"

"I'm not allowed to say."

"Who says you're not allowed—"

"I hurt Sissy, too."

Kerrigan scratched his head again. The lump felt hot to the touch now, and it was painful again. Not itchy. "I thought you said Sissy was your friend?"

"She is, but she's such a goodie two-shoes sometimes. The instructions didn't say we had to make our poster boards 3D, but she went ahead and made hers 3D because she loves to show off in front of everyone. It's only because her daddy's an engineer, and he helped her. And she still got extra credit even though everyone knows she didn't do it by herself."

Kerrigan pulled out one of his handkerchiefs and wiped his brow. He felt flushed all of a sudden. "What did you do to Sissy?"

"One night, after gymnastics, I snuck back into our classroom and ripped up her poster board. It was the night before the project fair and she was really excited to show it off, but she couldn't because it was in like a bazillion pieces."

The girl let out a satisfied chuckle. She was enjoying this.

"It's not very funny, young lady. It's not very funny at all. I have to be honest with you, these are some really terrible things you did. I'm afraid your act of penance has to be fairly serious. Is there anything else you think you should tell me?"

Kerrigan thought he heard whispering again. More than one voice. "Are you talking to someone in there, young lady? Is someone in there with you?"

"No."

"Is there anything else you wanna tell me?"

"I said no."

"Are you sure? You're here now. This is your chance to get everything off of your chest. Start off fresh."

She said nothing.

"Alright, I think it's time we say the Act of Contrition then. Do you remember it, young lady? Young lady?"

"What?"

"The act of contrition—do you remember it?"

"No."

"Alright, that's okay. If you don't know it by heart you can read it. There's a card hanging—"

"I don't feel like it."

"Young lady . . . it's very important you say the Act of Contrition. It's how we show God we're sorry for the things we've done. If we don't show God we're sorry, then he might not forgive us. You don't want that, do you?"

The girl was quiet, but Kerrigan wasn't ready to give up on her. Something deep inside him told him he needed to see her through the confession, release her from her sins. It was his duty as a priest.

"We can do it together," Kerrigan said. "All you have to do is repeat after me."

"I said no!" The girl's swelling voice echoed through the church.

"Why not?"

The girl suddenly began to weep. "I . . . I can't."

Kerrigan felt another chill pass through his body, but he soon felt warm again. Too warm. More sweat formed on his brow. He loosened his clerical collar for some relief. "Sure you can."

"I . . . I have to go now. Before—"

"Before what?"

"I gotta go."

"Wait just a second!" Kerrigan pleaded. "Let me just recite the prayer of absolution so God can forgive you your sins. It'll just take a second."

"I . . . don't . . . want . . . it!"

"Okay. Alright. I hear you. Loud and clear. How about a quick blessing then. It'll only take a second. Yeah?"

She said nothing again. She only groaned through the screen. She sounded very agitated. Kerrigan considered letting her go. It wasn't his place to force people, only to guide them through the process. But something told him not to let her go without completing the sacrament, as if her soul depended on it. Kerrigan decided to recite the absolution in Latin and slip it by her. It wasn't by the book, but it was probably better than nothing.

"Alright, here we go." Kerrigan made the sign of the cross. "In the name of the Father, and of the Son, and of the Holy Spirit." Kerrigan bowed his head and drew from his memory. It had been a while since he said any prayer in Latin, let alone the prayer of absolution. "Deus, Pater misericordiárum, qui per mortem et ressurectiónem—"

"DON'T YOU TRY THAT SHIT WITH ME, PRIEST!" the girl howled through the screen, so loud and ferocious Kerrigan's bones rattled like a locomotive had just thundered by. The sound was more animal than human, a piercing, guttural shriek no young girl could possibly have made, even with drugs or powerful stimulants. This was something else.

Kerrigan was frightened so badly he leaped out of his seat and slammed his head against the light fixture again, shattering the plastic shell encasing the bulb into dozens of pieces. The light went out, and Kerrigan was left in darkness. The girl was still inside the booth, breathing, huffing and puffing now, like an animal through a snout.

Then she burst out of the confessional and ran out of the church, her heavy, thumping footsteps echoing behind her. Kerrigan heard the doors slam. She was gone.

Kerrigan, still in darkness, his back against the wall of the confessional opposite the screen, could barely breathe. His heart pounded in his chest like a mallet against a drum. Not since his days in Vietnam, when bombs and bullets struck down men standing right next to him, had he felt so vulnerable and afraid.

Something outside the confessional squealed like a rusty playground swing swaying aimlessly on a cold winter day. A few moments later, when Kerrigan worked up the courage to stick his head out of the curtain sealing off the confessional, he saw the ornate byzantine lamps just outside swaying back and forth.

CHAPTER 5

Kerrigan, staring down at a patch of cockles growing along the trail, pulled in deep, heavy drags from yet another Marlboro Red. The hand he used to hold the butt of the cigarette trembled so violently ashes sprinkled into the damp earth below. Although Kerrigan didn't realize it, the cigarette was barely the length of the matchstick he used to light it.

Carmichael was standing just behind Kerrigan. He gave Kerrigan a moment to gather himself after telling his frightening story. But now he tried to get Kerrigan's attention. "Nathan."

Kerrigan failed to respond. He continued to look down into the cockles, pulling on his cigarette.

"Nathan!"

Kerrigan took another drag and coughed. He dropped the cigarette butt and continued to cough violently into his elbow.

"I was trying to tell you," Carmichael said. "You're not supposed to smoke the filter."

Kerrigan leaned against a nearby oak tree until his coughing fit ran its course. Once it settled, he hacked up a mouthful of phlegm, cocked his head back, and spat the wad of sputum out into the cockles. Carmichael grimaced at the sight.

"Are you alright?"

Kerrigan nodded. "Yeah, I'm fine. I'm sorry about this, Monsignor."

"Sorry about what?"

"I shouldn't be smoking around you."

Carmichael scoffed. "Never mind that."

"No, I mean it." Kerrigan wiped a string of spit dangling from his chin. "I know you went through hell to quit."

"We both did. Forget it, kid. Come on." Carmichael grasped Kerrigan's arm and tugged him away from the cockles. "Let's go. We can watch the weeds grow another time, hmm? When the weather's better."

Kerrigan followed Carmichael's lead. By then, he'd given up trying to convince the Monsignor they should turn back.

"This girl," Carmichael said. "Whatever it was on the other side of that screen. Did you find out who she was?"

"No. I tried to, though. I asked around, checked with some of the policemen I know from the church. Asked them if they heard anything about a tire slashing at one of the schools. Nobody knew anything. So, either this girl isn't from around here, or . . . ."

"She made it up."

Kerrigan looked at Carmichael and shrugged. "I don't know, Monsignor. That's quite a yarn for a young girl to spin, isn't it?"

"Yes. Yes, it is."

"It didn't sound like she was lying, I can tell you that."

Kerrigan gazed down at the trail beneath their feet. Though the rain had quit for the moment, the wind picked up, swirling the leaves on the ground. When Kerrigan looked back up, he noticed more of the black birds he spotted earlier. They were taking refuge in some of the trees lining the trail. They were quiet, watchful.

"Surely, you don't suspect it was the Armenian girl who came to visit you in the confessional?"

Kerrigan shook his head. "I don't know. I mean, how could she? She hasn't moved or spoken in years. No, this was something else. Something else entirely."

"So why did you go back?"

"Go back where?"

"To the Armenian girl. Why did you go back to her?"

Kerrigan stopped in place. "I don't understand. What are you asking?"

"You said you went back to her because of what happened in the confessional."

"That's right."

Carmichael cleared his throat. His voice scratched slightly. "Well, if you didn't think it was the Armenian girl who came to see you at the church that night, what made you go back to her?"

"Come on, Monsignor. You don't really think this was a coincidence?"

"I'm just wondering what one has to do with the other. It's not clear to me, Nathan."

Kerrigan sighed. "You weren't there. You didn't hear what I heard. The church shook, Monsignor. The lamps twenty feet above my head were swinging back and forth like there was an earthquake or some . . . some bomb went off. Whatever it was, it was powerful, and it was bold. Waltzed right into a house of God, into the confessional booth, and mocked our most sacred sacrament. Like it was nothing. I haven't been back since. I keep telling the guys I have a stomach flu."

"Nathan, I understand something came to see you that night in the confessional booth. Something sinister. But what does it have to do with the Armenian girl?"

"Can't you see it?"

"Explain it to me."

Kerrigan shifted on his feet. He opened his mouth to speak but then closed it. He was tongue-tied again. "Well . . . I . . . that's how I knew that this . . . this could be real. That there really is something evil out there."

Carmichael shook his head, disapprovingly.

"What?"

"Come on, Nathan. There's surely more to it than that. Isn't there?"

Kerrigan looked down at the ground. He tried to look back up at Carmichael, into his green-blue eyes, but couldn't. Instead he retreated to the opposite edge of the trail and lit another cigarette as he looked out into the trees.

"Nathan?"

"Yeah?"

"What that girl said about switching sides. About secrets. Those weren't just off-handed remarks, were they?"

Kerrigan took a heavy drag from his cigarette. Rather than exhale immediately, he pulled the smoke deep into his lungs and let it linger for a while. "I don't know, Monsignor. Don't we all have secrets?"

"Well, yes. Of course. We've all got our peccadillos. But secrets . . . they're the same as lies, Nathan. You know that. Okay in small doses, necessary on occasion. But like those weeds back there—let them grow out of control and they'll just destroy everything else that's good."

"I know. I know."

Carmichael stepped toward Kerrigan. "Then why won't you talk to me? Of all people, after all these years, all we've been through, by God, you should know you can talk to me. Whatever it is. I've nothing but love for you."

Kerrigan, still facing the trees, fought back tears. Despite his effort, a single tear formed and rolled down his cheek. He could hear Carmichael breathing behind him.

"You know," Carmichael said. "That man, whose confession you heard, just before that girl came to see you. I'm afraid that's you right now. Sharing what you're comfortable with and leaving the rest for another time. But what good would it have done if that man had never mentioned his gambling problem? Hmm? What good would it have done him? His family? What good would it have done anybody?"

Kerrigan wept. He couldn't hold it back any longer. His cigarette, still burning, fell to the ground. "I don't know how I let it come to this. I just don't know how I let it come to this."

Carmichael whispered just behind Kerrigan. "Talk to me, Nathan. I'm right here."

"I can't."

"Why not?"

"I don't know." Kerrigan wiped his nose with his white handkerchief. "I . . . I'm scared."

125

Kerrigan expected a response, but there was nothing. Only silence. "Monsignor?"

Kerrigan turned around and saw that he was alone. He felt his heart skip a beat. He quickly looked both ways, searching desperately for his mentor, but saw nothing. Carmichael was nowhere to be found. "Monsignor? Monsignor?"

"Come on!" Carmichael hollered from a distance. Kerrigan saw Carmichael several yards ahead, disappearing into a light fog. He seemed to be moving at a rather brisk pace.

"Where are you going?"

"There's roses! Red roses! Come on, Nathan!"

Kerrigan whispered to himself. "Red roses?" Carmichael was no longer in sight. "Wait! I'm coming! I'm coming!"

* * *

Kerrigan had to round several bends in the trail before he spotted Carmichael in front of a rosebush, and when he arrived he was out of breath and wheezing. He came to a stop just behind the monsignor, hunched over with his hands pressed against his thighs for support. Carmichael was busy admiring the flowers, which were so red it looked like someone dipped their petals in crimson-colored paint. He picked one of the flowers and brought it up to his nose.

"Roses . . . in the middle of the woods?" Kerrigan muttered, between heavy breaths. He was still collecting his breath. He'd never seen a wild rosebush before.

"Can you smell them, Nathan?"

Kerrigan shook his head. "I can't even breathe."

Carmichael looked at Kerrigan and grinned. His eyes had a lively glow to them.

"Don't you . . . don't you have mass later?" Kerrigan asked.

Carmichael ignored Kerrigan. He took another moment to smell the rose he'd picked. "Beautiful, aren't they?"

"Yeah, sure. I've never been much of a flower guy."

Carmichael grinned again. "They remind me of my mother and father. My mother adored red roses. My father, the hopeless romantic he was, he brought them home when he knew she was angry with him."

Having caught his breath, Kerrigan stood up slowly. He recalled what little Carmichael had said about his parents over the years. Although Carmichael rarely spoke of them, Kerrigan knew they'd died protecting him from the Nazis when they had occupied Poland. Carmichael's father, a Scottish merchant, had moved his family to Poland in pursuit of a business opportunity a year or two before Hitler and Stalin invaded the country. After the Nazis landed, Carmichael's parents arranged for him to be smuggled safely back to Scotland but were captured before they could escape. Carmichael learned many years later that his mother and father were executed in the middle of the street by a pair of German soldiers, beaten and then shot to death while friends and strangers watched helplessly from balconies and rooftops.

"Your parents . . . to tell you the truth, I almost forgot . . . you never really—"

"For years I wished I could forget." Carmichael turned toward Kerrigan and rested his hands on his cane. He was still holding the rose.

"To spare yourself pain?"

"I didn't see them die, Nathan. Not in the flesh. I was always grateful for that. But I saw it in other ways."

Several birds cawed, the sounds echoing through the woods. Kerrigan noticed a growing number of black birds in the trees along the trail. They were agitated, like something was stirring them. The birds were all around them.

"Did you blame God?"

"In those days, Nathan, I wasn't sure there was one."

"I didn't know that."

"These were frightening times, desperate times. People just about everywhere were beginning to wonder where the hell He was. Why He didn't just strike those lunatics down with bolts of lightning or heart attacks or whatever. It was only natural. The world was falling apart."

Kerrigan crossed his arms. He listened intently. He couldn't recall the last time Carmichael was so forthcoming about his personal life. When it came to such matters, Carmichael had always been a man of few words.

"What about you?" Kerrigan asked.

"I didn't know what to think. What I did know was that my parents were murdered in cold blood by two men, two human beings. Men who walked the earth, breathed the same air we're breathing now. Men with hearts, minds, consciences. I blamed them. Hated them as a matter of fact. Not just for murdering my mother and father, but for everything. For ruining my life."

"So, what happened?"

"For years, nothing. I went nowhere, did nothing except wallow in my own grief and self-pity. And then one day . . . one day the most amazing thing happened."

Carmichael handed Kerrigan the red rose. Kerrigan gazed down at the flower, unsure what he was supposed to do with it. He decided to hold it at his side. Carmichael gently wrapped his free arm around Kerrigan and eased him forward again.

"I was living on the streets of Aberdeen. Had been for months. This one hot summer day—scorching hot, Nathan, so bad they were finding people dead in the street. I managed to scrounge up enough money, begging, to buy myself a pint of beer—"

"Begging?"

"That's right. I was an alcoholic. Homeless. On the streets. Lost. Alone. Had been that way for years by then."

"I had no idea."

"That's because I never told you. Haven't told anyone. Had no reason to until now. Anyway, I walked into a bar with my cup full of coins and ordered a nice, cold beer. When it came, I sat there drinking in silence, staring down at the bar top, feeling sorry for myself. As usual. Then this man with a slick haircut, a sharp business suit, and a briefcase takes the seat right next to me, orders a beer of his own. Didn't take him long to realize I was living on the streets. Probably smelled it. Anyway, he took a good look at me and he asks, 'What the hell's wrong with you?' In Polish. I told him what happened to my mother and father in Poland, how those . . . those bastards ruined my life. He gulped down his beer and pulled out this black and white photograph from his wallet. It was a family—they were smiling together in front of a church. Looked like they were celebrating a first communion or a confirmation maybe. He pointed to one of the small boys in the photograph and said it was him. Said he was the only one left."

Kerrigan twisted the stem of the rose between his fingers. "It was his family?"

"He told me he was also in Poland during the occupation. Wasn't home when the Nazis brought his family in. His father had sent him out for bread and eggs. He came home with the bag of groceries in his hands, found the door broken down, the apartment in shambles, his family gone. And he never saw them again."

"My God."

"I asked him. I said, 'look at you. You're successful. You've made it. Made a life for yourself. How did you do it?' You know what he said?"

Kerrigan shook his head. "No."

"He said, 'I forgave them. I forgave them.' Like it was nothing. Now me, I shook my head, dismayed. Couldn't believe it. Found the idea preposterous, as a matter of fact. 'They don't deserve to be forgiven,' I said. 'They killed your family, our families, in cold blood, for no reason other than they were born somewhere else.' He said, 'the hell with what they deserve or don't deserve. I did it for me, and you should too.' He slid over a hundred pounds, winked at me, and left. I never saw him again. Never even got his name. What I realized years later, Nathan, was that if it weren't for that man, I never would have made it. Never would have found my way back to God. If it weren't for him, I certainly wouldn't be standing with you here, now."

"You forgave those men?"

"Not right away. It took some time, some doing. But eventually I grew tired of spending every waking moment consumed with this terrible anger. This hatred, this resentment.

Tired of spending my days dreaming about the life I should have had, the one I deserved. Tired of not being able to go anywhere or do anything without swallowing a pint of whiskey first. I realized, Nathan, that I was wasting the very life my mother and father died saving. And that if I was going to try to start living a life worthy of their sacrifice, then by God I had to let go of all that anger and self-pity. It was just like the man said, forgiving those men was as much for me as it was for them."

As Kerrigan considered Carmichael's story, the black birds suddenly cawed all at once, as if to warn of an approaching predator. Kerrigan looked around to see what might be agitating the birds, but he saw nothing, only birds—many more than before. The birds got so loud Kerrigan and Carmichael stopped to investigate.

"What's got them so riled up?" Kerrigan asked.

"I don't know."

"What are they, ravens?"

"Nah." Carmichael was looking up at the trees. "They're crows. Black crows. Maybe there's a fledgling on the ground somewhere—"

"Look out!"

One of the crows dove out of its tree like a suicide bomber and streaked toward the priests, passing them so closely Kerrigan felt a cool rush of air blow across his face. He ducked to avoid being struck.

Just as quickly as the first, another crow swooped out of the trees and clipped Carmichael's ear. Kerrigan saw a drop of blood fall to the ground. Before they could react, birds were attacking from all directions.

"Come on!" Kerrigan hollered. He clutched Carmichael's arm and pulled him forward, but Carmichael could only move so quickly. The birds continued their assault. It seemed they were focused more on Carmichael, aiming for him. Kerrigan tried to swat at the birds and keep them away.

"What the hell is wrong with these birds?" Kerrigan cried out.

Carmichael lost his footing and fell to his knee. He moaned with pain. Kerrigan knelt down next to him, so he could help him back onto his feet.

Kerrigan shouted over the deafening roar of the birds: "Are you alright?"Carmichael nodded. With Kerrigan's assistance, he leaned into his cane and stood back up. Together, the two priests scurried down the trail until they were free from the assault. When they were, they took a moment to catch their breath and stared back toward the birds.

"What the hell was that?"Kerrigan asked. He was wheezing, bent over again with his hands on his knees. He was more out of shape than he'd realized, and he couldn't help but wonder whether the cigarettes were at least partly to blame. Carmichael, who was several years older, seemed to be breathing just fine.

"Your ear," Kerrigan said.

Carmichael reached for his right ear.

"No, the other one."

Carmichael touched his left ear and looked at Kerrigan blankly. He shrugged his shoulders. "What about it?"

"You're bleeding. One of the birds got your ear."

Carmichael touched his ear again and looked at his hand. There was no blood. "I'm alright, Nathan. Don't worry."

"What the hell got into them?"

"Worms. Look." Carmichael lifted his cane and pointed it toward the ground beneath the trees. Hundreds of those black crows were on the ground now, digging at the dirt with their beaks. Kerrigan needed to squint to see them, but Carmichael was right—the ground was writhing with earthworms. Hundreds, if not thousands of them. The heavy rain had brought them up from the soil.

"I've never seen so many worms in my life," Kerrigan uttered.

"I've never seen so many birds."

Kerrigan smiled. He was still hunched over, wheezing. "Neither have I." Carmichael approached Kerrigan and extended his hand. When Kerrigan took it, Carmichael helped him stand up straight. Despite his appearance, Carmichael was surprisingly strong. It seemed he still had some of that fighter's spirit left in him.

Several birds shrieked behind the two priests, startling them. When they turned toward the sound, they saw two of the birds fighting over a large earthworm, each with an opposite end in their beak. Hundreds of others were still picking at the ground.

"How about we get a little farther away from these damn birds?" Carmichael asked.

"Amen."

With that, the two priests continued to walk the trail, leaving the birds and the worms they were eating behind them. And for a little while, all they did was walk.

"So now what?" Kerrigan eventually asked.

"You were going to tell me what happened when you went back to the girl."

"I was?"

"Weren't you?"

"Yes. Yes, I suppose I was."

* * *

Less than a week after his encounter in the confessional booth at Saint Michael's, Kerrigan had just finished the six o'clock mass he said at the diocese's small chapel every weeknight, and was sitting in the sacristy, praying the rosary. The incident had shaken him badly. The knot in his stomach refused to go away, and he could barely sleep through the night. He'd managed to give away each of his shifts in the confessional since, but he could sense his colleagues were beginning to wonder whether there was more going on than a stomach bug.

His eyes closed, the set of rosary beads his mother had given him years before she died weaved through his fingers, Kerrigan tried to focus only on the prayer he recited inside his head, one passage at a time. But hard as he tried to drown it out, he could still hear the thundering voice he'd heard in the confessional days earlier, the one that rattled his bones and shook the church around him. The dreadful voice repeated inside his head like a recording set on a playback loop. "DON'T TRY THAT SHIT WITH—"

"Excuse me!" someone called out to Kerrigan from the doorway. Kerrigan jumped straight out of his chair, dropping his mother's rosary beads onto the floor. It was one of the young men Kerrigan hired to man the rectory's telephones during evening hours. "I'm sorry, Father K. I didn't mean to—"

"Forget it, kid. It's not your fault. I was just praying the rosary, and I . . . what's up?"

"A man called for you at the rectory. I asked for his name and number but he hung up on me. He said it's urgent."

"Alright, thanks Christopher."

"You're welcome, Father."

Kerrigan walked toward the doorway and watched the young man leave. As he made it to the end of the hallway, he turned back toward Kerrigan. "Hey, Father?"

"Yeah?"

"Are you alright?"

"Yeah, yeah. My stomach's on the fritz, but I'm fine. Go on now."

The young man gave Kerrigan a small smile and walked away. Kerrigan watched until he was out of sight and waited to hear one of the church's doors open and close. Once he did, Kerrigan headed back into the sacristy and sat down at a wooden desk with an old rotary telephone on it. He lifted the cradle from the receiver and dialed a number he had written down on a crumpled sticky note. The line rang.

"Yeah," a gruff voice on the other end said.

"It's Father Kerrigan."

"She just left. She was dressed for work."

Kerrigan looked over his shoulder. "And the boy?"

"He's there. Just him and the girl. Wouldn't be calling you otherwise."

Kerrigan sat there quietly, watching the pendulum on an old grandfather clock swing back and forth.

"You there, Padre? Otherwise I got shit to do."

"I'll be right there."

Kerrigan heard the line go dead and slowly returned the telephone receiver back onto the cradle. He looked at the grandfather clock and continued to watch the pendulum swing.

* * *

As Kerrigan pulled his Impala into the parking lot outside of Harout's apartment complex, he spotted the man who'd phoned him leaning against the facade of the large building, just outside the main entrance. The man held a cellphone in one hand and a burning cigarette in the other. He took a drag and tapped his foot impatiently. Kerrigan had caught traffic on the way.

Kerrigan parked the car near the entrance and turned off the engine. Before he opened the door, he looked out the windows and over his shoulders. He waited for a young couple to make their way into the apartment complex and then stepped out of the car. He closed the door gently, so it didn't slam too loudly. Then he adjusted his overcoat and approached the man.

"Where the fuck you been?" the man barked. He was dressed in dark navy coveralls and heavy boots. His name, C. Charles, was embroidered on his uniform. He was one of the building's maintenance men.

Kerrigan looked over his shoulders again. "Keep your voice down, will you?"

Charles jingled a large set of keys hidden somewhere inside his uniform. "You got the money?"

Kerrigan made sure they were alone again and reached into his overcoat for his wallet. He pulled out a crisp, one hundred dollar bill and handed it to Charles. Charles took the bill and held it up to the sunlight, to make sure it was real. Then he stuffed it into one of his pockets.

"The situation hasn't changed?" Kerrigan asked.

"No. She only left about an hour ago. She was dressed for work and shit, like I said."

"Thanks." Kerrigan proceeded to walk toward the entrance, but Charles grabbed his shoulder and stopped him in his tracks. Kerrigan looked at him.

Charles blew a puff of cigarette smoke right into Kerrigan's face. Kerrigan winced and turned away.

"Gimme another hundred," Charles demanded.

"That's not what we agreed. What? You forgot already?"

Charles took another puff from his cigarette and shook his head. "I don't give a shit what we agreed. I want another c-note. This is some shady shit. I don't like it. I could lose my job."

"This only occurred to you now?" Kerrigan asked. Charles just looked at Kerrigan, waiting. "If I say no?"

"I think you can use your imagination, can't you Padre?"

Kerrigan, biting his tongue, reached back into his wallet. Something had told him to bring more money, just in case. "Real nice," he mumbled. "Hustling a priest. That's good. Real slick."

"Don't get all high and mighty with me, Padre. How do I know you're a priest, anyway? Just 'cause you got that collar on don't mean shit."

"You reached me at the church, didn't you? Asked for Father Kerrigan? Huh?"

Charles shook his head, smugly. "Whatever, man. I don't know what you got planned up there. Maybe you're going up there

137

to fuck that boy in his ass. Maybe the girl too—maybe you like it when they're nice and still. Maybe I should call the police."

Kerrigan grinned at Charles and then punched him right in the throat. As Charles clutched his neck and gasped for air, Kerrigan pinned him against the building. This time, he didn't bother looking over his shoulders. "Say something like that again, to anyone, and I'll take a lot more from you than money. And suppose you're right . . . suppose I'm really not a priest. You think that works in your favor? We understand each other?"

Charles, still gasping for air, nodded desperately. Kerrigan let go and watched him crumple down to his hands and knees. Kerrigan took out a fifty dollar bill and let it fall onto the ground next to Charles.

Kerrigan stepped past Charles and headed into the building. "Have a blessed day, now."

As Kerrigan made his way to the corridor leading to Harout's apartment, doubt crept its way into his mind again. He wondered if he should just turn around and walk away. He'd already done everything he could. No one could say otherwise. Harout's mother didn't want his help, and it was wrong of him to go behind her back. Very wrong. He knew it. Yet he trudged toward the apartment anyway, one deliberate step at a time. His stomach tightened. His earlobes pulsated with each beat of his heart. Sweat rolled down his brow. He couldn't just turn around. He needed to know.

In front of unit 241B, Kerrigan took a deep breath and kissed the crucifix hanging from his neck. Like his rosary beads, the crucifix was also a gift from his mother. She'd given it to him while she was ill with cancer and told him to never lose his faith. He knocked on the door and stepped back. Then he waited. Silence lingered for a long, painful moment, then Kerrigan heard footsteps approach cautiously from the other side of the door.

The door opened as far as the chain lock allowed. Harout looked out into the corridor through the crack and saw Kerrigan. Just from Harout's face, Kerrigan could see that things weren't going well. Heavy bags hung from beneath Harout's eyes. His face had narrowed from weight loss. His dark hair was longer and unkept. Kerrigan hoped he wasn't too late.

Without saying a word, Harout closed the door enough to unfasten the chain lock and open it. He turned and walked through the beaded curtain. Kerrigan stepped inside and pulled the door closed behind him. He followed Harout to Marianna's bedroom. Her white bedroom door was closed.

Just before he entered, Harout looked back at Kerrigan. "She is much worse now, Father." A tear rolled down Harout's cheek.

Kerrigan nodded. Harout opened the door and stepped aside. Kerrigan hesitated. He took in another deep breath and made a sign of the cross. Then he walked into the bedroom. Harout did not enter with him.

"You're not coming?"

Harout shook his head. "No."

Kerrigan nodded. Harout pulled the door closed and left Kerrigan alone with Marianna. Kerrigan looked at her. Like before, she was quiet, lying completely still in her bed. Lifeless. Frail. Only now she was connected to an artificial respirator, which whooshed and hissed as it pumped air in and out of her lungs. Kerrigan thought about Delaney and what he had said. It was true—Marianna, an innocent young woman, one who'd never had a chance to discover herself, was on her deathbed. And it would take nothing less than an act of God to bring her back.

"God help us," Kerrigan uttered. As the sight of Marianna sunk in, Kerrigan smelled cigarettes again. He wondered if the smoke from Charles' cigarette clung to his clothing, but the smell was too fresh. Too sweet. It was so potent he was convinced smoke was leaking into the room from somewhere. He looked around for a potential source, but there were no ventilation grates or open windows. Kerrigan shrugged it off and reminded himself he wasn't there to investigate secondhand smoke; he was there to see if there really was a demon lurking inside the lifeless girl before him, her chest rising and falling with each stroke of the mechanical pump powering the artificial respirator. But as he approached her bedside, the odor grew stronger, more sweet. It was as if someone was smoking in the room that very moment. Only that was impossible, because there was nobody else. Just him and Marianna.

Kerrigan tried to ignore the smell and reached into the pockets of his overcoat. He removed three items he'd brought with him: a small, wooden crucifix that hung over the doorway to his quarters back at Saint Michael's, a travel-sized shampoo container filled to its brim with holy water, and a small, portable sound recorder. He set each of those items neatly onto the nightstand next to Marianna's bed.

Then, he took a deep breath, closed his eyes, and prayed to himself. When he finished, he pressed the record button on the recorder and looked down at Marianna. Though much of her thin face was obscured by the breathing apparatus fastened to her mouth with medical tape, it was painfully clear there was little life left in her. Her eyes were fixed and reflective, like glass. Her skin appeared dry, papery. She was even more frail than before, her arms and wrists so thin and delicate they looked as though they might snap as easily as twigs. Kerrigan guessed she weighed less than ninety pounds. It was a wonder she was still alive.

Kerrigan picked up the wooden crucifix and lowered it carefully toward Marianna's forehead. When he was within an inch of contacting her delicate skin, he paused. Doubt flooded his mind again, reminding him he had absolutely no business being there. But Kerrigan quieted those thoughts. He rested the crucifix gently onto Marianna's forehead and left it there. Nothing happened. Marianna did not suddenly howl in pain; her skin did not sizzle. She just lay there still, quiet.

Kerrigan reached for the holy water next. He carefully unscrewed the plastic cap of the shampoo bottle and poured some of the water on his thumb and index finger. He took back the crucifix and smeared a sign of the cross onto her forehead with the holy water. Her skin felt alarmingly thin against the hard skull beneath it. Kerrigan did the same to her wrists and feet. Still, there was nothing. Marianna was motionless, quiet. Like a wax figure.

Kerrigan set the shampoo bottle back down onto the nightstand and took a step back. With a hand under his chin, he thought carefully about what to do next. His doubt lingered, reinforced now by his failure to invoke a response. Suddenly, the absurdity and inappropriateness of his presence in Marianna's room became impossible to ignore. A part of him couldn't help but wonder whether he had finally lost it, whether the problem was him, not Marianna. And yet he thought back to Harout, his conviction. His raw love for his sister.

Kerrigan gathered himself and proceeded. He removed one last item from his overcoat—a travel-sized copy of the Rite of Exorcism. He was keenly aware that use of the Rite was strictly forbidden without express permission and approval from the presiding bishop, but he also knew such permission would not be granted without a proper investigation and documented evidence of possession. Such things would take time, time Marianna very likely did not have.

"God help us," Kerrigan uttered once more, looking up at the ceiling. He opened the small book to a page he earmarked earlier—the prayer to Saint Michael the Archangel. He checked that the recorder was still recording, and began to recite the lines.

"O glorious Prince of the Heavenly Host, Saint Michael the Archangel, defend us in the battle and fearful warfare that we are waging against the principalities and powers, against the rulers of this world of darkness, against the evil spirits. Come thou to the assistance of men, whom Almighty God created immortal, making them in His own image and likeness and redeeming them at a great price from the tyranny of—"

Kerrigan thought he saw Marianna move, but realized it was just her throat, which swelled and contracted with the work of the ventilator. He cleared his own throat and continued. "Redeeming them at a great price from the tyranny of Satan. Fight this day the battle of the Lord with thy legions of holy Angels, even as of old thou didst fight against . . . fight against Lucifer—"

The smell of burning cigarettes tickled Kerrigan's nose again, distracting him. It was even stronger than before, closer. Kerrigan rubbed his nose and proceeded. "Even as of old thou didst fight against Lucifer, the leader of the proud spirits and all his rebel Angels, who were powerless to stand against thee, neither was their place found anymore in Heaven. And that great dragon was cast forth, the ancient, who is called the—"

The lamps on both sides of Marianna's bed flickered. Kerrigan coughed. The smell was even stronger, so potent and thick he tasted it on his lips and felt it scratch the back of his throat. His cough got worse. The lights flickered again. Within seconds, Kerrigan was coughing so hard he could barely catch his breath. He was suddenly dizzy and nauseous. He turned away from Marianna and leaned against the nearest wall to steady himself. The copy of the Rite fell to the floor.

Kerrigan groaned. "Oh. Oh God!" His stomach sank. He cupped his hands over his mouth and ran straight out of the bedroom. He burst into the small bathroom just outside and locked the door behind him. Inside, he collapsed to his knees in front of the toilet and vomited into the bowl.

As he caught his breath, Harout knocked on the bathroom door. "Father? Are you okay?"

Kerrigan lifted his head out of the bowl so his voice didn't echo. "Yeah kid, I'm fine. Just give me a couple of minutes, alright?"

"Are you sure?"

"I'm okay. I'll be out in just a minute. Alright?"

"Okay."

Kerrigan waited for Harout to step away from the bathroom and sunk his face back into the bowl. When he felt a little better, he flushed the toilet and stood back up. He felt less nauseous, but his stomach ached and his esophagus burned with acid. He knelt over the sink and washed his hands. As he let his hands soak under the warm water, he gazed into the small round mirror above the sink and the pale face staring back at him.

"You're losing your mind," he mumbled to himself. "You're losing your goddamned mind."

* * *

Kerrigan splashed his face with cool water. He looked into the mirror again and noticed he, too, looked worse for wear. Dark circles were forming beneath his eyes. He looked and felt exhausted. He thumped his chest and let out a small belch. Then he stepped out of the bathroom. Harout looked at him from the kitchen, a dish towel over his shoulder. He looked worried.

"Are you okay, Father? Some water or something?"

"No, no. I'm alright. Been fighting a stomach bug."

"Are you finished?"

Kerrigan stood there and looked at Harout. He wasn't sure. Without saying anything, he turned around and headed back toward Marianna's bedroom. He looked back at Harout one last time, then stepped through Marianna's door and closed it behind him. As soon as he let go of the door handle, he heard something behind him. A wheezing sound. "Jesus!"

Marianna was on her side, hanging off the bed. Her body pulled dangerously on the respirator tube. Her bedsheets were on the floor, and she was dressed in a delicate nightgown made of satin or silk. The dress was so thin Kerrigan could make out her spine through it. He wasn't sure, but he thought she'd had on a hospital gown earlier.

Kerrigan ran to Marianna's bedside and rolled her gently back onto the bed. When she was on her back again, he noticed one of her arms was raised. It was raised just like it was the first time he saw her, only her small hand was crumpled into a strange pose, like she was grasping at something. Her fingers were so long and thin they looked more like those of a woman in her eighties than a teenager. Kerrigan grasped her arm and gently pushed it down. Then he checked the respirator tube to make sure it was connected properly. He didn't quite know what to look for, but he saw her chest rise and fall, which gave him some comfort. He knelt down and retrieved the bedsheets from the floor.

When he stood back up with the sheets in his arms, both of Marianna's arms were in a different position. Instead of resting at her sides, her hands were pressed against the small of her belly, one on top of the other. As Kerrigan stared in shock, Marianna's eyes suddenly opened. She coughed. Kerrigan lost his footing and fell backwards against the wall behind him. Marianna's cough quickly grew violent. It was loud and raspy, as if her lungs were full of fluid. Panicked, Kerrigan ran to her but didn't know what to do. He tried sitting her up so she wouldn't choke on the fluid, but the moment he placed his hands on her shoulders, Marianna vomited blood into the respirator and gurgled. Kerrigan looked back down at her hands, and screamed.

Marianna was bleeding profusely from her torso. Although Kerrigan didn't notice it before, a white handkerchief, much like the one he had given to Harout the night they met, was clenched between her fists. Only the handkerchief was stained with bright, red blood. Marianna was pressing it into her belly as if to put pressure on a large, gaping wound, her grip so tight her knuckles were paper white. Blood oozed from her belly onto the mattress beneath her.

Marianna gasped for air and choked. Blood flooded her respirator and began to spill out, running down her face in long streaks.

"God!" Kerrigan uttered. He rushed back to her and lifted her up. He tilted her torso forward to clear out some of the blood, but she continued to choke and gasp.

Kerrigan screamed desperately for Harout. "Harout! Harout! Call 911! Call 911 right now!"

There was no response. Marianna struggled in Kerrigan's arms. She choked and gasped so violently that her frail body convulsed with surprising strength. Blood continued to ooze from her mouth and run down her face. The white handkerchief was soaked, completely red.

Kerrigan cried out for Harout again, but there was still no response. He feared his voice wasn't carrying beyond the closed bedroom door. He didn't want to leave Marianna, but there was no other choice.

Kerrigan pulled the respirator off Marianna's face and lifted her off the bed. Despite his panic, he was struck by how light she felt in his arms. He laid her down on the floor next to the bed and rolled her on her side so she wouldn't aspirate. Blood dripped onto a white area rug beneath her.

"Hold on!" Kerrigan charged toward the bedroom door and burst through it. He ran straight to the kitchen, but Harout wasn't there. "Harout! Harout!"

There was only silence as Kerrigan searched the apartment. He ran past the kitchen and into a short hallway that led past two additional bedrooms. Both doors were closed. He ran into the first bedroom. It was empty. He burst into the second and found Harout kneeling in prayer with a set of rosary beads wrapped around his hands. Alarmed by the sudden intrusion, Harout turned toward Kerrigan with wide, startled eyes.

"Call 911 right now and tell them to send an ambulance right away! Right away! Then meet me in your sister's bedroom!"

Harout only looked back at Kerrigan, expressionless, frozen.

"Hurry!"

Harout sprung up from the floor and followed Kerrigan into the kitchen. Kerrigan ran straight back to Marianna's bedroom and found the door closed. He tried to open it, but it wouldn't budge. Kerrigan twisted the knob, but the door was locked from the other side.

"Stay back!" Kerrigan hollered at Harout, who was standing just behind him with a cordless telephone pressed up against his ear.

Kerrigan backed away from the door and then rammed his shoulder into it. The door buckled, but did not give. Kerrigan tried a second time. The door cracked down the middle, but remained closed. He tried a third time, putting even more distance between him and the door. The door finally gave way and flew open, slamming into the adjacent wall. Splinters flew across the room.

What Kerrigan saw next took his breath away. Marianna wasn't on the floor like he'd left her. She was back in her bed, tucked neatly beneath her bedsheets. She was wearing a hospital gown, not a nightgown. She was quiet, peaceful. The respirator was attached to her mouth and working perfectly. Neither the bedsheets nor the area rug was soaked with blood. There was no blood anywhere. None at all. Kerrigan just stood there in disbelief.

Harout approached Kerrigan. The telephone was still up against his ear. "Father?"

Kerrigan didn't respond. He couldn't. He just looked at Marianna, watching, stunned, as her chest rose and fell with the respirator.

"Father?"

A voice on the other end of Harout's telephone spoke. "911, what's your emergency?"

Harout looked at Kerrigan for instruction. "Father?"

Kerrigan finally looked back at him. "Tell them you made a mistake." His voice was flat, distant.

Harout told the woman on the phone he dialed 911 by mistake and hung up. He looked back at Kerrigan. "Are you okay? Father?"

Kerrigan suddenly charged toward Harout and pinned him against the wall opposite Marianna's bed. The framed photograph of Marianna Harout had shown him the night they met fell to the ground, face up. The glass inside shattered. "What the hell is this, huh? What are you trying to do to me?"

Harout barely tried to wriggle free. He was in shock. Kerrigan screamed at the top of his lungs. Spit flew from his mouth. "Is this some kind of joke? Huh? A sick fucking joke?"

Harout said nothing. He only shook his head.

"You used the handkerchief I gave you. Huh? Positioned her that way when I was in the bathroom? How did you know? Huh? How the fuck did you know?"

Harout looked even more confused than he already was.

"The white cloth I gave you! To blow your fucking nose!"

Harout shook his head back and forth. "No, Father. No."

"Where is it, then? Where is it?"

"I don't know."

"You're lying!"

Harout burst into tears. He kept shaking his head.

Kerrigan looked down and noticed Harout's feet were dangling inches above the ground. His hands still clenched around Harout's throat, Kerrigan glanced over his shoulders and looked at Marianna; she was still lying quietly and undisturbed in her bed. He looked back at Harout and let go. Harout slumped onto the floor and sat against the wall. He was still crying. Kerrigan took one last look at Marianna and ran straight out of the apartment.

CHAPTER 6

"Here, let me," Carmichael said. Kerrigan was trying to light another cigarette, but couldn't get it. His hands were shaking too badly. Carmichael took the matchbook and helped him. When the cigarette was lit, Kerrigan took in a lungful and breathed the smoke out into the rain that had started again moments earlier. The rain was accompanied by a light fog, which steadily filled the empty spaces between the trees. Kerrigan couldn't recall the last time he'd witnessed such dramatic shifts in the weather in such a short period of time, except perhaps during his time in the jungles of Vietnam. It was as if the sky was alive, its mood swinging wildly from one moment to the next.

"Where did you run off to?" Carmichael asked.

Kerrigan let out a heavy breath and took another long drag from his cigarette. He was mindful this time not to smoke the filter. "I didn't stop until I got all the way back to the car, and then I drove like a madman to the first gas station I could find. Think I even ran a couple of lights."

"What for?"

"Cigarettes. Bought two cartons with the change left in my pockets after I paid that fucking janitor. Then I smoked in the car until I stopped shaking. Burned through two packs before that happened. After that I was sick to my stomach."

Kerrigan scoffed, then shook his head. He raised his Marlboro Red for Carmichael to see. "That's how this started. And I can't stop. I can't even slow down."

Carmichael patted Kerrigan's shoulder. "Don't worry. You'll put them down again."

"I don't know, Monsignor. I'm not sure things will ever be the same for me."

As he and Carmichael traveled deeper into the trail, Kerrigan noticed the woods surrounding it had grown denser. The thicker foliage drowned out more light, and it seemed the trail grew darker with each step they took. Kerrigan looked at Carmichael as he walked. Even though he was managing the trail just fine, there was no denying Carmichael had lost ground since Kerrigan saw him last. The folds of skin around his face and neck had a cold, grayish tone to them. He looked sickly. Kerrigan worried about him, and regretted letting so much time pass without reaching out. Despite everything, he was glad they were together.

"You know there's one thing I just can't wrap my head around," Kerrigan said. "For the life of me I just can't make heads or tails of it."

"What is it?"

"What's he after?"

"The devil?"

"Yes . . . what does he gain from this? He's not communicating through her. He's not spreading fear. There's no message. He's just hiding like some . . . some coward while her body wastes away. If she dies, it'll be like he was never even there. So what's the fucking point?"

Carmichael shuddered, like he'd felt a draft.

"What's the matter?" Kerrigan asked.

"I just remembered something I haven't thought of in years, Nathan. Years."

"What is it?"

"You asked me before if I've ever been near an exorcism."

"And you said no."

"Perhaps that wasn't entirely accurate."

Kerrigan stopped dead in his tracks. Carmichael, who had insisted on carrying the umbrella this time, took a few steps before he realized Kerrigan was behind him. He saw Kerrigan standing in the rain and pulled him back under the umbrella. Together, they continued to walk the trail.

"It was ages ago," Carmichael said. "When I was a young priest, not long after I made it out of the seminary. I'd forgotten. Somehow I'd forgotten all about it."

"What happened?"

Carmichael appeared lost in thought for a moment. "I had just been assigned to Saint Stephen's in Georgetown. It was my very first assignment. I can still remember how nervous I was. Hadn't done more than a couple of masses, not much else. The pastor there—his name was Jordan Walsh, Monsignor Walsh, actually. He was a steady, Irish priest. Took quite a shine to me from the beginning, though I never understood why. He and I had absolutely nothing in common; Monsignor Walsh loved his sports, and me . . . I could hardly tell the difference between a football and a soccer ball. He also loved his beer, which in those days I was trying to stay away from. But this Monsignor Walsh, I'll never forget him. He was the holiest priest I've ever known, Nathan. His faith was absolutely unshakeable.

"Anyway, one day I'm tidying up in the sacristy at Saint Stephen's and Monsignor Walsh comes in, asks me to ride with him to some nursing home in the city. I forget the one—it's been closed for many years. An elderly gentleman there just had himself a massive heart attack, and the doctors were afraid he wouldn't make it, had the nurses call for a priest in case he went. We rode in Monsignor Walsh's car, but for all his gifts the man had absolutely no sense of direction. He made a few wrong turns, we hit traffic. When we finally arrive at the nursing home, we're informed by a pair of nurses that we were too late; the man had just passed, maybe ten, fifteen minutes ago. I'm feeling very anxious now. He hadn't said anything, but I knew he was going to ask me to anoint the man. At the time, I hadn't much experience with the dead, hadn't developed the stomach for it. The nurses escort us to the man's quarters and he's there, lying still in his bed, lifeless, his mouth hanging open. You could see he only just passed—there was still some blue left in his cheeks, his lips. There were no family members, no friends. Only nurses, busy removing tubes and wires, wheeling away machinery. The monsignor, he stands at the man's bedside. Me, I'm at the foot of the bed. As I suspected he would, he asks me to anoint the man. And so I began, stumbled through the first couple of verses but then I settled into a rhythm. I remember feeling proud of myself, actually. For the first time I finally felt like a priest."

Thunder rumbled faintly in the distance. The storm persisted.

"And then—I shiver at the thought of this, Nathan, even after all these years—this man, who we were told had passed away, whose heart had stopped beating according to the machinery, who was cool to the touch, he howls. Not like a man, Nathan. Like an animal. Angry. Rabid."

Kerrigan himself felt a shiver run up his own spine. He couldn't help but think of the voice he heard in the confessional.

"So loudly, I was told, that other residents of the facility heard it from their rooms, even with their doors closed. And not one second later, before my mind could even register what was happening in front of me, he's lunging at me, his eyes wide open, focused. His long, yellow teeth clenched. I'm in a state of total shock, standing there like a statue, and before I know what's happened this man's hand is clasped around my wrist, so tightly, Nathan, I worried he might just crush my bones. Somehow, I don't know, in the confusion the chain around my neck broke, my crucifix fell to the floor. One of the nurses handed it to me afterwards."

Kerrigan shuddered. The hair on the back of his neck stood on end. "My God."

"And just like that, Nathan, he went limp. Like someone flipped a switch or yanked a plug. I pulled away, and he fell backwards onto his pillow. And I'll never forget this, but a rush of air escaped from his mouth, so loud it sounded like someone in the room cut open a car tire. We all heard it—me, Monsignor Walsh, the nurses still in the room. And then he was gone again, this time for good. The nurses—they hooked him back up to the machines just to make sure. He was gone. A few minutes later, this smug, young doctor comes in, insists it was just a muscle spasm and nothing more, that we all needed to calm down. The prick."

"But this wasn't just a muscle spasm?"

"Not a chance in hell. We all saw it, we all knew it. Even the nurses—when that doctor left, they told us they'd seen muscle spasms before, but never anything like that."

"You must have been scared out of your wits."

"Oh, I didn't sleep through the night for months, Nathan. Not for months."

"So what do you think it was?"

Carmichael scratched the pocket of gray razor stubble on his chin. "I really didn't know what to make of it. But Monsignor Walsh—he had a view, a belief, and he was absolutely sure of it. So sure, I'm certain he would have bet his life on it."

"What was it?"

"He didn't tell me right away. As a matter of fact, we didn't even talk about it in the car on the way back to the church. I remember him asking if I was alright, and in response I lied, said I was. But that was it. It wasn't until a week or two after that he told me."

"Why?"

"I think he knew how unsettled I would be, how any young priest might be, really. But eventually I confronted him in his office at the rectory, told him I couldn't stop thinking about what happened. Asked him to tell me what he thought. I knew he knew something. And he knew I knew. He told me he was sorry he had brought me. He said that if he had known, he wouldn't have."

A single bird cawed in the distance. Both priests looked toward the sound.

"Known what?"

"He said there was a demon hiding inside the man. That this demon was this close—" Carmichael pinched his index finger and thumb together, as if to sprinkle salt into a pot of chicken soup. "—this close to dragging the man's soul down with him into the bowels of hell, condemning it for eternity. And that when I anointed the man, we snatched the man's soul from this demon's cold grip and yanked it back toward the light at the very last moment, just before it was gone forever. That it was this demon, angry for snatching the man's precious soul away from him, who lunged at me across that bed with one last breath from the man's flesh and blood before he faded away."

Kerrigan stopped short again. Carmichael turned around and covered him with the umbrella.

"What's the matter?" Carmichael asked.

"Are you trying to tell me he's after her soul? Her soul's in danger?"

Carmichael shook his head. "I can't know that any more than you can."

"But it doesn't make sense. How could God let that happen? What if you didn't make it to the nursing home in time? What if you were stuck in traffic another five minutes, another fifteen?"

"I asked Monsignor Walsh those very same questions. You know what he told me?"

Kerrigan looked on eagerly. "What?"

"He said, God didn't allow anything to happen. He made sure we were there when we needed to be. That when it comes to such matters, God always makes sure the right people are where they need to be, when they need to be, even if it means bending some of his own rules."

"What rules?"

Carmichael shrugged. "I don't know. He told me that this man was a sinner, one who committed several mortal sins for which he neither confessed nor expressed remorse. That when I prayed that his soul be commended into the hands of the Lord, for his sins to be forgiven, God was there, waiting, and he answered."

Kerrigan felt his nerves acting up again. "Do you believe it?"

Carmichael put his free arm around Kerrigan's back and urged him forward again. Carmichael seemed intent on remaining in motion.

"Well, I was a young priest, Nathan. Ordinarily I would've been inclined to believe anything such a seasoned priest might tell me, especially one as sturdy as Monsignor Walsh. Yet, like you, I suppose I was still a bit of a skeptic when it came to the preternatural. I think I felt how you do now, that there was enough evil roaming the earth that we didn't need inspiration from ghosts and goblins."

"So, you didn't believe it?"

"I wanted to know more. I went back to the nursing home. On my own, a few weeks after that man passed away, I had coffee with the nurses who were in the room with us when it happened. What they told me was that this man had only been admitted to the nursing home a few months earlier. He was a transfer from another home, one they threw him out of because he was picking on some of the other residents. They said there was a rumor floating around that he was a Nazi sympathizer, that he made a habit of insulting Jews. That in the weeks before his death, he became increasingly isolated. He mocked residents who gathered to pray the rosary. He ranted about God, Jesus, the Catholic Church and all its puppets. They told me they would often find him up all hours of the night, rambling to himself in German, pacing from one end of his quarters to another, even though weak legs bound him to a wheelchair most of the time. That many of the nurses who knew him had sneaking suspicions there was something very wrong with him."

"But Marianna's not a sinner, Monsignor," Kerrigan interjected. "Not in that way. She hasn't even reached the age of majority."

"I know. But we can't understand the devil's motivations any more than we can understand God's. You know that. To answer your real question—do I believe now, as we're standing here, that we yanked that man's soul from Satan's cold grip, that this wasn't just some once-chance-in-a-thousand muscle spasm? I really don't know. Even now, after all I've seen and lived through, I still don't know. But I'll tell you what."

"What?"

Carmichael looked Kerrigan dead in his eyes. "Either way, I'm glad we were there."

Kerrigan took a moment to let Carmichael's remark sink in. When it did, he stopped and stood in the rain. He shook his head.

"What?" Carmichael asked.

"I know what you're doing."

"What am I doing?"

"You're still trying to convince me to do it. To be in the room with her. That's why you're dragging me through the woods, in this terrible fucking weather."

Carmichael approached Kerrigan. "Nathan, I'm just trying to understand why you refuse to be. I'm trying to understand what you are so afraid of. Because I've never seen you this afraid. Of anything."

Kerrigan scoffed. "We've been over this already, Monsignor. If you don't think facing the devil is enough to be afraid of, then I don't know what to tell you. Goddamnit, if you're so fucking courageous, maybe you should be in the fucking room."

"Nathan—"

"You know, just this once, can't you spare me your fucking lectures and your fucking stories and just listen to me? I told you what I need, I know what I need—"

"I'm not trying to lecture you, Nathan, I'm just trying to "

"Jesus Christ, Monsignor!" Kerrigan's voice echoed through the woods. "Will you talk to the bishop for me or not? Because if the answer is no, I have to figure something else out. And I certainly don't have time to wander around the woods without a clue as to where the fuck we're going."

Carmichael said nothing in response. He only stood there silent, looking at Kerrigan with eyes that somehow continued to convey patience and understanding. And love. Kerrigan immediately felt awash with shame.

"God, I'm sorry," Kerrigan uttered.

"It's alright—"

"No, it's not." Kerrigan felt his hands trembling again. "I'm . . . I'm not myself."

"It's alright, Nathan. It's alright."

Kerrigan reached into his pocket for another cigarette. Despite his trembling hands, he managed to light it himself. He took in several drags, one after another, until the nicotine took the edge off again. "I'm a mess, Monsignor. I'm a goddamn mess."

The rain suddenly slowed to a mist, and then stopped altogether. Carmichael looked up into the sky through the small spaces between the branches and trees above him, and folded his large umbrella. "Shall we keep going?"

Kerrigan smiled and nodded. He didn't know what else to say or do. For a little while, all the two priests did was walk. It was Kerrigan who eventually broke the silence. "It's so quiet here. I think I forgot what quiet sounds like."

"It's nice, isn't it?"

"Yeah. It is. So, Bishop Gailey, if you do talk to him, he won't be easy to convince, will he?"

"No. I'm afraid not. Myron's a good man, there's no question about that. But he is stubborn as a doornail. As he's gotten older, it's only gotten worse."

"You think you can change his mind?"

"I can only promise that I will try. If I talk to him."

Kerrigan nodded. "Right."

"There is something I've been thinking about all morning."

"What is it?"

"Well, knowing Myron, I can't help but wonder how you were able to convince him to approve the exorcism so quickly. I know he wouldn't have done that if he feared there was any doubt this is a genuine case."

Kerrigan looked at Carmichael and then out into the trees surrounding the trail. The two priests kept walking.

* * *

As Kerrigan waited to be summoned into Bishop Myron Gailey's personal study, he had to make a conscious effort to keep his hands steady. He had been waiting in the office of the Diocese for nearly an hour without a cigarette, and was dying for another one. Though he was tempted to step outside for a quick smoke, he knew he could be called in at any moment and didn't want to risk keeping the bishop waiting. Starting the meeting off on the wrong foot was the last thing he needed.

Even before he spoke to Carmichael in the woods, Kerrigan was well aware Gailey was a tough bishop. The man was a both a traditionalist and a disciplinarian, notorious for his insistence on compliance with old rules and practices most younger priests had abandoned long ago. Gailey solidified his reputation soon after he took on the role, insisting, for example, that his staff write letters and notes by hand, even for mass mailings, and despite the fact they'd been using computers for decades. Kerrigan, who had known Gailey many years himself, kept these characteristics in mind when he'd prepared for the sit down. He knew it would take some doing to convince Gailey not only that he should approve Marianna Petrosian's exorcism right away, but that he should see that it was expedited.

"Can I offer you something to drink?"

Kerrigan's neck snapped toward the older woman standing just in front of him. He was so lost in his head he didn't notice her trying to get his attention.

"I'm sorry," the woman said. "I didn't mean to give you a fright."

"No, no. It's my fault."

"Alright, well, can I offer you something to drink? I know it's been a while. The bishop's been on the phone all morning. We have bottled water and seltzer if you'd like something. We used to have soda but Bishop Gailey made us get rid of it. Too much sugar."

"No. No, thank you. I'm fine." Kerrigan summoned a smile. The woman smiled back and returned to her desk. He thought about how badly he wanted a cigarette instead. By then, it had been a little over a week since he'd been in Marianna's bedroom, and he was already burning through two packs a day. He was ingesting more smoke than food or water.

"I hope he's ready for you soon," the woman said. "I can see he's still on the phone."

"That's quite alright. I've got nowhere else to be today." Nowhere else in the world, Kerrigan thought. Nowhere at all.

The woman smiled another small smile and went back to work. She was writing something. The office was so quiet Kerrigan could hear her pencil scratching, even from several feet away.

A few minutes later, Gailey emerged from his personal study and approached Kerrigan. "Father Kerrigan!" The bishop's voice sounded a bit more gruff than Kerrigan remembered.

Kerrigan rose from his seat and reached for Gailey's hand. He kissed Gailey's ring. "Your Excellency. Thank you for seeing me."

"Of course, Nathan. Of course. I'm sorry to keep you waiting so long. I worried you might not be here when I got out."

"No, no, that's okay."

"I wouldn't have blamed you. I've been on the phone with the Vatican all morning, unfortunately."

"The Vatican?"

Gailey nodded, then gestured toward his study. "There's a lot going on, Nathan. More than you know. Please, go in and have a seat. You'll have to excuse me just another moment. I need to use the restroom."

"Of course."

Gailey held open the door to his study so Kerrigan could enter. After Gailey left, Kerrigan looked around. The walls of the large office were covered with mementos and photographs. Gailey had spent many years traveling from one corner of the globe to another on countless special missions and assignments. Kerrigan saw photographs of Gailey taken in Africa, Israel, Jerusalem, Thailand, and Italy. There were photographs of Gailey standing next to Pope Francis, Pope Benedict XVI, and even Pope John Paul II. Kerrigan was still admiring the pictures when Gailey stepped back into the study. Gailey saw him looking at them and smiled.

"It looks like there's few places you haven't been, your Excellency."

Gailey chuckled. "I keep telling myself the next trip will be my last, and yet, somehow, there's always one more."

"Do you have another trip planned?"

"Have a seat, Nathan."

Kerrigan sat in a leather armchair in front of Gailey's large, mahogany desk. Gailey sat in his.

"Actually not," Gailey said. "Unfortunately, there are pressing matters here I must attend to, and on top of that the holidays will be upon us before we know it. Speaking of my travels, let me get you something to drink. I think you'll enjoy this."

"Uh, no . . . no thank you, your Excellency. I appreciate it though."

Gailey waved his hand at Kerrigan dismissively and headed over to a liquor cabinet in the back corner of the study. From there, he removed a decanter filled to the top with liquor the color of maple syrup. Kerrigan assumed it was whisky—in addition to his other qualities, Gailey was known to have an affinity for whisky. Gailey poured a healthy amount of the golden-brown spirit over ice cubes and handed Kerrigan an ornate glass. Kerrigan could hear the ice crackling.

"If what you told me over the phone is true, Nathan, then I think we could both use a drink. Am I right?"

Kerrigan nodded. He secretly worried the whisky might irritate his empty stomach, but he went along anyway. Gailey put the decanter away and then sat back down on his chair.

"Cheers," Gailey said. He held up his glass.

Kerrigan held up his. "Cheers."

Gailey swallowed down his drink in one large gulp. Kerrigan started with a small sip.

"Wow," Kerrigan said. "This is very smooth."

"Isn't it? You know where I got it?"

"No."

"Columbia. About five years ago, now. The guards at the airport almost took it away from me. There was a man there in one of the villages we were assisting. Very poor people, Nathan. Very poor. We were helping them set up wells for drinking water. This man made his own whiskey in barrels, but couldn't anymore when the water dried up. Once we got it flowing again, he made a batch and gave me that bottle as a token of his appreciation. Just so happens I decided to open it last week. Felt like a good time. Would you like another?"

Kerrigan looked down at his glass. It was still three-quarters of the way full. "No, I'm still working on this one, but thank you, your Excellency. It's very good."

Gailey smiled. He took his glass back over to the liquor cabinet and left it there. After that, he returned to his desk and dropped into his leather chair. He swiveled the chair and stared out the window overlooking the main road just in front of the office of the Diocese. On the other side, there was a playground full of children from a Catholic summer camp; the children were running around. Gailey watched as they hollered and laughed. He looked pensive.

"Tell me about the girl, Nathan."

Kerrigan leaned forward in his chair. "Her name is Marianna Petrosian, your Excellency."

"She's Armenian?"

"Yes. She's very young—she turned fourteen not long ago. She lives with her mother and brother in Lawlry Heights."

"How did you get involved? This family—you mentioned they don't belong to Saint Michael's?"

"No. They belong to Saint Matthew's. It was the girl's brother . . . his name is Harout."

"The resurrection," Gailey said to himself. "Beautiful name."

"He came to see me at the church one night, asked me to have a look at his sister. He told me she is possessed by the devil. I was skeptical, of course."

"What about the mother? Tell me again why she wasn't the one looking for a priest?"

Kerrigan sighed. "It's complicated, your Excellency. Her mother's a very holy woman. Maybe too holy. In this case, I believe her faith has blinded her. She can't accept that God would allow this to happen. Not to her daughter."

"And her father?"

"He's dead. He was killed in action in Iraq. He enlisted in the Marines after 9/11. Felt indebted to the country."

Gailey groaned. He shook his head in disgust. "That lousy war. Going there was a grave mistake. A grave mistake."

"Your Excellency . . . I realize this is a delicate matter and there are procedures we have to follow, but there's a time element to this you need to understand. This girl—Marianna—she's gravely ill. As a matter of fact, she's . . . she's dying."

"How long?"

"It's hard to say, your Excellency. The doctors think she's on borrowed time now. Could be a couple of weeks. Maybe more. Maybe less. I'm not a doctor, but I can tell you she's very, very weak. In just the couple of weeks I've known her, her condition has deteriorated significantly. She was breathing on her own when I met her, but she's on a ventilator now."

For the first time since he sat down, Gailey turned away from the window overlooking the children and faced Kerrigan head on. "You were a doctor once, weren't you?"

Kerrigan shook his head. The question surprised him. He had never discussed it with Gailey and rarely shared those personal details with others. "No, not quite. I never finished my residency. I enlisted in the Marine Corps the year after I graduated medical school, and after that I found my way to the priesthood."

"I see." Gailey cleared his throat. "What's wrong with the girl? Physically? You said something about catatonia?"

"Yes. She's in a catatonic state now. She doesn't speak. She doesn't move. She doesn't respond to medication. The doctors are calling it a treatment-resistant case. It's rare, but known to happen. When it does, the outcomes usually aren't good. But I have to be honest with you, your Excellency."

"What about?"

"I don't think it's catatonia at all. I think it's all just a ruse. This demon—for some reason he's hiding there in plain sight. What he's after, I just don't know."

Gailey sighed, then crossed his arms tightly. Kerrigan could see he was genuinely disturbed by the news, that it weighed on him. While Gailey could be rough around the edges, he still cared about people. "We are living in troubled times, Nathan. I don't know why or how we got here, but here we are nonetheless. I suppose now it's just a matter of what we do with it."

Kerrigan gazed back at Gailey, his head slightly tilted. "I'm not sure what you mean, your Excellency."

"I am afraid this isn't an isolated incident. It's a scourge. Cases just like this one are sprouting up all over the place, and the Vatican can't train enough exorcists to keep up. That's why I've been on the phone with them all morning. You are the fourth priest just this year to come to me requesting approval for an exorcism."

Kerrigan slowly leaned back into his chair, his mouth open. The news shocked him.

Visibly restless, Gailey stood up, folded his hands behind his back, and approached the window overlooking the playground. "They're going after our children, Nathan. Some even younger than this poor girl we're talking about right now. Some as young as the little ones out there."

Kerrigan looked out the window. The children were very young, at most five or six. He looked at Gailey and saw the worry weighing on him. He carried it in his shoulders, which were uncharacteristically hunched forward. Gailey was a tall, proud man.

"The other cases," Kerrigan asked. "Did you approve them? The exorcisms, I mean."

Gailey turned back toward Kerrigan and looked at him with eyes which suddenly seemed large and glossy, like he'd had one drink too many. "All three, Nathan. I approved all three."

Gailey walked back over to the liquor cabinet and poured himself another drink. "You want another? I'm having one."

"No, thank—"

"Have one anyway."

Kerrigan looked down at his glass again. It was still three-quarters full. Before Gailey turned around, Kerrigan tilted back his head and swallowed the rest in a single gulp. The liquor burned on its way down his esophagus, but felt surprisingly warm and comforting in his stomach.

Immediately after, Gailey was there with the next round, only this time he neglected to fill the glasses with ice first. He sat back down and waited for Kerrigan to lift up his new glass. When Kerrigan did, both priests took down the second drink in one gulp.

"Were they successful, the exorcisms?" Kerrigan asked.

"So far we think two of them were. Now it's just a matter of watching those children very closely until we're sure."

"And the third?"

"The third—and please, Nathan, I know this goes without saying, but I must say it anyway. Nothing we discuss here today leaves this room."

Kerrigan nodded. "Of course."

"The third . . . the third is still underway." Gailey looked down at his watch. "As we speak, as a matter of fact. It's been going on for months now."

"Months?"

"Yes. I'm told the demon is . . . persistent."

Kerrigan could barely believe what he was hearing. This was not a world he spent time in or thought about. "My God. I've heard some rumors here and there, but this, I had no idea."

Gailey shook his head and groaned in dismay. "I know about the rumors. They're not helping anything."

Gailey sat for several moments. He folded his hands and rested his chin on top of them. "Nathan, we must tread very, very carefully here. Very carefully. If this Armenian girl . . . if she's as weak as you and the doctors say she is, on a respirator and such, an exorcism might very well kill her, might it not? Have you considered that?"

"I have, your Excellency. Very much so."

"And?"

"If we do nothing, she'll be dead soon anyway. With the exorcism, at least we'd be giving her a chance."

Gailey sounded utterly exhausted. "It is imperative we are not mistaken. Do you understand? Tell me how you know this is what you think it is."

Kerrigan pulled his chair forward and leaned in closer to Gailey. He was waiting for this question. He'd rehearsed his response over and over. This was his chance to get Marianna help before it was too late, and he knew there wouldn't be another. "The truth is I didn't believe it at first. I didn't want to. Looking back, I think it's because I didn't want to be involved. But now . . . now I don't have any other choice. I saw something. I saw something, and it cannot be explained any other way."

"Tell me what you saw."

"At first, nothing. Now, I don't know what this demon's up to, but he doesn't want to be seen or heard. He doesn't speak, he doesn't move. He's just hiding there inside her, dormant. Waiting, I suppose. For what, I don't know. Before me, the only other person he showed himself to was the boy. Her brother. I believe now that's only because he knew no one would believe him if he talked. I certainly didn't believe him. Not right away. Neither did his own mother. Then I suppose I got close enough, too close maybe, and he blinked. He revealed himself. Tried to ward me off."

"Revealed himself how?"

Kerrigan hesitated. He considered one last time whether he should go any further. "It spoke to me, your Excellency. Said

something out loud I haven't heard in more than forty years."
Kerrigan shook his head. "It's still hard for me to believe. At first, I
didn't know what it was saying because it was speaking in Italian.
I was so shocked Marianna was speaking at all, the words didn't
even register, not right away. It was only after a couple of verses
that I realized I'd heard those words before. It was a lullaby. An
Italian lullaby. 'La Nina Nanna.'"

"A lullaby? Couldn't she have heard it in school, Nathan?
Kids study Italian in middle school, don't they?"

"It's not the language that's significant, your Excellency.
Something happened to me in Vietnam, something that's haunted
me my entire life."

Gailey rested his elbows on his desk and leaned in closer.

"It was '73. I was five and a half months into my six-month
rotation as a combat medic. Another two or three weeks and I was
going to be transferred to a field hospital, away from combat. I was
counting down the days."

Kerrigan shuddered. Memories from those days flooded
into his mind—the sound of bullets tearing through flesh and
shattering bone; the blood-curdling screams of men set ablaze with
napalm; the cold, empty expressions of the deceased. "Anyway, at
the last minute my squadron was assigned to accompany a sweep for
North Vietnamese troops spotted mobilizing somewhere a couple
of miles west of Cigar Island. At that point, we were already in Chu
Lai, close enough that we could make our rendezvous on foot. We
walked through the jungle for two days straight. The first day was
fine, dry, not too hot. We were tired but in good spirits otherwise.
But the second day . . . the second day it rained like cats and dogs.

Started in the morning and just wouldn't let up. By the afternoon we were all spent. Our uniforms were soaked, covered in mud. We were cold, miserable, exhausted. We needed to rest, badly, but there just wasn't any time. We had to make the rendezvous point and were already behind because of the weather. So we kept going. We kept going, but some of the guys, they got sloppy. They just couldn't take the cold and the wet and the mosquitos anymore, and so they started charging through the jungle like locomotives, cutting down branches with their machetes. Making noise. Too much noise. The rest of us, we were just trying to keep up. Then the shots rang out. Three or four of them, just like that. We all hit the deck, buried our faces in the mud, hid behind trees, bushes, whatever we could find. Me . . . I was down in the mud."

Kerrigan paused and gauged Gailey's expression. He was listening intently.

"These were rifle shots. The rest of my guys, they start yelling. They're trying to find the sniper. But he's camouflaged, hidden. And the jungle—it was wet and dark so you couldn't see a damned thing. I'm still on the ground, keeping my head down, and after a while I realize I'm lying in a pool of blood. Bright red blood mixed in with the dark brown mud. I'd seen that mixture before. My first thought is that I'd been hit, but I didn't feel any pain. I look to my right and I see two of my squadmates on the ground, one just behind the other. They were both lying on their backs in the mud. They'd both been hit. Now, all I want to do is run over to them, but I can't because shots are still ringing out, from both sides now, and I know that if I so much as lift my head I take a bullet in the skull. I'm the medic—I'm not supposed to take chances. So I wait, and I wait, and I wait. Finally, we hit him. The sniper. He fell out of the tree he was hiding in and into a marsh below, broke some branches on the way down. I hear the all clear and I'm off running. I come up on my guys and then I'm frozen. Just standing there, shocked. They were both bleeding from the upper right portion of their chests. The wounds, they looked identical. Exactly the same."

Kerrigan placed his left hand against the right side of his chest, gesturing the approximate location of the wounds.

"And then I realize what happened. Those guys—they were buddies. They were walking in single file when the shots rang out. They were about the same height, the same build. It was one bullet, tore right through both of them. I knew right then I couldn't save them both. They'd been shot through the chest with a high-powered rifle, at a relatively close range. Both of the wounds were sucking wounds, the worst I'd seen. Wounds I would have to plug up very quickly. They were both dying. Fast. There just wasn't enough time. There just wasn't enough time. So I had to choose. Quickly. Either I focused on one of them or they both died. It was that simple."

Gailey cringed. He looked down at his desk and shook his head.

"Now that's nothing new," Kerrigan said. "That's part of a combat medic's responsibility. That's triage—you prioritize the ones you can help, and the rest—you have to let them go. That's what I was trained to do. But these were two men, men I'd spent months with in that jungle . . . and their wounds were exactly the same. Neither was more likely to survive than the other. I tried . . . tried to find something to distinguish the two, something I could point to when I faced their mother or father and explained why I chose the other guy. But there was nothing. Nothing at all. So how do you choose? How do you choose who lives and who dies? Do you flip a coin? What do you do?"

Gailey leaned forward. "Nathan, I'm not sure there's—"

"I chose based on the color of their skin," Kerrigan uttered. "That's how I did it. On the color of their skin."

"What do you mean?"

"One of those men was white. Italian. Private Rizzo. Giovanni Rizzo. We used to call him 'G Riz.' English was his second language so he had this heavy, Italian accent. The guys were always on his case about that. He wouldn't stop talking about how he was going back to Italy after the war to find a beautiful Italian bride from Palermo. God, he made us laugh. The other man was black. His name was Darnel Davis. Private Davis. We didn't have a nickname for him. Fact is the guys weren't kind to him—he was the only black soldier in our squadron, and the guys weren't exactly thrilled about it. He was risking his life, same as everyone else, but they treated him like an outcast. Darnel sensed it, so he kept to himself mostly. I didn't know much about him except that he came from a large family in Alabama."

A loud whistle sounded across the street. The children were being rounded up. Playtime was over.

"You saved the white man?"

"No. I chose Darnel Davis. Private Davis from Alabama. That's who won the coin toss."

"Why him?"

"Because he was black. It occurred to me while I stood there agonizing over which of the men I should attend to, if I

174

chose Private Rizzo . . . ." Kerrigan's voice trailed off. "If I chose Private Rizzo—"

"You would be accused of choosing a white man over a black man."

Kerrigan nodded. "You remember how it was back in those days, don't you? People everywhere thought we were sending the blacks over there to die. That's what popped into my head as I stood over those two men. I saw myself on the front cover of the New York Times, the white combat medic who chose to save a white man over a black man, all else being equal. And so I tended to Private Davis from Alabama and left Private Rizzo to die, choking on his own blood."

Gailey reached into one of his desk drawers and pulled out a tissue box. Kerrigan took a tissue and wiped tears from his eyes.

"You didn't let anyone die, Nathan. That wasn't up to you. You saved a man's life. Had it been a lesser man in your shoes, both men might have died."

"I know a decision had to be made, your Excellency. And I thank God I was able to make one in time. But even after all these years, I still wish it wasn't a selfish one."

Gailey only looked at Kerrigan. It seemed he didn't know what to say.

"Anyway," Kerrigan went on. "While I was tending to Private Davis, Private Rizzo spoke. It started just as a mumble. He was nearly dead, his brain surely starved for oxygen. But he managed to get out a few words. In Italian. I wasn't fluent in the language at the time, but I recognized enough of the words that I was able to write some of them down later. After I was sent home about a year later, I went to see Private Rizzo's father. Felt I owed him that. He told me Giovanni was reciting verses of an Italian lullaby his family had used for generations, that Giovanni's mother sang it to him when he was just a boy and gravely ill with meningitis. He said she passed away a year or so before Giovanni did, of cancer. It was the same lullaby Marianna recited to me in her bed. It knew. Saw through me like an open book. Saw my greatest regret, and threw it right in my face."

Gailey covered his eyes with the palm of his hand and shook his head. He was visibly troubled by Kerrigan's tale. After a few moments, he stood up and paced behind his desk. "Have you any other proof, Nathan?"

"I'm afraid not, your Excellency. I tried, but this demon's much too smart for that."

"What about the boy? You said he saw something. What was it?"

"He's only spoken of dreams and visions, in vague terms. The truth is I haven't pressed him very hard because I imagine what he saw is as troubling to him as what I saw is to me."

"What about the mother?"

Kerrigan shook his head. "She still can't see a thing."

"But she approves?"

"Yes. I'm not sure she's crazy about the idea, but at this point she's willing to try anything. She has a sister. She's a nurse. She's been a huge help."

Gailey walked back over to the window overlooking the children. He watched as they were being herded into the school across the street.

"Nathan, do you realize what you're asking of me, of the church?"

"I do."

"Do you?" Gailey turned toward Kerrigan and looked at him with serious, piercing eyes. "You're asking me to approve an exorcism on your word alone. If this goes forward and something goes terribly wrong, if this poor girl doesn't survive the ritual, they'll blame you. They'll blame both of us."

"I understand, your Excellency."

Gailey looked out the window again and watched as the last of the children shuffled back into the building. "I'm going to make the call immediately. Based on the condition of the girl, I want this to go forward as soon as possible. I'll make sure the urgency is understood."

Kerrigan sprung up from his chair. "Thank you, your Excellency. Thank you."

"We'll need a doctor there for the ritual. Have you someone in mind?"

"Yes. Yes, I do."

"Good. I'll leave that to you. In the meantime, as soon as I find out who will lead the ritual, I will put him in touch with you."

"Okay, good. I'll bring him up to speed, introduce him to the family, whatever he needs."

"Good, good. You'll also want to prepare yourself, Nathan. Familiarize yourself with the Rite. Sit for confession. It's very important you sit for confession. I'll have some materials prepared for you. You won't have as much time as you should, but I'm afraid this is the situation we find ourselves in. God help us."

Kerrigan was frozen in place. Gailey was still speaking, but none of the words registered.

"What's the matter, Nathan?"

"I'm . . . I'm not sure I understand, your Excellency. Why should I sit for confession, familiarize myself with the Rite? I thought you said you were going to call for an exorcist."

"Yes."

"So . . . why would—"

"This is not a one-man job, Nathan."

"No, I understand that, your Excellency, but—"

"I'll be lucky to get one exorcist. You heard what I said before?"

"No, of course. Of course. But . . . uh . . . I just thought . . . wouldn't it be better if we got someone with more experience to assist?"

"How many priests do you think have such experience?"

Kerrigan was tongue-tied. His thoughts raced wildly, looking for a response that might persuade the bishop otherwise, but couldn't find one. "It's just—there's got to be someone better suited than me."

"How so?"

"Well . . . someone with experience. Someone who's assisted with an exorcism before. Someone who's seen—"

"You're not understanding me."

"With respect, your Excellency, I'm just not cut out for this. If we could just find someone else—"

"Nathan, you just don't understand what we're up against. We're already spread dangerously thin. Now experience is helpful, sure. But so is familiarity with the case, the family. I cannot ask for two men. Besides, waiting for another exorcist to free up will only serve to delay things. We're on borrowed time now, aren't we?"

"What if I—"

"Enough!" Gailey approached and placed his hands on Kerrigan's shoulders. Kerrigan smelled the whiskey on his breath. "There is no one else, Nathan."

Kerrigan's heart pounded through his chest. He could feel the heat in his face, and he was damp with sweat.

"I don't know if I can do it, your Excellency."

"That's fear talking. I understand you're afraid. Lord knows I would be too. But I have to believe God brought you and the girl together for a reason. And now he's calling on you to see this through."

CHAPTER 7

"And you know what he said to me just before I left?" Kerrigan asked Carmichael. "He said, don't worry, Nathan. I will keep you in my prayers." Kerrigan chuckled, angrily. "Sure, your Excellency, that's just great. Fantastic. You're forcing me to square up with the devil himself, but I don't have to worry because you're going to mention me in your daily prayers. Give me a fucking break."

Kerrigan looked over and realized Carmichael wasn't by his side. He wheeled around to find Carmichael was several yards behind him. Carmichael was standing in the middle of the trail, his hands resting on his cane. For the first time that day, Kerrigan saw judgment in Carmichael's eyes. He could see it even from afar.

"What?" Kerrigan asked.

"You lied to him."

"I had to, Monsignor."

"He put his trust in you. Was willing to risk his reputation, the church's. And you betrayed that trust."

"I did it for the girl, Monsignor. I did it for Marianna."

"Now you're lying to me."

Kerrigan shook his head. "No. I'm not."

"Yes, you are."

"What was I supposed to do?" Kerrigan's voice swelled. "I had no proof. I had one shot to convince him she needs the exorcism, and needs it now. One shot."

"So why not tell him what you really saw in that bedroom? Why not tell him the truth?"

Kerrigan had no response. He turned away instead. The fog was thickening around him.

Carmichael approached Kerrigan from behind. "Because it meant something to you, didn't it? Didn't it mean everything?"

"I don't know what the hell you want from me."

Carmichael placed his hand on Kerrigan's shoulder. "I want you to talk to me, Nathan."

"I've been talking to you! All fucking morning I've been talking to you!"

"No . . . you haven't. You've been talking around me. Telling me just enough so that I can't ask you the questions that matter."

"Are you kidding? That's all I've been doing is answering your questions. I asked just one, and I still don't know what the answer is."

"I'm trying to help you. Can't you see that?"

Kerrigan pulled away from Carmichael and stomped from one side of the trail to the other. The fog grew even thicker still, swallowing the priests. "Goddamnit. I don't understand this. I'm doing everything I can for this girl. Everything I can. If it wasn't for me she wouldn't even be having the fucking exorcism. Now she has a chance at least. So what if I told a white lie to get her there?"

"This was no white lie, Nathan. You know that."

"Christ Monsignor, haven't I done enough? Why is everyone insisting that I be there for the exorcism? I don't have any expertise. I have no experience. I don't bring anything to the table. Not a thing. I didn't . . . I didn't ask for this."

Kerrigan looked at Carmichael and saw he was still standing there, calm, patient. The judgment he saw in Carmichael's eyes just a few moments earlier was gone.

"Nathan, from the moment we met this morning, the moment I smelled those cigarettes on your clothes, I knew I wouldn't be speaking to the same Father Kerrigan I've known all these years. The priest who cares more for others than he does himself. Who spends the little free time he has volunteering at soup kitchens and visiting children's hospitals. That Father Kerrigan wouldn't be content with doing just enough. He would see this through to the very end, no matter the cost."

Kerrigan shook his head. He walked away from Carmichael and stared despairingly into the fog. It was nearly waist high, so thick he could barely make out his own feet.

"What is it, Nathan? What was it this demon showed you in that bedroom?"

Kerrigan said nothing in response. He stared out blankly into the fog, his mind cycling through images of Marianna withering like an aging flower in her bed, of Harout being slapped across the face by his mother, the bloodstained handkerchief Marianna clenched against her belly.

Carmichael approached again and placed his hand beneath Kerrigan's chin, lifting Kerrigan's head until their eyes were aligned. "It's just me, Nathan. Just you, me, and the trees. Even the birds are gone. For now, at least."

Kerrigan gazed into Carmichael's eyes. He was close enough now that he could see and appreciate their subtle beauty, their depth, the swirls of greens, turquoises, and deep blues, these eyes that had been looking at the world far longer than his. If there was anyone in the world who might understand, truly, it was Carmichael. Kerrigan knew it. He knew it, but he just couldn't face it.

The fog was closing in, rising. Kerrigan felt like he was suffocating. His hands trembled again, his heart pounded against his sternum.

"I . . . I can't," Kerrigan moaned.

"Yes, you can."

"No, I . . . I . . . I don't want to."

Kerrigan hunched over. He couldn't catch his breath.

"Breathe, Nathan. Breathe. It will pass. You've been through this before."

"I can't . . . I can't breathe."

"Just hold on, Nathan. Let it pass."

Kerrigan felt pain surge beneath his breastbone now, like an elephant was standing on his chest. He didn't realize he was doing it, but he was backing away from Carmichael, one shaky step at a time.

"Please," Kerrigan begged. "Please stop."

"You can do this, Nathan. You have to."

"Please, Monsignor. Just . . . just let me be."

Carmichael took a single step toward Kerrigan, but Kerrigan flinched like a frightened animal. "Nathan—"

"Stop!" Kerrigan cried out. He was desperate, now. Afraid. His breaths were shallower, more rapid. "Please, just stop. I can't breathe. I can't breathe."

Carmichael reached out for Kerrigan. "Nathan—"

"Stay away from me! Stay back."

"Nathan, I'm just try—"

"I can't breathe!" Kerrigan was panicking now, white as a ghost. He was wheezing loud enough that Carmichael could hear it. "I can't breathe!"

"Nathan—"

Kerrigan turned and took off running as fast as he could. He ran up the trail and disappeared into the fog.

Carmichael cried out after him. "Nathan! Nathan! Be careful! The fog! The fog!"

Kerrigan ignored Carmichael's pleas and ran as fast as he could. With each yard he covered, the fog rose, thickened. Before long he was wading in it. Carmichael continued to shout, but his voice sounded distant, faint.

After sprinting for several yards, Kerrigan ran out of breath and slowly came to a stop. The fog was so thick and heavy he could no longer make out the trail in front of him. As he tried to catch his breath again, he reached into his pocket for his pack of cigarettes but couldn't find it. He checked his pockets, but they were empty. He patted himself down all over, feeling for the pack. "No! No, no, no, no, no . . . ."

He searched everywhere, but the pack just wasn't there. He realized it must have fallen out of his pocket during his dash through the woods. He couldn't see the ground through the fog. It was too thick. Desperate, he dropped down to his hands and knees and felt around. "Not now! Please, not now!"

Kerrigan crawled around the earth in search of the pack, his hands and knees wet from the damp soil beneath him. He searched frantically, but he felt only leaves and stones.

Kerrigan heard someone whisper his name. The sound was faint, muffled. He shot up onto his feet. Birds fluttered around him. The fog was just below his neck now. "Monsignor? Monsignor? I'm right here." He listened for a response, but there was nothing at first. Moments later, he thought he heard Carmichael call out to him again. The voice was more distant. "Monsignor! Monsignor! Where are you?"

Kerrigan heard another whisper. He turned in the direction of the voice and followed it into the fog.

"Shit!" Kerrigan groaned. He'd tripped over something big and hard and toppled over. He tried to break his fall with his hands, but he was suddenly tumbling downhill. He gained speed at a terrifying pace for several yards before crashing into a tree. His head slammed violently against the thick trunk, disorienting him. He moaned with pain.

Kerrigan was lying on his back in thick, wet mud. Dark, shadowy trees, barely visible through the thick, murky fog, looked down at him. He tried to lift his head up and get his bearings, but the movement made him dizzy. A sharp pain radiated from his neck and shoulders. Wincing, he lay back down. He couldn't see the trees anymore.

Kerrigan heard something hiss. He hoped it was just his imagination, but he heard it a second time. Louder. Closer.

He tried to move, but couldn't. His eyes just grew heavier and heavier. . . .

* * *

. . . . "HISS!"

He woke up slowly now, irritated by the water droplets pinging off his helmet.

"Hiss!"

Private Nathaniel Kerrigan lifted his head from the cold, wet ground and rolled slowly and carefully toward the hissing sound. His squadron had only stopped to rest a half hour earlier. The trees and brush above were shedding moisture from a large rain storm earlier. The men sleeping beneath them were sweating under the hot Vietnamese sun.

Careful not to make any sudden movements, Kerrigan scanned the earth around him and looked over to the black soldier sleeping a few feet away. He saw nothing out of the ordinary, only dirt and heavy vegetation which swayed gently in the slight breeze. He let gravity pull his eyelids closed again.

"Hiss!"

Kerrigan's eyes flew back open. There was no doubt now; there was a snake nearby. He scanned the area again but didn't see anything. Then, he looked up and spotted the snake wrapped around a tree branch just a few feet above his head. He knew from the bands of gray-black and cream he was staring at a cobra. He shifted his body and turned toward his squadmate.

"Billy!" Kerrigan whispered, hoping to wake the soldier from Tennessee. "Billy!"

The cobra hissed again, as loud this time as the whistle from a small air compressor. Kerrigan looked up at the snake and saw it dangling from the branch, sampling the air with its long, forked tongue. It swayed from side to side like a pendulum.

Kerrigan whispered louder this time. "Billy!" His squadmate stirred, but only scratched his nose and turned from his back to his side. The cobra continued to sway back and forth as if in search of something, it's tongue flickering like a candle in the light breeze.

Kerrigan considered reaching for his sidearm, but feared it would require too large a movement. The cobra slowly lowered itself from the branch. Kerrigan felt his hair stand on end. He spotted a twig he could reach easily and grabbed it. With a small flick of his wrist, he tossed it at Billy. The twig struck the Marine right in the nose and startled him awake. Instinctively, the young man from Tennessee reached for his pistol.

The commotion agitated the cobra. Kerrigan watched with wide eyes as the serpent lifted its head and displayed its menacing hood.

"Hiss!"

Kerrigan resisted the overwhelming urge to get up and run; he knew he was much too close to outrun a strike. He looked over to his squadmate and saw Billy reaching for his M-16.

Kerrigan frantically shook his head back and forth. He whispered as loud as he could without further rousing the snake. "Billy, no! No!"

But Billy was oblivious, his eyes trained only on the snake. He lined up for a shot. Kerrigan tried again to flag his attention. "Billy, no! Your machete! Use your machete!"

Billy slid his finger over the trigger and used his thumb to disengage the safety.

"No!"

But it was too late. Private Billy Caldwell from Tennessee pulled the trigger and fired multiple rounds at the snake. The sound cracked through the air like a thunderclap. Blood misted all over Kerrigan's face and got into his eyes. Dozens of birds shot up into the air. What remained of the cobra dangled from the branch like a limp rope.

Kerrigan wiped his eyes and face with his sleeve. Though relieved, he awaited the inevitable onslaught. Seconds later, he and Billy were surrounded by their squadmates, each with their rifles cocked. They were white as ghosts, startled awake.

"It's okay guys," Kerrigan said. "It was just a snake. Came right up on me."

"What snake?" one of the squadmates demanded.

"Where the fuck is it?" another barked.

"Right there." Kerrigan pointed to the limp carcass dangling from the branch. It was sliding off.

"What the fuck's going on here?" an angry voice growled from beyond the circle of Marines surrounding Privates Kerrigan and Caldwell. It was their lieutenant—Jeffrey R. Rosenthal.

The lieutenant punched through the circle of men. He was shirtless, his torso shiny with perspiration. He held a pistol in one hand and a bottle of moonshine in the other. "What the fuck happened?"

Billy bowed his head. He knew he was in for a licking.

"It was a snake, sir," Kerrigan explained. "A monocled cobra. Right there on that branch. I tried to squirm away, but it was about to strike. Private Caldwell shot the snake before it did. Saved me, sir."

"Son of a bitch!" Rosenthal grunted. "Do you realize what the fuck you just did? You just broadcast our position to every goddamned Charlie within five miles of his hellhole!"

"Billy had no choice, sir. The cobra—it—"

"How many rounds did you fire at that fucking snake?" Rosenthal demanded, looking at Billy. Spit flew from his lips.

Billy only shook his head, too frightened to get any words out.

"How many fucking rounds did you fire at that snake, Private?"

"I . . . I don't know, sir."

"Well, I counted at least fifteen. Fifteen rounds to drop a snake not even a yard away? Huh?"

Billy just sat there silently.

Rosenthal ripped the M-16 from Billy's arms. He removed the ammo clip and turned it sideways for the men to see. "You see this?" He turned back toward Billy. "You emptied half the fucking clip! On a snake barely a yard away!"

"I'm sor—sorry sir."

"You're sorry?"

"Yes, sir."

"Do you even have a brain inside that thick black skull of yours? Do you think before you act? Can you even do that?"

Billy said nothing. He only looked down at the ground.

"It happened so fast, sir," Kerrigan said. "The snake—it was about to strike—"

"Shut your mouth, Kerrigan! I'm not talking to you, am I?"

"No, sir."

"No. I'm talking to this here young man they sent all the way from Tennessee. Real fine specimen they sent us."

Rosenthal raised the ammo clip once more for the men to see. "Bullets are for Charlie! Not snakes. Understand?"

Each of the men nodded their heads. Billy nodded too, but Rosenthal bent down and got in his face. "You understand me, Private?"

"Y-y-yes sir. Yes sir."

"Alright then, boys. Saddle up. We move out in ten."

The Marines collectively moaned and groaned. They weren't happy. Not at all.

"We just got here," one of them protested.

"Don't look at me, fellas," Rosenthal retorted. "These two fucksticks compromised our little slumber party. Can't risk staying here. We've got ground to cover anyway."

Rosenthal flashed Billy one last dirty look and stormed off. The rest of the men, still moaning and groaning, dispersed and made their way back to their belongings.

"Thanks a lot, dickheads," one of them grunted.

The cobra's bloody carcass slid off the branch and fell right into Kerrigan's lap, startling him. "Shit!" He grabbed the snake and tossed it out into the brush.

"I'm sorry," Billy said.

"For what? You saved my life. I don't carry any antidote. The guys know that. As a matter of fact, you may have just saved some of their lives, too."

"How do you mean?"

"I'm the medic, remember? If I go, there's nobody around to patch people up."

Billy nodded, still subdued. Kerrigan could tell his nerves were still raw. Things hadn't been easy for him since he'd arrived. He was the first and only black Marine in the squadron, and the men had been less than kind to him. It was shameful. Kerrigan, however, had befriended him.

Kerrigan stood up and collected his gear. He walked over to Billy and extended his hand. "Thanks Billy. I owe you one."

"You don't owe me nothin'."

Billy took Kerrigan's hand. Kerrigan helped him up on his feet. He looked into Billy's eyes and nodded. "Yes, I do. Don't worry about the guys. They'll get over it."

"I dunno. They ain't like me much. It's plain to see."

"Give it time. They'll warm up."

Billy shrugged his shoulders. He seemed doubtful. "The lieutenant, he always drinkin'? I smelt it on his breath again."

"It's been getting worse. This jungle—it can wear people down after a while."

"It wear you down?"

"I manage best I can, same as everyone else."

"How?"

"I like to read, mostly."

"Watcha read?"

Kerrigan reached into one of his bags and removed a pocket version of the King James Bible, bound in camouflage.

"I lost mine," Billy said.

Kerrigan tried to hand him the bible. Billy shook his hand at him.

"No sir. I can't take it from you."

"No, but you can borrow it. Only if you want. I'm not trying to convert you or anything. I'll leave that to chaplains."

Billy looked at the book, then took it from Kerrigan and tucked it in his rucksack. He smiled at Kerrigan. Kerrigan patted him on the shoulder.

"Come on," Kerrigan said. "We should go. Before the guys get even more pissed."

* * *

Kerrigan's squadron had been marching for six or seven hours without a break. They were headed north toward the Bến Hải River to meet with another squadron and escort a group of four-man reconnaissance patrols assessing enemy activity just south of the demilitarized zone. From their current position, it would be at least another two hours before they reached the rendezvous point, and the men weren't in particularly good spirits.

Per Lieutenant Rosenthal's orders, the men were spread out along a horizontal axis, almost in V formation, in groups of three or four. The most recent intelligence report had indicated the area they were passing through was relatively quiet, but the men all knew the Việt Cộng had a knack for appearing from thin air, killing several Marines before a single one of them could be spotted.

"This is fuckin' bullshit," said Private Danny Mitchell, a twenty-one-year-old from Staten Island, New York. "Why do we have to walk all this way? Why don't they send another crew? Someone closer. My feet are fuckin' killing me."

"All of our feet are killing us, Mitchell," said Corporal Allan P. Houser. Corporal Houser was Rosenthal's second-in-command.

He was rough around the edges, but a good man nonetheless. He genuinely cared about the men under his command. Kerrigan had grown very fond of him. "And, as usual, you're the only one complaining. Guess that nickname the guys gave you ain't so far off the mark."

Kerrigan, who was marching just behind Mitchell, watched him bump Billy's shoulder and mumble something to the black soldier under his breath. Mitchell, like the rest of the men, blamed Billy for ruining their nap, and they made no effort to keep their resentment a secret.

"To answer your question, Mitchell—"

"What question?"

"Christ, kid." Houser chuckled. "I hope for your girlfriend's sake—that is, one, if you make it out of this hellhole alive and, two, she's still your girlfriend when you do—that your dick isn't as short or inadequate as your memory apparently is."

The Marines chuckled.

"Why us? Well, it's us because there ain't nobody else. Far as I know, nobody's this close to the river, except for us and that mortar squad from Alpha Company. But I'll tell ya the truth, boys. I don't like these recon missions any more than you do. Me—I'd rather be sent straight into a gunfight. That way at least I know what I'm getting into, and at least I can kill me some Charlie."

"Amen," Mitchell said.

"Hey, at least we ain't humping mortars," said Private Jeffrey Campbell of Pennsylvania, who enlisted in the war much to the consternation of his father, the mayor of his local town. Rumor had it Campbell's father pulled strings in Washington to get his name removed from the draft, but he enlisted anyway to avoid being called a draft dodger. "Those things are heavy as fuck."

"Those mortar squads aren't the only ones carrying heavy loads," Houser said. "Kerrigan, tell your esteemed colleagues what it's like to hump all that shit on your back through this majestic paradise."

Houser was referring to the oversized rucksack Kerrigan carried on his back and the rest of his heavy medical equipment. Kerrigan hauled two-three times the weight the other grunts did.

"It's not so bad, sir."

"Not so bad?" Houser asked.

"No, sir. I've gotten used to it."

Houser let out a hearty chuckle. "You see that, guys? Y'all can learn a lot from this here Private Kerrigan. He doesn't complain. He doesn't ask questions. He carries out his orders expeditiously and without hesitation. Hell, if more of you were like Private Kerrigan, I reckon we might just wrap this fuckshow up and get our asses out of this bush in no time. Y'all should think about that."

Mitchell leaned into the ear of the last Marine in their four-man group, Private Oscar T. Guzman, a twenty-six-year-old hispanic. Mitchell and Guzman were particularly close. "Are those bags really that heavy or what?"

Guzman shrugged. "How should I know?"

"Speaking of humping," Houser said. "Y'all need to slow down with the hookers. I mean it. Too many grunts coming down with the claps, getting shot up with their hands in their pants, scratchin' their nutsacks. Besides, you get used to that tight, South

Vietnamese pussy, when you go home to your sweetheart it's gonna feel like you're slinging your hotdog down a hallway."

"He has a point," Guzman said, nodding his head.

"Shit! I never thought about it like that," Mitchell added.

"Hey, Kerrigan. I've been meaning to ask you . . . what's your position on all that?"

Kerrigan lifted his head toward Mitchell, who was ahead and to his right. He was keeping an eye out for snakes as he navigated the terrain. He was still rattled from the encounter with the cobra earlier. "I don't know what you mean."

"What I mean is every time we make a run for some boom-boom, you never come. You just stay behind and read that bible of yours. I mean, you musta read that thing a hundred times by now."

"Leave him alone," Campbell said.

"I'm just sayin'," Mitchell said. "Some of us need to blow off steam."

"Some of us don't like paying for pussy," Guzman added.

Mitchell scoffed. "The fuck you talking about, Guzman? You buy more pussy than all of us, combined."

"That's because I'm a horny bastard. Doesn't mean I like paying for it."

Campbell chuckled. "You're a cheap Charlie, Guzman. You don't like paying for anything. Not for a round for the guys once in a while like everyone else does, not for your child support . . . ."

"Oh, shit!" Mitchell cried out.

"Hey, fuck you, Campbell!" Guzman retorted.

Campbell slapped Mitchel high five. "No thanks!"

"Hey, we still didn't get an answer from Kerrigan," Mitchell said.

Kerrigan heard Mitchell, but declined to respond.

"Maybe he don't like Vietnamese pussy," Guzman said. "It does smell different. Anybody notice that?"

"I was thinking maybe Kerrigan doesn't like pussy at all," Mitchell said.

"That's enough, boys," Houser grunted. "Quiet down."

The men approached a break in the trees. Houser took a knee and signaled for the men to shelter in place. While Houser went ahead to see what was on the other side, Billy crouched next to Kerrigan.

"You alright, Billy?"

"Yeah, I'm alright."

"Good."

"I was wonderin' though. About that nickname."

"What nickname?"

"Mitchell's. Corporal said something about a nickname."

Kerrigan smiled. "Oh. They call him 'Bitchell.' Because he bitches too much."

Billy chuckled. Kerrigan couldn't recall seeing him laugh before, and he was glad to see it.

From up ahead, Houser whistled and signaled for the men to push forward toward him. As they approached, they saw the break in the trees was followed by a marsh. Houser and Rosenthal were waiting at the edge of the marsh. Neither Kerrigan nor anyone else could hear what they were saying, but it was clear they were having a serious discussion.

"Fuck me," Mitchell groaned. "Don't tell me we're walking through that shit."

"I dunno man," Guzman said. "Rendezvous's gotta be on the other side. I don't think we can just go around. Look how far it goes."

Kerrigan looked at the marsh. It stretched as far as he could see in both directions. "I think Guzman's right. We're gonna have to pass through."

Mitchell groaned again. "Nobody said anything about passing through another marsh, man."

"Dude, it's a fuckin' jungle," Guzman retorted.

Kerrigan watched closely as Rosenthal and Houser spoke. They had summoned one of the radio operators. Something wasn't right.

"Whataya think's happenin'?" Billy whispered to Kerrigan.

"I'm not sure. We're not too far now. They're probably trying to make contact with the mortar squad."

"How long you been out here?"

Kerrigan looked back at Billy. "Where? Here? In the jungle?"

"Yeah."

"Two and a half years."

"I heard the guys say you enlisted. That true?"

Kerrigan nodded. "That's true." He took a sip of water from his canteen. Like the others, he was worn out, and thirsty.

"They drafted me. My family don't think I should be fightin' this war. My daddy says our country ain't deserve my life."

"How do you feel about it?"

"Me? I don't think on it much. Right now, alls I concern

myself with is stayin' alive. Figure I can think on everythin' later."

Kerrigan nodded. He reflected for a moment how hard it must be for black soldiers like Billy to fight for a country that expects them to stand at the front lines of a questionable war yet sit at the back of the bus. The hypocrisy was both insolent and shameful. Kerrigan had had his doubts going in, and those doubts only intensified. He couldn't wait to go home and get back to finishing his residency.

Kerrigan looked back over to Rosenthal and Houser. They had just folded up a map. Houser headed back toward them.

"What's the word, Corporal?" Mitchell asked.

"Nobody's heard from the mortar squad," Houser said. He removed his helmet and scratched his head. He did not look happy.

"Shit!" Guzman uttered. "How long?"

"They missed a check-in about an hour ago. Nobody's been able to reach them since."

"So, what now?" Mitchell asked.

"We keep going. Proceed to the rendezvous. Once we get there, we wait."

"But sir, what if Charlie wiped out the other squad?"

Houser grimaced and shook his head. "Relax, Mitchell. We got no reason to assume that yet. They've been having comm issues in this area all week. Get your asses up, boys. Looks like we're wading through the muck."

"Fuck!" Mitchell groaned. "I knew it. I fuckin' knew it."

* * *

"Keep your gear high above your heads!" Houser shouted at the men. "We don't know how deep this cesspool is."

Rosenthal was sending the men into the marsh one group at a time, spreading them out in three separate directions. He chose four men to stay behind and provide cover until the first group made landfall on the other side. Because the marsh was at least fifty yards wide and dense with vegetation, he knew it would take the men some time to make it across, and he didn't want to leave them exposed without cover.

Kerrigan looked out into the tree line on the other side. The jungle seemed oddly quiet. He didn't say anything, but the idea of entering the marsh made him nervous. The marshes were typically hotbeds for disease, and they were too far north to count on a helicopter evacuation if someone came down with something serious.

Houser made his way into the marsh first, his M-16 high above his head. Mitchell stepped in behind him.

"Fuck, it's cold!" Mitchell groaned. He inched into the marsh like a child might the frigid ocean.

Houser turned back around and clutched Mitchell's forearm, pulling him in. "Get your ass in here and shut the fuck up!" Once Mitchell was in, Houser shoved his arm away.

"Ah, it's fuckin' thick," Mitchell said. He was already waist-deep in it. "It's like fuckin' quicksand or some shit."

"Shut your goddamn mouth!" Houser screamed at him. "I'm not gonna tell you again."

Guzman stepped in behind Mitchell, without complaint.

Kerrigan inched in next, waist-deep after only three or four steps. While Mitchell was exaggerating about how cold the water was, it did have a bite to it, especially after the heat of the jungle.

Kerrigan felt it sucking on his legs. He turned around and saw Billy right behind him, also wading through the muck without complaint.

"Stinks like somethin' died in here," Guzman whispered. "Somethin' definitely died in here."

Kerrigan smelled it too. There was something decomposing in the marsh, which only increased the likelihood the water was carrying harmful bacteria.

"We should keep moving before we die in here," Campbell joked. Nobody laughed.

"It's getting really deep, Corporal," Guzman said. He was on the shorter side, and the waterline had already reached his neck. "Should I keep going?"

"Keep going until you can't," Houser said. "Or find another way."

Kerrigan, neck-deep himself now, looked left through a small break in the vegetation. He saw other men from the squadron pressing ahead. The water seemed shallower where they were.

"Boss!" Guzman whispered. He reached a wall of vegetation he would need to wriggle through. Houser nodded at him to proceed. Unable to peel the greenery out the way with his hands, Guzman turned sideways and squeezed through. The rustling sound echoed over the surface of the water. One by one, the rest of the Marines followed.

As Kerrigan neared the wall of vegetation, he heard buzzing. He held his rucksack as high above his head as he could and wriggled through the vegetation. A branch from one of the plants scratched his cheek and drew a few drops of blood. On the other side, he found Houser, Mitchell, and Guzman huddled together, staring toward the noise. It was much louder.

The Marines were looking down a path surrounded by walls of vegetation. In the middle of the path, directly ahead, there was an enormous dark cloud hovering ominously above the murky water like a bad omen. It was mosquitoes—more mosquitoes in one place than Kerrigan had ever seen in his life.

"Jesuchristo," Guzman uttered.

"No!" Mitchell protested. "No way. Let's go back."

Kerrigan felt a mosquito buzz in his ear. He shook his head to shoo it away.

"They're gonna eat us alive!" Mitchell exclaimed.

"How many you think that is?" Campbell asked. He had just emerged from the greenery, right behind Billy.

"I dunno," Guzman said. "Millions?"

Campbell shook his head. "No way. Thousands definitely. Maybe a hundred thousand."

"It doesn't matter how many fuckin' mosquitos there are!" Mitchell groaned. He was getting louder. "It's too many. We'll all come down with malaria if we walk through that shit. We should double back and find another way."

Kerrigan winced as a mosquito bit him in the neck. Though Mitchell wasn't one of his favorite people, he couldn't help but share the younger Marine's concern. Walking through the cloud of mosquitoes was a serious health risk.

Houser was quiet. He stared into the hovering mass, calculating. Kerrigan understood the predicament they were in— they couldn't see the rest of the men through the heavy vegetation and had to assume they were pressing forward. The last thing they wanted was to fall behind. Rosenthal would be furious.

"We keep going," Houser said. "I don't like it any more than you guys do, but as far as I'm concerned we're sitting ducks in this fucking cesspool, and I want us out ASAP. Just move through it, fast as you can."

Mitchell grunted.

"Shut up, Mitchell! Alright? I'll take the lead," Houser said. He held his rifle even higher above his head and pressed forward into the dark cloud. Guzman went next, followed by Mitchell. Kerrigan and the others brought up the rear.

Kerrigan watched as Houser and Guzman walked through the mosquitos. Within seconds, the backs of their necks were covered with dozens of mosquitoes, and they groaned and flinched with pain from the onslaught of bites. By the time Kerrigan entered the cloud, there were mosquitos all over his face. He kept blinking to keep them out of his eyes. Men on either side of him moaned and groaned with pain. They were being eaten alive.

"There's too many!" Mitchell cried out. "There's too many. We have to go back! We have to go back! Ah, son of a fucking bitch!"

"Just keep moving," Guzman said. He was just behind Mitchell.

Kerrigan cringed as a mosquito landed on his nose. He watched with crossed eyes as the mosquito bit him. He wanted so badly to just drop his gear into the marsh and swat the mosquitoes away.

The sound of a snapping tree branch cracked through the air. The men froze in place as thousands of mosquitos buzzed around them. The sound was deafening. The men watched feverishly as Houser pushed forward to investigate.

"Fuck, there's one in my ear!" Mitchell protested.

"Shut up!" Guzman said.

"It's in my fucking ear! Fuck! I can't do this! I can't do this!"

"Shut up, man!" Guzman pleaded. "You're gonna get us killed!"

Kerrigan looked back at Billy. He was standing there silently, but trembling. There were mosquitos all over his face.

"Fuck this!" Mitchell cried out. He dropped his rifle and gear into the water and headed back where they came from. His movement echoed dangerously through the marsh. "I'm goin' back! I'm goin' back!"

Houser snapped back around with wide, angry eyes, and watched furiously as Mitchell sloshed through the water. As Mitchell squeezed his way past Kerrigan, the ominous crack of an AK-47 pierced the air. Something struck Mitchell from behind and his body arched backwards. His mouth wide open, he looked at Kerrigan for a fleeting moment and then went limp. His body dropped abruptly and he sunk into the marsh. Guzman reached out for him.

"FALL BACK!" Houser screamed. "FALL BACK!"

The trees on the other side of the marsh lit up like Christmas trees with muzzles flashes from AK-47s. Bullets rained down on the men from all angles, splashing violently into the water like pellets from a hailstorm. The Marines, panicked and neck-deep in the brown water, dropped their weapons and gear and scattered in all directions to avoid the incoming gunfire. Guzman was still reaching for Mitchell's sinking body when a bullet tore through his shoulder, blowing a fine mist of blood into the air. The impact stunned him and left him frozen. Kerrigan noticed he wasn't budging and pulled him away.

"No! I can't leave him!" Guzman protested. Mitchell was below the surface now. Pools of bright red blood floated to the surface like oil on water. "He's fucking drowning!"

"He's not!" Kerrigan said.

"Look at the bubbles, man! He's drowning! He's fucking drowning!"

"He's dead, Guzman! We gotta go!"

A grenade went off a few feet away, spraying water and blood into the air. Kerrigan dove beneath the surface, thrashing as bullets cut through the water around him. He rose to the surface and found himself surrounded by vegetation. Guzman was nowhere to be seen. Nor was anyone else.

"Oscar!" Kerrigan whispered. "Billy!"

There was nothing, only the terrible sounds of rifle shots and men screaming for their lives.

Bullets showered down on Kerrigan again, cutting through some of the vegetation around him. He dove below the surface without a breath. He kicked violently and tried to swim his way to safety, but the heavy, viscous water dragged at him. It was like swimming in motor oil. Not a moment later, a bullet ripped through his left calf. He howled from the pain while still below the water and drew water into his lungs. He surfaced, flailing in the water and gasping for air. Blood from his wound bubbled up, pooling around his torso.

The gunfire abruptly ceased. It was eerily silent. Kerrigan grabbed a rod of bamboo to steady himself. He stood still and listened. The quiet was interrupted by stealthy splashing. It sounded like multiple men had entered the marsh.

Kerrigan's heart raced. As quietly as he could, he moved through the water, pulling himself from one plant to another in an effort to keep pressure off his wounded leg. One of the plants he grabbed snapped suddenly under his weight, and he was sucked beneath the water. When he surfaced again, he spotted a Việt Cộng soldier waist-deep in the marsh, three or four yards away. The soldier saw Kerrigan. He shouted in Vietnamese and lifted up his AK-47. Kerrigan watched frozen as the soldier lined his weapon up for a shot.

Kerrigan dove through a wall of vegetation as gunfire erupted around him. He went below the surface again, tumbling this time like clothing in a washing machine. Bullets zipped through the water around him. He kicked desperately to escape. Out of breath, he surfaced, treading water. His injured leg, burning with pain, was failing. He couldn't stay afloat. He was drowning.

From behind, someone grabbed Kerrigan by the neck. Kerrigan fought to break free, but the man was too strong. The Việt Cộng soldier Kerrigan encountered a moment earlier exploded through nearby greenery and lined up for another shot. This was it, Kerrigan thought. He closed his eyes and waited.

Three pops went off next to his head, the sounds excruciatingly loud. A body fell into the water. Kerrigan opened his eyes and saw the man with the AK-47 sink into the marsh. The man still holding him had done the shooting.

"I got you," the man said. "I got you."

Kerrigan looked over his shoulder. Both of his ears were ringing. "Billy?"

"Yes, sir."

Kerrigan turned to look at him but slid below the surface again. Billy pulled him back up. Voices yelled out in Vietnamese. More water sloshed. There were more Việt Cộng, and they were closing in.

"Billy, you gotta go. I can't walk. Just go, take care of your—"

Before Kerrigan could get another word out, Billy knelt over and lifted Kerrigan over his shoulder with surprising strength and proceeded to carry him out of the marsh.

More Vietnamese voices echoed. They were closer, still.

"They're coming, Billy! They're coming! I'm just slowing you down. Let me go and get your ass out of here."

With Kerrigan's heavy weight on his shoulder, he pressed forward, one step at a time. He squeezed through the greenery and made it to the bank of the marsh.

"Billy, get down!"

Another Việt Cộng soldier emerged from the marsh and opened fire. Billy screamed in pain, and Kerrigan fell with him. They rolled and slid down a slope slick with mud. When Kerrigan came to rest at the bottom of the slope, Billy wasn't there.

Kerrigan stood slowly, looking for Billy. He tried to climb the muddy slope, but his injured leg burned like fire.

Two more Việt Cộng soldiers emerged over the crest of the slope and opened fire on him. He dove through nearby shrubbery. As bullets continued to spray around him, he hobbled desperately into the jungle. He didn't look back.

* * *

Kerrigan limped for at least a hundred yards before he stopped to rest, panting and shaking. He leaned against a tree trunk to take weight off his wounded leg. The adrenaline sustaining him had faded, and the pain intensified. As far as he could tell, he'd lost the two Việt Cộng soldiers who'd opened fire on him from the top of the slope, but he couldn't be certain.

After Kerrigan had caught his breath, he bent down to examine his wound. He pulled up his pant leg and poured water from his canteen over it. Once he washed most of the blood and mud away, he could see it was just a flesh wound; a round had entered the meaty part of his calf and passed clean through. He reached instinctively for his medical supplies, but remembered he had dropped his rucksack into the marsh after the shots rang out.

A blood-curdling scream pierced the air. Kerrigan wheeled around toward the marsh. It sounded like Billy. "I'm coming," Kerrigan uttered. "I'm coming."

Kerrigan reached frantically for his knife and cut off one of his sleeves. He knelt down, bit down on the handle of the knife, and tied the sleeve around his injured leg. His teeth digging into the knife, Kerrigan tugged on the knot with all his strength, tightening it. The pain was unbearable.

Billy screamed again. Gunfire erupted. Water splashed. Việt Cộng soldiers shouted at each other.

Kerrigan shot to his feet. "I'm coming. I'm coming." His leg was still bleeding. Knife in hand, he headed back toward the marsh.

A heavy fog suddenly rolled in. The jungle was dead quiet again. Kerrigan used the fog as cover and moved slowly. With each step, his leg burned with excruciating pain.

Kerrigan made it back to the muddy slope. He spotted a trail of blood and followed it back to the marsh. His knife held high, he stepped back in. His leg stung as it contacted the water. He moved slowly, careful not to make noise. Following a trail of blood on the surface, Kerrigan came to a body and turned it over. It was Corporal Houser. He had been shot in the forehead. Kerrigan closed Houser's eyelids and retrieved his dog tags.

Kerrigan suddenly heard rippling water and ducked next to Houser's body. Two Việt Cộng soldiers were turning over other floating bodies, making sure they were dead.

Kerrigan heard more water ripple to his right. A third Việt Cộng soldier was wading right toward him, a machete in one hand and an AK-47 in the other.

Kerrigan quickly squeezed through a row of tall reeds to escape. On the other side, he was overwhelmed with the stench of rotting flesh. It was the same smell Guzman had picked up earlier, only much stronger. Kerrigan was horrified to see two dead Marines hung like scarecrows on rods of bamboo. Hundreds of flies and mosquitos circled the two corpses. Kerrigan, shocked by the image, nearly forgot the immediate danger he was in. He heard Việt Cộng soldiers shout and snapped toward the voices. The three soldiers huddled together disbanded, with one heading straight toward Kerrigan.

Kerrigan scanned desperately for an escape, but the soldier was too close. With nowhere else to go, Kerrigan squeezed himself between the decomposing corpses and hid. The odor from the rotting corpses was so overwhelming he could taste it. He struggled to remain motionless.

Not one, but two Việt Cộng soldiers pushed through the reeds and stopped just in front of the dead Marines. They looked up at the corpses and laughed. Kerrigan held his breath and struggled to remain still as his injured leg was threatening to give way.

Another Việt Cộng soldier shouted in the distance. The soldiers rushed toward the voice, creating ripples that pushed tainted water up into Kerrigan's nostrils. Kerrigan coughed. One of the soldiers turned back, listening. Kerrigan remained as still as possible. The soldier moved on.

Kerrigan was about to move when he heard a hissing sound. It was close, right above his head. He froze in place.

The snake hissed again, louder this time. Kerrigan couldn't see it, but he knew it just was above him. Using only his eyeballs, he watched, terrified, as a long, black snake slithered down one of the dead Marine's arms and slipped into the water just in front of him. It skimmed weightlessly across the surface until it disappeared into the greenery. His heart pounding, Kerrigan heaved a sigh of relief as he moved away from the corpses and moved deeper into the marsh.

He entered a pocket of water free of vegetation. It was red with blood and filled with the floating bodies of his fallen squadmates. Some were bobbing facedown like Corporal Houser had been; others were face up, staring emptily at the gray sky above. Kerrigan broke down in tears.

Then someone coughed. Kerrigan saw a Marine sprawled out over a log.

"Billy!" Kerrigan whispered. He waded toward him. "Billy!"

Billy was barely conscious. His breaths were shallow and labored. Kerrigan spotted an exit wound on the upper right portion of Billy's back. Blood oozing from the hole bubbled with each of his heavy breaths. It was a sucking wound. With each breath, Billy was drawing air into his chest cavity, making it more difficult for him to breathe. Without immediate intervention, he would suffocate.

"Alright Billy, I got you. I got you. Just stay with me."

Kerrigan looked for a path out of the marsh. He knew that if Billy's wound dipped below the surface, water would be drawn into his chest and make matters even worse. He had no choice but to carry Billy over his shoulder.

"Alright, here we go." Kerrigan took in a deep breath and lifted Billy with everything he had. Kerrigan's legs sank into the mud under the weight. The pain in his leg was excruciating. Yet, one step at a time, sweating and gasping for air, Kerrigan carried Billy toward dry land. He pushed through greenery, navigated around the floating bodies of his fallen comrades, and forced his way through water so deep that he tiptoed to keep his nose above the surface.

When Kerrigan reached the edge of the marsh, he set Billy down and tended to his wound. Billy was still breathing, but his lips were turning blue. Kerrigan heard a noise and looked up. A Việt Cộng soldier cracked him over the head with the butt of his rifle. When his vision cleared, he realized that he and Billy were facedown in the mud, surrounded by Việt Cộng soldiers who had their weapons trained at their heads. One of them smiled at

Kerrigan, raised his pistol, and pressed it into his temple. Kerrigan closed his eyes and waited for it to be over.

Gunfire erupted around him. A mist of blood enveloped him. Bodies thudded to the ground all around him. Shaking violently, Kerrigan opened his eyes. The Việt Cộng soldiers were all dead. Marines he did not recognize approached, their M-16s smoking. It was the mortar squad. They'd shown up just in time.

CHAPTER 8

"HISS!"

Father Kerrigan awoke gasping for air. He was still lying on the ground, face-up, at the bottom of the slope he'd tumbled down. He tried to lift his head off the cold, wet ground to get his bearings, but the movement made him dizzy.

The fog was still there, but it had receded. Now it rose only inches above the ground, just high enough that the snake could slither undetected.

"Hiss!"

It was closer now. Leaves near Kerrigan's torso rustled.

"Help!" Kerrigan whispered, hopelessly. "Somebody help!"

The serpent lifted its head just above the fog and sampled the damp air with its forked tongue. It swiveled back and forth as if in search of something, then looked right at Kerrigan. It was about to strike. Helpless, Kerrigan closed his eyes.

He was startled by a whipping sound, followed by dull thumps against the soggy ground. He opened his eyes and watched as a long shaft repeatedly struck the ground next to him. It was Carmichael. He was beating at the ground with his cane, scaring the snake away.

The serpent slithered between tall blades of grass into a small body of water. Relieved, Kerrigan laid his head back down.

"Thank God," he gasped. "Thank God. You got here just in time. You got here just in time."

Carmichael thumped his cane back into the wet earth and leaned on it. He was catching his breath. "You're alright, Nathan. It was just a mud snake. Sinister looking, but non-venomous."

Carmichael bent over and extended his hand. Kerrigan, still on his back, looked at the hand but shook his head. He was exhausted. "I can't do this anymore, Monsignor."

"We're not finished."

"I am. I'm done. I'm tired."

Carmichael kept his hand out. "We've come so far, Nathan. Makes no sense to turn back now."

"I can't do it anymore. I'm sorry, but I just can't. I don't even have my cigarettes. I lost them in the fog. I'll never make it without—"

"Nathan—"

Kerrigan shook his head, despairingly. "I can't, Monsignor."

"Nathan—"

"Please, no more. Not today. Not today—"

Carmichael shouted at Kerrigan. "Nathan!"

Kerrigan looked up and saw Carmichael was holding out a pack of Marlboro Reds. His pack.

"How did you find—"

"Almost tripped over them trying to find you." Carmichael slid one of the cigarettes out of the pack. "There's still a couple left. Now come on, let's go."

Kerrigan hesitated a few moments, staring at the cigarette. Then he took it and slid it between his lips. He felt for his matchbook, which he still had, and lit the cigarette. He took in several deep drags and blew the smoke out into the cool air.

Carmichael looked down at him. "Can you walk? Are you hurt?"

Kerrigan shook his head. "I'm alright. Just a couple of bruises I think."

Carmichael offered his hand again. Kerrigan hesitated a moment, then took it and stood up.

"Come on," Carmichael said. "This way."

Carmichael led Kerrigan back to the dirt trail. For a while, they just walked in a companionable silence.

The large trees made way for ferns rising above beds of blue and lavender hyssop. Kerrigan enjoyed his cigarette as he looked out at the shrubbery. The woods were surprisingly colorful. It was beautiful.

Birds cawed overhead, breaking the silence.

"Are they back?" Kerrigan asked. He was looking up into the trees. He heard fluttering, but saw nothing.

"Not all of them, I don't think. Seems like there are a few sentries."

More birds cawed. Kerrigan stopped and looked up. He saw a couple of the black birds move from one tree to another.

"Nathan?"

"Yes?"

"Are you going to tell me what happened to you or not?"

Kerrigan looked at Carmichael. Carmichael was looking at him with tender eyes. Sad eyes.

"It's only me, Nathan. By God, if not me, then who?"

"No one." Kerrigan looked at the ground. "That was the idea."

"Was it really? Oh, Nathan. What did you expect? Did you really think I would just run to Bishop Gailey without asking questions? You know me better than that."

Kerrigan didn't respond. He turned and looked into the trees. "I should have known."

"Should have known what?"

"But if ye will not do so, behold, ye have sinned against the Lord: and be sure your sin will find you out. I fooled myself into thinking that no longer applies to me."

Carmichael took a step closer to Kerrigan. Kerrigan heard him approaching but refused to turn around.

"For the longest time I was afraid the truth would come to find me. Lived with that terrible fear for years. Years. It was this constant pit in my stomach. But then . . . I don't know what happened, but I actually started to believe I'd outrun it. How naive I was. I never outran anything. It's been here with me all this time."

"Something happened to you in Vietnam. Didn't it?"

Kerrigan nodded. His hands trembled again. Tears began slowly trickling down his face.

"What happened?"

Kerrigan wept. Carmichael put his hand on Kerrigan's shoulder.

"Come on," Carmichael said. "We have to keep moving."

Kerrigan turned toward Carmichael but couldn't bear to look him in the eye. Carmichael noticed and gently lifted Kerrigan's chin.

"Talk to me, Nathaniel."

"I . . . can't."

"Yes, you can."

"I'm . . . afraid."

"What have you to fear? This demon, he already knows—"

"I don't care what the demon thinks."

"Who then? The world? Me?"

Kerrigan said nothing. He wept inconsolably. Carmichael grabbed Kerrigan's arms and pulled him forward. "You've nothing to fear, my son. For forty years, I've known you and watched you grow. I know how you live your life. I know what kind of man you are. There's very nearly nothing that can change that. Not today. Not ever. Do you understand?"

Kerrigan shook his head.

"Do you understand?"

Kerrigan looked at Carmichael, into his green-blue eyes, then nodded.

"Come on," Carmichael said, easing Kerrigan forward again. "We've got to go."

Kerrigan followed Carmichael's lead and the two priests continued along the trail. Kerrigan reached into his pocket for another cigarette and ripped another match from his matchbook.

When Carmichael noticed, he grabbed Kerrigan's hand and stopped him from lighting it. "Why don't you take a break? Hmm? Just for a little while?"

Kerrigan was caught off guard by Carmichael's gesture, but yielded. He slid the cigarette back into the pack and put it away.

"I didn't want to go, you know," Kerrigan said.

"To Vietnam?"

"I wanted to finish my residency, become a real doctor as soon as possible. I was still young and idealistic. I wanted to start helping people and change the whole world while I was at it. Change medicine at least. I was gonna be good at it, you know. Even then, I knew it. I thought I was born for it."

"So why did you go? To Vietnam?"

"It was my father."

"He made you?"

Kerrigan shook his head. "No, he didn't make me. That wasn't his way. But he was such a proud veteran. He loved this country. He believed in his bones that we have a duty to serve. He believed it so deeply it started to wear off on me. Who was I to go off and live out my dreams while so many others were dying over there? Even if the war was all wrong, it didn't feel right to just sit back and do nothing. I remember telling him I'd enlisted . . . his eyes lit up so bright, it was . . . I'd never seen him so happy or proud about anything, especially after my mother died. Then I told him I was going to be a medic."

"How did he take it?"

Kerrigan laughed. "Wasn't quite what he had in mind. But I didn't budge. Told him it was that or nothing. He didn't like it, but he saw I meant it, and you know, after a while, I think he actually began to see the value in it. And that was that. I trained as a combat medic, and then I was off to the war."

"Must've been frightening."

"It was. I remember trying to make peace with myself before I left, in case I didn't make it back. But boy, did I pray to

God that I did. I prayed every day. That's how I got close to him, you know. Then one night after a really hard day in the jungle, I made a pact with him, that if he brought me home alive and well enough, I would spend the rest of my life helping people."

"As a doctor?"

"As a doctor. That was always the plan."

"You turned out to be a fine combat medic, didn't you?"

Kerrigan looked at Carmichael and shrugged. "I did my job. That's all."

"Seems you did more than that."

"You've seen the article, haven't you?"

Carmichael nodded. "Yes, I saw it. Read your interview, saw your picture on the cover of that magazine."

The sky darkened as heavy clouds rolled in from beyond the horizon. The trail was suddenly darker than it had been all day. Kerrigan stopped.

"I hated that interview. I didn't want to do it. I wasn't going to do it. But they made me. Made a publicity stunt of the whole thing."

"There's more to that story, isn't there? That's what this is all about, isn't—"

Thunder rumbled for several moments, like God's stomach was empty.

"Do you hear that?" Kerrigan asked, looking around.

"Hear what? The thunder?"

"No."

Several black birds shot up from the trees and took to the sky.

"Easy, Nathan," Carmichael whispered.

"What is it?" Kerrigan heard growling and turned around. A wild dog stood in the middle of the trail, snarling and bearing teeth. Strings of saliva hung from its open mouth.

"We need to move," Kerrigan whispered.

"No! Stay still, Nath—"

The wild dog took off running and barrelled toward them. Kerrigan stepped into its path to protect Carmichael from the assault, but the dog ran right past him. The snarling dog catapulted itself into Carmichael, knocking him to the ground.

"Monsignor!"

Kerrigan ran to the dog and wrapped his arms around its body, ripping it off Carmichael and tossing it away. The dog landed on its feet and lunged at Kerrigan, sinking its fangs into his sleeve. Kerrigan tried to shake it off, but it wouldn't let go.

"Here!" Carmichael cried out. He held out his cane.

As the dog tugged at his arm, Kerrigan reached for the cane with the other. He finally grabbed it and began striking the dog as hard as he could. After several blows, the dog yelped and ran off into the woods.

Down on one knee, Kerrigan leaned on Carmichael's cane to get up. He turned to Carmichael and was horrified to see him clutching the side of his neck, with blood oozing between his fingers.

"Oh, Christ!" Kerrigan exclaimed. He ran toward Carmichael and dropped to his knees next to him. "Let me see!"

"I'm alright, Nathan. I'm alright."

"You're bleeding!"

Kerrigan tried to pull Carmichael's hand off the wound, but Carmichael pulled away. "Let me see it, Monsignor."

"It's fine. Just a scratch. I'm okay."

Blood was still oozing through Carmichael's fingers.

"It's not just a scratch. Here, take this." Kerrigan pulled out his white handkerchief. Carmichael took it reluctantly and pressed it against his wound. "Just keep pressure on it, okay? Stay right there."

Kerrigan stood up and took out his cellphone. He tried to dial out, but couldn't get a signal.

"What are you doing?" Carmichael asked. He sat up and watched as Kerrigan waved the phone around.

"I'm calling an ambulance, getting you the hell out of here. Do you know where we are? How do I even tell them where we are?"

Carmichael reached for his cane and stood up. "I don't need an ambulance."

Kerrigan kicked at the ground. "Son of a bitch! I can't get a goddamn signal!"

"Nathan, put the phone down."

"What?"

"We have to keep going."

Kerrigan got in Carmichael's face. "Keep going? Are you out of your fucking mind?"

"I told you I'm fine. Now let's go."

Kerrigan stared at the handkerchief. It was mostly red now, soaked through with blood. "You're not fine. You were just attacked by a dog and you're bleeding from your neck. You need stitches, antibiotics . . . probably a rabies shot."

Carmichael shook his head. "That dog doesn't have rabies, Nathan."

"How can you know that?"

"Because I've seen rabies."

"Goddamnit!" Kerrigan still couldn't get a signal.

"Stop, Nathan."

Kerrigan ignored Carmichael. He continued to pace up and down the trail, waving his cellphone around.

"Ouch!" Kerrigan cried out. Something struck his shin hard, right on the bone. It hurt like hell. Carmichael had struck him with his cane. "Why the hell did you do that?"

"Because you're not listening. And it's time to go."

"Monsignor, you're not—"

"I'm fine."

"But you're bleeding . . . we have—"

"No, I'm not. Not anymore."

"What are you talking about?"

"Look."

Kerrigan approached Carmichael and peeled the handkerchief from his neck. There were two small puncture wounds, but they were already scabbing over. Each of the wounds appeared superficial.

"You still need antibiotics. Rabies shots, too."

Carmichael approached Kerrigan and looked him square in his eyes. His expression was serious as a heart attack. "After."

"What if it comes back?"

"Another good reason to keep moving, isn't it?"

Kerrigan stood there, dumbfounded. He didn't know what to say. Carmichael started walking. His pace was brisk now, as if time was suddenly important.

A few yards ahead, Carmichael turned around. "I'm sorry about the handkerchief, by the way."

Kerrigan looked down at the once white handkerchief in his hand. The blood on it was drying, changing from bright red to dark crimson. He stared at it several moments before dropping it and leaving it behind him. Then he jogged up the trail until he caught up to Carmichael.

"Next time," Kerrigan said. "How 'bout I choose where we meet?"

Carmichael smiled at Kerrigan. Kerrigan smiled back.

"Fine," Carmichael said. "Fine."

Kerrigan looked around. The woods were quiet again.

"If what that article says is true," Carmichael said, "that makes you a hero."

"It's true. But I'm no hero."

"Why not?"

Kerrigan took in a deep breath and looked ahead. The trail appeared to go on endlessly.

* * *

"PSST!"

Private Kerrigan, asleep on his cot in the infirmary, slowly opened his eyes. He felt someone tap on his good leg.

"Yo, Kerrigan! Wake up."

His eyes still adjusting to the dim light inside the evacuation hospital, Kerrigan was only able to make out two blurry figures at the foot of his cot. When his vision finally cleared, he realized he was looking at Privates Guzman and Campbell, both were in wheelchairs and hospital gowns. Guzman's shoulder was wrapped in gauze. Campbell was holding two vanilla ice cream cones. The three Marines were at the 91st evacuation hospital in Chu Lai, just under a hundred miles south of where they were ambushed by the Việt Cộng days earlier.

"You want one?" Campbell asked.

"No, thanks," Kerrigan said, squinting toward a small clock hanging on the tent wall across from his cot. It was two-thirty in the afternoon. "What's going on?"

"What you got planned for tonight?" Campbell asked, licking his ice cream cone. The other was melting, with streams of ice cream running down his fingers.

Kerrigan sat up, careful not to disturb his wounded leg. It was still tender; due to infection from the bacteria in the marsh, the wound was healing slowly. An intravenous drip with antibiotics was still connected to Kerrigan's arm. "What do I got planned? What do you mean? I'll be here. Lying in bed. What else?"

"We're goin' out. To celebrate," Campbell added. There was a spot of ice cream on his nose.

"To celebrate? What's there to celebrate?"

Guzman noticed the ice cream on Campbell's nose and let him know by touching his own. His hands were still occupied with the two cones, so he wiped his nose on his sleeve.

"You tell him," Campbell said.

Guzman looked at Kerrigan. "They're writing you up for the Silver Star, brother."

Kerrigan sat up even straighter. "What?"

"Yeah—you're getting a medal," Campbell said. "We just heard. That's why we woke you up."

"For what?"

"For what?" Campbell scoffed. "Come on, Kerrigan. You know what you did. You saved our asses."

"I did what I was supposed to do."

"You're the only one who went back," Guzman said. "On a bum leg. You deserve it."

Kerrigan sat there silent a moment, processing the news. "What about Billy?"

"He's gonna be alright," Guzman said. "The surgery went good. He's going home."

"No, I know that. Are they giving him a medal, too?"

Both Campbell and Guzman looked at each other. They shook their heads and shrugged. It was clear they didn't know what Kerrigan was talking about.

"He saved me first. After I took one in the leg, I was gonna drown in that marsh, but he pulled me out. I've been telling everyone that."

Campbell and Guzman just looked at each other.

"If he's not getting one, I shouldn't be either."

"We didn't hear nothin' about Billy," Guzman said. "But for you, everybody already knows."

"What do you mean, everybody knows?"

"They're sending it through all the wires," Campbell said. He bit off the top of one of his ice cream cones. "Your name's gonna be on it and everything. The whole Corps is gonna know who you are now. What you did."

"Why would they do that?"

Campbell finished the cone and looked over his shoulder as if to make sure no one was listening. Then he leaned in closer. "Think about it, Kerrigan. White combat medic, wounded, risks his tail for a black Marine? Way things are goin', that's some pretty good public relations material. They're saying it'll help with recruitment or something. I dunno."

Kerrigan lay back on his cot and thought in silence. While a part of him couldn't wait to share the news with his father, the blatant racism disgusted him. It was one thing to watch others engage in such shameful behavior and another to be made a part of it. Kerrigan was beginning to wish he'd never enlisted.

"How's the lieutenant?" Kerrigan asked. Lieutenant Rosenthal had also been wounded in the attack, but had managed to escape the marsh and radio for help. Shrapnel from a grenade had sliced open Rosenthal's cheek, but he'd suffered no other injuries.

Guzman shook his head. "He's drinking like a fish. Won't talk to anybody. He blames himself."

"Where he's getting it?" Kerrigan asked.

"You know Rosenthal," Campbell said. "That prick's got friends everywhere."

Kerrigan shook his head. For weeks, he'd watched as the lieutenant slowly descended into what seemed like a very serious depression. This was sure to finish him off.

"Anyway," Guzman said. "He's gonna be there. He's the one who set it up."

"Where?" Kerrigan asked.

"I dunno, some bar in one of the villages. He knows the spot. It's not far."

"Are you nuts? I can't go to a bar. I can barely walk."

"Come on, man," Guzman retorted. "Don't be like that. I saw you walking around here with that nurse yesterday. Come out for a little while, get your ass out of that bed. Have a drink. It will be good for you."

"I can't drink," Kerrigan said. He looked over to his intravenous drip. "I still have antibiotics in my system."

"Don't worry," Campbell said. "Doc said you can have one or two. It won't kill you. We already talked to him."

Kerrigan lay there quietly. He really didn't want to go out, not in the slightest. Besides, the bars the guys liked to visit typically weren't just bars.

"Listen, you better come," Guzman said. "Otherwise the lieutenant's gonna be upset. He set the whole thing up, you know."

Kerrigan paused a moment. "What kind of bar? The kinds of places you guys go, that's not really my—"

"Don't worry, we know," Guzman said. "Just come out, have a drink."

"I don't know," Kerrigan said. "My leg—"

"What's to know?" Guzman asked. "Come on man. You deserve a night out. You're a hero now."

"It just doesn't feel right. It doesn't feel right."

"What doesn't feel right?" Campbell asked.

"Celebrating. Having a good time. With all the guys we lost . . . ."

Guzman grabbed Kerrigan's wrist. "I know, brother. I watched Mitchell sink underneath the water. He was my brother.

You were there. You pulled me away, saved my ass too. Mitchell's gone. They're all gone. I'm still here because of you. We're all still here. For now. But how long before one of us goes next? Huh? Nobody knows. That's why we gotta live a little. Come on. We deserve this. You deserve it, brother."

"Yeah, Kerrigan. Let us buy you a drink. It'll be fun. We'll have fun."

Kerrigan looked up at his intravenous bag and then down at his wounded leg. He hesitated a few moments, then nodded reluctantly in agreement.

* * *

Kerrigan stared at himself in the mirror as he slid his razor down the side of his face. He hadn't shaved since before the ambush, and his face and neck were beginning to itch from his short beard. As he rinsed off the blade under the faucet, he felt a small twinge of pain on his face and watched a sliver of blood ooze from his cheek. He started to wipe his cheek with a towel, then froze. Small as it was, the line of blood dripping from his cheek brought him back to the marsh, the sight of his squadmates floating facedown in the muck. It brought him back to the helicopter ride over the South China Sea, where he burned through reams of gauze stabilizing Billy's sucking wound. Kerrigan was lucky to be alive. Damn lucky. Perhaps Guzman was right. Perhaps it was time to live a little. Still, a lump formed in the pit of Kerrigan's stomach, solid as a rock. He wasn't quite sure why.

Kerrigan looked at the pistol and thigh holster Guzman and Campbell had brought to him earlier. They'd told him to strap it on and conceal it beneath his pants, just to be safe. He hadn't thought about it before, but he would have to strap it to his injured leg.

*　*　*

As instructed, Kerrigan met Guzman and Campbell at the rear of the evacuation hospital, near the loading area. A nurse, aware of the outing, pushed Kerrigan in a wheelchair. Outside, a convertible jeep was waiting with the engine running. Guzman and Campbell were already sitting inside, Guzman in the front passenger seat and Campbell in the back just behind him. An officer Kerrigan didn't recognize was in the driver's seat, tapping on the steering wheel. Kerrigan got out of his wheelchair and limped his way toward the jeep. He had considered taking a set of crutches with him, but decided he could manage without. He still couldn't believe he was leaving the comfort of his cot for a night out with the boys.

"You need help?" Campbell asked as Kerrigan approached the jeep.

"Nah, I got it." Kerrigan grunted with pain as he climbed inside. He immediately smelled alcohol.

"You want one?" Campbell asked. He held out a can of Budweiser. There were several empty cans on the floor.

"Not right now. Thanks."

Campbell shrugged his shoulders. "Suit yourself."

"Where's the lieutenant?" Kerrigan asked.

"He's already there," Guzman said. "He's been there a while with a couple other guys he knows. We're meeting them there. You got the piece?"

"Yeah," Kerrigan said. He looked at the lump bulging from underneath his pant leg. "I got it."

"That everybody?" the officer in the driver's seat asked.

"Yeah, muchacho," Guzman said. "Let's hit the road."

* * *

"You want a drag?" Guzman hollered out to Kerrigan from the front seat. The warm summer air blowing over the windshield and into their faces made it difficult for the Marines to hear each other unless they shouted. Guzman was smoking a Marlboro Red.

"No thanks!" Kerrigan shouted. "I don't smoke."

"What do you do, then?" Campbell asked. He took the cigarette from Guzman, pulled in a long drag, and blew the smoke straight up into the night sky. The breeze carried it behind the jeep along with a cloud of dust from the dirt road they were traversing.

"Those things will give you lung cancer, you know," Kerrigan said. "It's true. They're doing a lot of studies now that show—"

"I'll worry about lung cancer when I make it out of here alive," Campbell said. He looked at Kerrigan and smiled as he took another drag. "How 'bout that?"

Kerrigan went back to looking out into the night. The jeep rounded the crest of a hill not far from the coast. Kerrigan watched the moon shimmer off the waves rolling in from the South China Sea.

* * *

The dirt road led the Marines away from the coast and deeper inland. The view of the sea made way for rolling countryside, the moonlight occasionally glistening over rice paddies and other small bodies of water. On the horizon, narrow plumes of smoke from man-made fires billowed into the air. There were several villages spread out over the land.

The driver slowed the jeep as he passed over a portion of the dirt road flooded with rainwater from a rainstorm that had passed through earlier.

"How much farther?" Kerrigan asked. Campbell and Guzman were both asleep. They were already drunk.

"It's just up the road," the officer driving the jeep said.

Kerrigan sat quietly as the officer followed the dirt road downhill. They were close enough to the villages that Kerrigan could make out the individual huts and other structures. As he took in the night air, he thought about how risky this was, venturing out beyond the relative safety of the evacuation hospital. Out here, they were on their own.

The driver took a left turn and followed an even narrower dirt road over a wooden bridge. The bridge passed over a small marsh flanking one of the villages Kerrigan had spotted earlier. Under the moonlight, Kerrigan was able to make out a South Vietnamese man fishing in a canoe. The man lifted his rice hat and watched as the jeep crossed the bridge.

The driver followed the dirt road around a bend leading past several huts and into a marketplace—instead of huts, there were long, open shacks and some more permanent structures made from stone and mortar. The village was quiet, desolate. Other than the man fishing near the bridge, Kerrigan hadn't seen a soul. The huts and other structures were silent and dark, the only light that of the moon.

"Look out!" Kerrigan hollered.

The driver hesitated a moment but then saw the small figure dart out into the road. He slammed on the brakes. The wheels locked up tight and the jeep slid several feet before coming to stop in a thick cloud of dirt. Kerrigan held his breath until the cloud dissipated enough for him to see the boy was fine. The jeep had stopped in time. A woman from a nearby hut ran toward the boy, took his hand, and pulled him out of the street. Lit by the jeep's headlights, she flashed the Marines a scornful look that conveyed both disapproval and resignation. These people didn't want them there, Kerrigan thought. They only tolerated it because they were poor and needed the money.

"Thanks," the driver said, his voice trailing off. He'd been rattled. "I didn't even see him. I didn't see him. Did you? I woulda hit him."

"I barely saw him eith—"

"Where are we?" Guzman asked, yawning.

"It's just up ahead," the driver said. He drove toward a large hut decorated with colorful lights.

Kerrigan thought he heard the dull roar of music in the distance.

* * *

The roar grew louder as the jeep approached the hut. Kerrigan realized it wasn't just music he heard; there was a gasoline generator running just outside the hut.

"Here it is," the driver said.

"Yo, Campbell," Guzman said. "Wake up."

"What?" Campbell asked, his eyes still closed.

"Time to go, muchacho. We're here."

"Shit, alright."

Guzman hopped out of the jeep. Kerrigan and Campbell followed him. With his injured leg, it took Kerrigan a little while longer to climb out.

"Someone will be back in a few hours," the driver said to the Marines.

"Not you?" Guzman asked.

"No, not me. I'll be sleeping."

Guzman reached into his uniform and pulled out a ten dollar bill. He handed it to the driver.

"Thanks," the driver said. Then he made a three-point turn and headed back the way he'd come.

"Wow," Campbell said.

"Wow what?" Guzman asked.

"You're actually covering something for a change."

"Hey, fuck you, alright? Let's go."

Guzman and Campbell headed toward the door of the hut. Kerrigan hesitated, wondering again why he'd agreed to come.

"You coming or what?" Campbell asked.

Kerrigan stood there a few more moments, then limped his way toward the door.

* * *

Campbell pulled the door open and a thick cloud of cigarette smoke and loud Vietnamese dance music enveloped the Marines before they even stepped inside. Kerrigan's suspicions were immediately confirmed. This was no bar; it was a brothel. The place was crowded with prostitutes and Marines. The women were scantily clad in tiny miniskirts and revealing bras, some were completely topless. Some of the Marines were lounging around on sofas and red velvet chairs with faux gold accents. Others were getting lap dances. Women mingled with Marines in front of the bar area, where a young bartender was serving Saigon Tea. Even under the dim glow of the light bulbs hanging from the ceiling, it was clear all of the women were very young.

"Welcome," said a gentleman dressed in slacks and a striped, silk shirt. The gentleman's open collar displayed several gold chains.

"We're with Rosenthal," Guzman said.

The gentleman nodded and motioned for the Marines to come inside. It seemed this was an exclusive affair.

Guzman and Campbell headed straight for the bar. Kerrigan followed nervously. As he looked around, he felt someone touch his arm from behind. It was one of the women.

"Some tea?" the woman asked Kerrigan. She rubbed his shoulder.

Kerrigan smiled nervously. "No . . . no thank you."

The woman stared at Kerrigan, waiting.

"I'm okay for now," Kerrigan said.

"Dude," Guzman whispered in Kerrigan's ear. "You can't just turn her down. You just got here. Get one and then buy her one. That's how this works."

"You didn't tell me we were going to a brothel."

"You need to relax, man. What did we talk about, huh? Enjoy yourself for a change."

The woman tugged on Kerrigan's shoulder again, then leaned in closer. She gazed at him with large, watchful eyes heavily lined with light blue eyeliner; her lips were covered with bright, red lipstick. She had on a short miniskirt and a translucent satin shirt. Her black, lacy bra showed through. The other women seemed to be made up similarly. Kerrigan found it a bit much.

"Okay, I'll take a tea," Kerrigan said. He reached into his pocket for his wallet. "Would you like one, too?"

The woman smiled and nodded. Kerrigan noticed she had a silver tooth.

"How much?"

"One dollar."

Kerrigan pulled out a one dollar bill.

"Each," the woman said.

Kerrigan hesitated, then pulled out another dollar. When he handed her the money, the woman signaled for the bartender and shouted at him. He quickly fixed up the drinks and set them down in front of her. She took hers and swallowed it down in one gulp. She waited for Kerrigan to do the same. When he did, he almost choked on it. It tasted like rubbing alcohol. Kerrigan had never been much of a drinker. Though his family had its share of problems, drinking wasn't one of them.

The woman rubbed Kerrigan's shoulder again, looking at him with eager eyes. "Another one?"

"No . . . not right now. Thank you, though."

The woman pouted and blinked at him. He noticed her eyelashes were incredibly long. Unnaturally so. "You want massage? Come with me?"

Kerrigan felt his heart skip a beat. He was feeling terribly uncomfortable now. A large part of him wanted to run straight out of the hut, but he was painfully aware there was nowhere for him to go without a ride back to the evacuation hospital. "No. I'm sorry . . . I just . . . I can't."

The woman frowned at Kerrigan and walked away, moving on to the next prospect. Just as he was about to let out a sigh of relief, he was propositioned by yet another woman. Only this one looked different. Unlike the others, she wore neither lipstick nor eye shadow. She didn't need to. Her deep, dark eyes needed no window dressing. She was naturally beautiful. She too wore a short miniskirt, but her blouse was dark-colored and opaque.

"Hello," she said.

"Hi," Kerrigan said, so nervous he could barely look at her.

"Hello, sweetheart," Guzman said. He swooped in and kissed the woman's hand. She smiled at him.

"You guys here for party?"

"We're here to celebrate," Guzman said. He pointed to Kerrigan. "This man is a hero."

"Oh," the woman said. She stepped in closer to Kerrigan and cradled his arm. He could feel her soft breast pressing against his shoulder. "I like hero."

"Oh shit! The short-stop from Brooklyn made it!" A large Marine Kerrigan didn't recognize hollered and approached Guzman. The Marine's arm was in a sling—it seemed most, if not all of the Marines in the hut were patients from the evacuation hospital. Kerrigan hadn't met many of his fellow patients because his wound had kept him confined to his cot, but he recognized a few faces. Guzman and the Marine hugged each other and chatted.

"Glad you can make it," the large Marine said.

"No way I was missing this. Where's Rosenthal?"

"He went back there with four girls three fuckin' hours ago. Nobody's seen him since. I wouldn't be surprised if he doesn't come out until morning. He was so fucked up he didn't even know his name."

Guzman's eyes bulged. "Four girls? Jesuchristo. How much is that gonna cost?"

"Are you kidding? He's not paying a dime. He put this thing together so we're all pitching in."

As Kerrigan eavesdropped, the woman tugged on his arm and pulled him closer to the bar. Without asking, she signaled for the bartender, who quickly put together two more Saigon Teas. Kerrigan reached into his wallet and gave the woman her two dollars. Like the woman before her, she drank her tea in one gulp. This time Kerrigan did the same. While it still tasted like rubbing alcohol, the second seemed to go down a little more smoothly than the first.

"What your name?" the woman asked Kerrigan. She removed a cigarette from her handbag and lit it. She took a drag and exhaled the smoke up into the air.

"Nathan. What's your name?"

"Mai Lan," she said, then began to giggle at him. She had caught him glancing down at her breasts through the blouse. He hadn't even realized he was doing it. "You like?"

Kerrigan blushed. "Your name? Yes. It's very lovely."

The woman giggled again. She puffed on her cigarette again and offered Kerrigan a drag. He shook his head to say no, but she brought the cigarette up to his lips and held it there until he reluctantly tried it. Up until that moment, Kerrigan had resisted experimenting with cigarettes because he feared becoming his father who, at his worst, couldn't go an hour without smoking half a pack. Kerrigan always worried such a crippling addiction might hinder his career as a trauma surgeon, which would require him to perform surgery for several hours at a time without a break. Yet, he couldn't help but notice how sweet the cigarette tasted on his lips. Like raisins. He closed his lips around it and pulled. Immediately, he coughed. Violently.

Mai Lan chuckled, then handed Kerrigan another tea. "Here, drink."

Still coughing, he chugged the drink without hesitation. When his cough settled, he reached for his wallet.

"No," Mai Lan said. She put his hand on his arm, stopping him. "This one on me."

"Thank you."

Mai Lan tossed her long, silky hair over her shoulders and looked at Kerrigan seductively. "You come with me. We go in back room." Mai Lan looked over at a beaded curtain near the back of the hut.

Kerrigan smiled nervously and turned away from her, unable to look into her eyes. "I'd like to. I really would. But I can't do it."

Mai Lan tilted her head. "What's a matter, you scared?" She rubbed his arm. "First time?"

Kerrigan felt himself redden. "Uh . . . well . . . it's not . . . I just . . . I don't know. The truth is I don't think this is right. Any of it."

"Ah, you have religion?"

Kerrigan smiled. He wasn't sure someone like her would understand, but she clearly did. He thought for a moment about the reasons he stayed behind when his squadmates ventured out into Vietnamese villages and towns to visit bars and brothels like this one. These women weren't selling their bodies because they wanted to; they either needed the money or were forced into it. It was no secret Vietnamese women were being sold into the trade in disturbingly large numbers, often at the hands of their own mothers or fathers. And yet the Marines exploited them anyway. To be a part of that went against everything Kerrigan believed in. Even worse, he knew it was something for which he could never forgive himself.

"Something like that."

"Ah, me, no religion. Why you come then?"

"I came for my friends."

Mai Lan nodded toward the area of the bar behind Kerrigan, where Guzman and Campbell had been only a moment ago. "You're friends. Gone."

Kerrigan quickly scanned the space for Campbell and Guzman, but they were nowhere to be found. He felt a pit in his stomach again.

"Look," Mai Lan said. She pointed at the beaded curtain. One of the women was pulling Guzman through it. "Your friend leave you. Now you only have me."

* * *

Mai Lan remained at Kerrigan's side after his squadmates had gone behind the beaded curtain. Surprisingly, she hadn't propositioned him further. Instead, she listened as he told her all about his life, why he volunteered for the war, the horrible things he'd seen since he got there, and what he planned to do if he made it home. Kerrigan worried the Saigon Teas were making a rambler out of him, but Mai Lan listened intently, and in response shared her own personal story. Struck by her maturity and intelligence, Kerrigan worked up the courage to ask her why she worked as a prostitute. He couldn't help but feel she was capable of much more. She told him she did it for her family, who lived in a nearby hut. Her family was desperately poor, barely able to keep her many younger brothers and sisters fed. Working the hut was one of the few ways to make money, and she was the only one both old enough and young enough to do it. Kerrigan couldn't think of anything more selfless or unfortunate. Mai Lan, like so many other young Vietnamese women, was just another casualty of the disastrous war in Vietnam. Kerrigan felt terribly sorry for her.

"Another tea?" Mai Lan asked, after a short period of silence.

Kerrigan shook his head. He'd already consumed too many. "No, I can't. I shouldn't. I'm still on medication."

"Wooooooo!" someone whooped. Kerrigan looked over to the beaded curtain and watched as Guzman and Campbell emerged with two women in tow. They saw Kerrigan at the bar and headed over with their ladies behind them.

"Yo, Kerrigan!" Campbell said. He was clearly drunk, barely able to stand up straight. He looked over to the woman cradling his arm. "This guy's a hero."

The woman smiled at Kerrigan.

"What's the deal?" Campbell asked Kerrigan.

Kerrigan looked at Mai Lan, then back at Campbell. He shrugged his shoulders.

Campbell leaned into Kerrigan's ear. "She sweet on you or something? Eh?"

"We're just talking."

"Yeah sure," Campbell uttered. He waved his hand at Kerrigan dismissively as he ordered another drink.

"I don't think I'll be able to touch my dick for another week," Guzman said. He kissed the woman next to him on the cheek and thanked her for a lovely time. As she walked away, he leaned against the bar between Kerrigan and Campbell. "Man. That was fuckin' unbelievable."

"Did you remember to pay her?" Campbell asked.

"Hey, fuck you!" Guzman groaned. "I paid her. She was worth every penny, too. Holy shit. My legs . . . they're numb. How you doin', Kerrigan? You havin' a good time?"

Kerrigan looked at Guzman and considered the question for a moment. The truth was he was very much enjoying his time with Mai Lan. There was something about her. "I'm doing alright."

Guzman patted him on the shoulder.

Kerrigan felt a sharp pain rail through his wounded leg. He moaned, leaned against the bar, and tried to shake it off. He realized he had been on his feet all evening. It'd been hours.

"What's the matter?" Mai Lan asked.

"It's just my leg. It's still healing."

"Oh no," Mai Lan exclaimed. She pointed at Kerrigan's leg. There was a spot of blood soaking through his pants.

"Ah, shit. Son of a bitch."

Mai Lan took Kerrigan's hand. "Come."

"No, I told you . . . I can't. I can't do that."

"For your leg."

Kerrigan looked down at his leg. The spot of blood had already grown. It was spreading. "I'm fine. Don't worry."

Mai Lan tugged on Kerrigan's hand and looked at him straight in his eyes. Kerrigan noticed again how beautiful she was, particularly under the warm glow of the light above her head. Her hand felt small inside of his, but also warm and safe. "It's okay."

"Go with her!" Guzman whispered into Kerrigan's ear. Kerrigan looked at Guzman while Mai Lan pulled on his hand. "Do you really want to die not knowing? This could be your last chance. Go!"

Kerrigan turned back toward Mai Lan. She kept pulling. Kerrigan didn't realize it, but his legs were moving beneath him.

CHAPTER 9

Father Kerrigan vomited into a bush along the side of the trail. Carmichael was behind him. Kerrigan stood up and wiped his mouth with his sleeve. "I don't know if I can do this."

Carmichael took Kerrigan's arm and pulled him forward. "We're almost home. Just a little farther."

"I need a . . . I need a cigarette."

Kerrigan pulled out another cigarette, lit it, and took in a drag. Carmichael let him be this time. Though Kerrigan only opened the pack that morning, there were just a few cigarettes left.

"I knew I shouldn't have gone through that curtain," Kerrigan said. Tears rolled down his cheeks. "I didn't know what was going to happen, but I knew it was wrong. I knew it. And I went anyway."

Carmichael stopped in place. "What now?"

Kerrigan looked ahead and saw a large, fallen tree blocking the trail.

"That didn't fall too long ago, Monsignor. Look at the trunk. The wood's still green."

More of the birds cawed overhead. It seemed as if they were following the priests.

Kerrigan shook his head. "Why don't we just go back? It's getting late now anyway."

"No. We'll go around."

Carmichael headed toward the fallen tree. Kerrigan smoked for a moment and then followed.

* * *

As Kerrigan passed through the beaded curtain, he could hardly believe his own eyes. Mai Lan led him through a narrow corridor, passing several doorless rooms. Each of those rooms was occupied with a Marine and prostitute having sex in the open for everyone to see. The moans and groans were loud enough to drown out the music playing from the other side of the hut. Mai Lan, unfazed by the scenery, pulled Kerrigan forward.

She led Kerrigan all the way to the end of the corridor and brought him into a vacant room. Like the others, the room was lit only by candlelight and furnished with a small cot and makeshift vanity table. The walls were made from staffs of bamboo which were tied together loosely, allowing busy shadows from the adjacent rooms to show through. As Kerrigan stood next to the cot, Mai Lan reached above the entrance to the room and lowered strands of a beaded curtain tucked above the door frame. While Kerrigan was thankful for the additional measure of privacy, he still felt incredibly exposed and nervous. More nervous than he'd felt in his entire life.

Mai Lan took his hand and led him to the cot. She sat him down onto it, walked over to the vanity table, and gazed into the mirror. She brushed her hair, then removed a necklace. Then she turned around, knelt down in front of him, and unfastened his boots. She helped him swing his legs onto the cot, so he could lie down flat. She was careful and delicate. She stood in front of him; and, without saying a word, she pulled off her blouse and unfastened her bra, letting it fall to the floor. Her small, supple breasts exposed, Mai Lan straddled Kerrigan's torso, careful not to disturb his wounded leg.

Looking up at her, Kerrigan saw she was even younger than he suspected earlier. Very young.

But, Kerrigan lay there frozen, like a deer in headlights. Mai Lan looked at him, her silky hair cascading over her shoulders. Despite her youth, she was calm and measured, in control. This wasn't her first time.

She reached down and unbuttoned Kerrigan's shirt. When she finished, she pulled the shirt away and tossed it onto the floor. Though Kerrigan remained still, his body trembled and his heart thumped in his chest. Mai Lan lay on top of him and planted gentle kisses on the base of his stomach, just below his navel. She made her way up his torso. Her lips were soft as velvet, her breath warm.

Kerrigan's body tingled all over. His breath grew more rapid and shallow. Mai Lan hovered over his face now, her lips just above his. Kerrigan wanted to kiss her. But Mai Lan made her way back down toward Kerrigan's stomach again, planting those soft kisses as she went. Her long, black hair tickled the sides of his stomach.

She hovered over an obvious bulge in Kerrigan's pants now, and unfastened his belt buckle, tugging to loosen it. Kerrigan's breath was ragged, his body writhing with anticipation and raw desire. Mai Lan pulled his belt through the loops in his pants and tossed it aside. She started to unzip his pants.

Kerrigan, so aroused now he could barely remain still, closed his eyes and grabbed at his own chest, moving his hand up toward his neck. He felt something hard. It took him a moment to realize it was his crucifix, the one his mother had given him before she died of cancer.

Kerrigan bolted upright, shoved Mai Lan away, and jumped off the cot.

"I can't do this," he cried out. "I can't do it."

Mai Lan was still on the cot, her eyes wide, her hand over her mouth.

"I'm sorry," Kerrigan said. "I didn't mean to scare you. I . . . just . . . it's wrong. You understand? It's wrong for me to . . . you're just a girl. You don't belong here. I don't belong here. None of us do."

A tear rolled down Mai Lan's cheek.

"No, no, no, no," Kerrigan said. "It's not you. It's not—"

Mai Lan jumped to her feet, sprung toward Kerrigan, and wrapped her arms around him. She kissed his cheek. As she pulled away, she noticed the crucifix hanging from his neck and cupped it in her hand.

"Religion?" she said.

Kerrigan smiled. "Yeah, religion."

Mai Lan smiled back.

Kerrigan reached for his wallet and pulled out all the money he had. "Here."

"No," Mai Lan said. "No."

Kerrigan took her hand, put the money in it, and closed her fist around it. "Please. For your family. It's not much."

Mai Lan looked down at the money in her hand, then back at Kerrigan. She leaned in and gave him another soft kiss on the cheek.

"Ah!" Kerrigan yelled. Another surge of pain passed through his wounded leg. He looked down and saw the circle of blood soaking through his pants had grown even larger. The wound had opened up. "Shit."

Mai Lan saw the blood and helped Kerrigan sit down on the cot.

"No, it's okay. I just have to get back to—"

Mai Lan waved her finger at Kerrigan, scolding him. "Wait. You wait here. I be right back."

She opened a drawer in the vanity table and quickly slipped on a thin, white nightgown, made from translucent, delicate fabric. Then she walked out of the room and disappeared. Kerrigan looked down at his leg—the wound was still bleeding through his pants. Blood was dripping onto the floor. He feared he'd opened some stitches.

Mai Lan returned with a small wooden bowl filled with water. She set the bowl on the floor and rummaged through the drawers of the vanity table. She removed a large, white cloth—a handkerchief—so clean and pristine it looked brand new. Mai Lan unfolded it. She got down on her knees in front of Kerrigan, tucked his injured leg under her armpit, and carefully rolled up his pant leg. She worked slowly and deliberately, like she'd done this before, too.

Then something popped, and the room lit up bright white like someone had just taken a photograph. A gunshot. Instinctively, Kerrigan checked behind him but saw nothing. When he turned back around, Mai Lan was on her feet, backing away unsteadily. Her mouth wide open, she clutched at her belly with her fists like she was nursing a terrible bellyache. Behind her hands, bright red blood spread through her gown in a large, growing circle. She looked at Kerrigan. And she went down.

* * *

By the time Kerrigan caught her, Mai Lan had already fallen to her knees. As Kerrigan looked into her dying eyes, he was horrified to realize that the gun strapped to his thigh had gone off while she was tending to his wound. He'd forgotten it was there.

Mai Lan's head relaxed against Kerrigan's arm and blood continued to spread across her filmy white nightgown at an alarming rate. "No!" Kerrigan whispered in horror. "Oh God, no!" He kneeled down and laid her gently on the floor. He tore the nightgown down the middle, exposing her torso. Mai Lan's hands, which were still pressed against her wound, shook violently as blood oozed through her fingers. Kerrigan searched desperately for something he could use to put pressure on the wound to slow the bleeding. Something white caught Kerrigan's eye. It was the handkerchief. Mai Lan had dropped it. Kerrigan reached for it and tried to press it against Mai Lan's belly, but her hands wouldn't budge. He had to pry them away.

Kerrigan pleaded with her to cooperate. "It's okay. It's okay. Please, you have to let me help you."

When he was able to lift her hands high enough to see the wound, his heart sank. The bullet had entered just above Mai Lan's navel. Given the close range, Kerrigan knew the damage was likely catastrophic.

Kerrigan cried out. "Oh God! Oh my God, what have I done? What have I done?"

He backed away from Mai Lan in a state of utter panic and shock.

"What the fuck happened in here?" someone cried out.

The voice startled Kerrigan. A Marine he did not know was standing in the doorway, naked. He was holding a pistol. Kerrigan returned to Mai Lan and pressed the white handkerchief against her wound. She barely reacted.

Another Marine stuck his head in through the beads. "Holy shit! What happened?"

"It was an accident," Kerrigan said. "My gun . . . it just . . . it just went off. I don't know why it—" He turned toward the two Marines standing in the doorway. "Go call for help! Please! I need to get her out of here. Go! Now!"

The two Marines just looked at each other.

Kerrigan screamed at them. "Please, go! Please!"

Mai Lan suddenly cried out in pain. She began to mumble incoherently. Her body shook uncontrollably. She tried to speak, but Kerrigan couldn't understand her. She was in shock.

"Please, just hold on." Kerrigan pressed the handkerchief into her wound even harder, but it wasn't enough. Mai Lan was losing too much blood—it was pooling on the floor beneath her and spilling into the cracks in the floorboards. The handkerchief was no longer white but bright red.

Kerrigan heard a woman scream behind him. One of the other women poked her head through the curtain and saw him with Mai Lan on the floor. News of what happened was quickly spreading.

"Jesuchristo!" someone screamed from over Kerrigan's shoulder. It was Guzman. He entered the room out of breath. More women followed behind him.

Mai Lan suddenly coughed up blood all over her chest. It had pooled in the back of her throat and was spilling over the sides of her mouth. She was choking. Kerrigan looked on in horror.

"No, no, no, no . . . ." He lifted Mai Lan into his arms and tilted her forward to clear the blood from her airway. She looked at him momentarily with wide, terrified eyes. Then she went limp in his arms.

"Mai Lan? Mai Lan?"

Kerrigan laid her down and pressed his ear against her chest. He heard nothing. "No! No! Please, God, please!" He leaned over and began chest compressions.

"What the fuck happened?" another Marine asked. It was Campbell.

Kerrigan ignored him. He focused on counting the compressions in his head.

More women pushed their way into the room. Kerrigan heard them scream and cry.

"What the hell are we gonna do?" Campbell asked.

"I don't know," Guzman said.

"We have to get back to the evac!" Kerrigan said. "We gotta get her back to the evac, now!"

Another Marine rushed into the room. "We're gonna have to get the fuck out of here. The locals know something's up. They're trying to come in. I don't know how much longer we can hold 'em off."

"Are they coming back for us?" another Marine asked.

"Yeah, Danny radioed in."

"Get these ladies out of here!" Campbell hollered. "Get them out!"

Kerrigan was still working on Mai Lan. He paused for a moment and listened to her chest. Still no heartbeat. He felt someone touch his shoulder. It was Guzman.

"She's gone, man," Guzman said. "It's not your fault, it was . . . it was an accident."

Kerrigan shook his head and kept going. "No, she's not. If we get her back to the hospital, I can fix this. I can fix—"

"Come on, brother. You know that's not gonna happen."

Kerrigan looked at Guzman desperately. "Oscar, please! Help me. She's just a kid, for Christ's sake. I can fix this, but I can't do it here."

Guzman only stood there, watching hypnotized as Kerrigan compressed Mai Lan's chest. Kerrigan was pressing harder and harder with each compression. But Mai Lan's eyes were empty and her body limp.

"Come on, please! Please!"

"What in the fuck is going on here?" a loud, gruff voice shouted. It was Rosenthal. He was standing in the doorway, shirtless and armed with his own sidearm. A long, stitched-up gash streamed along his cheek.

Everyone in the room quieted as Rosenthal walked in. The only sounds were those of Kerrigan working on Mai Lan, the floorboards creaking with each of his chest compressions. The men watched wordlessly.

Rosenthal approached, so drunk he nearly fell over. He stopped in front of Guzman and grabbed his shirt collar. "What the fuck happened?"

Guzman shrugged his shoulders. "I dunno . . . I wasn't here. His gun went off or somethin'. I dunno."

Gunshots went off outside. Screams filled the air.

"We gotta go!" one of the Marines yelled. "They're coming in with broomsticks and knives now. We don't have time."

"Son of a fuck!" Rosenthal groaned. Spit flew from his mouth. He reeked of alcohol.

"They got a couple of jeeps on route—they'll be here in a few minutes," a Marine said.

"Alright," Rosenthal ordered. "Everyone get the fuck out of here. We're leaving."

Rosenthal walked over to Kerrigan and Mai Lan and stood over them. "That's enough, Kerrigan."

Kerrigan ignored the lieutenant. He continued with the compressions on Mai Lan's chest. He was pressing so hard that some of Mai Lan's ribs had cracked beneath his hands.

"I said, that's enough!"

Kerrigan didn't respond. He kept working on Mai Lan.

Rosenthal reached down and grabbed Kerrigan's arm. Kerrigan turned and slugged Rosenthal right in the face, opening up his wound and knocking him to the ground. Kerrigan went back to work on Mai Lan. He looked up at the ceiling and pleaded with God. "Please! Please! God! Help me, please!"

"You son of a bitch!" Rosenthal gritted. He charged at Kerrigan and wrapped his arm around Kerrigan's neck, prying him away from Mai Lan's lifeless body.

"No!" Kerrigan yelled. "Let me go! Let me go!"

Kerrigan pushed his feet off the ground and slammed Rosenthal into one of the bamboo walls behind them, breaking through it. Kerrigan and the lieutenant thrashed among the debris.

"Guys, stop!" Guzman cried out.

Rosenthal overpowered Kerrigan and pinned him to the floor. He struck Kerrigan in the face several times in rapid succession, bloodying his nose. Blood poured into Kerrigan's eyes.

Kerrigan kneed Rosenthal between the legs. Rosenthal gasped for air and fell over. Kerrigan ran straight back toward Mai Lan, but Rosenthal grabbed him from behind and slammed his head against the vanity table, disorienting him. Dizzy, Kerrigan was unable to fight back as Rosenthal pinned him against another wall. Rosenthal drew his pistol and pressed it into Kerrigan's forehead.

"You got some balls on you!" Rosenthal screamed furiously. "Some fuckin' balls."

"Please, Lieutenant. Let me help her. Please."

"Now you listen to me you fuckin' stupid, cocksucker—"

"Please—we can't just let her die. She's just a kid."

"We can't just let her die? We can't let her die? We didn't do shit. You did this. Ruined a perfectly good evening, too. Look at what you did." Rosenthal peeled Kerrigan off the wall and forced him to look at Mai Lan. She was on the ground, still, covered in her own blood from head to toe. Several of the Vietnamese prostitutes were at her side, sobbing over her. "She's fuckin' dead. You understand me?"

"I can help her if we get her back to the evac, I can fix this. I can fix this. There's still a chance—"

Rosenthal pinned Kerrigan against the wall again and struck him several more times, splitting his forehead.

"Pease, God! Let me—"

"God? God? I'll show you God." Rosenthal jammed his pistol into Kerrigan's forehead even harder. "Here's my fuckin' God. You wanna see yours right now? Hmm? Ask him why He didn't stop that pistol from popping off?"

"Lieutenant, please," Guzman pleaded. He was still in the room. "Stop this. We gotta go."

"Last chance, Kerrigan," Rosenthal said. "I'll leave you right here. Won't even think twice."

More gunshots went off outside. There were more screams.

Kerrigan looked into Rosenthal's crazed eyes, then at Mai Lan's lifeless body. Then he nodded. Rosenthal let him drop to the floor.

CHAPTER 10

Kerrigan, his cigarette smoldering in his hand, was sitting on a tree trunk at the edge of the trail. "And just like that, we left. The guys, they carried me out a back door and loaded me into one of the jeeps. I couldn't even talk. I couldn't even move. There was an angry mob outside. We had to go."

Kerrigan winced with pain. For the second time that day, he'd forgotten about the cigarette smoldering in his hand and let it burn his fingertips. He dropped the cigarette into the dirt and ground it out with his foot.

"And as we were pulling away, I heard this—" Kerrigan choked on the words. "We heard this terrible scream. This piercing, ghastly scream. Different from all the others. And I knew. I knew. It was her mother. She said they lived close by."

Carmichael stood there quiet. For the first time all day, it seemed he didn't know what to say.

"I didn't see her die," Kerrigan said. "But I know she didn't leave that hut alive. Not unless God came down from the heavens and took back my sins. She died choking on her own blood. And I just left her there."

Kerrigan sobbed into his hands.

"Is that what you think, Nathan? That you left her there for dead?"

Kerrigan sprung up onto his feet and thumped himself on the chest. "She died because of me! I killed her."

Carmichael shook his head. "No. That's not what happened. It was an accident."

"She was just a girl, Monsignor. Barely a teenager. Innocent. I was the adult. I was supposed to be responsible. I was supposed to protect her. Not take advantage of her. And she died because I . . . because I was tempted."

"Nathan, I—"

Carmichael suddenly looked pale and gray in the face.

"Are you alright?"

Carmichael's breaths were suddenly heavy. Beads of sweat congealed on his brow. He took a step forward and fell to his knees.

"Monsignor!"

Carmichael waved his hand at Kerrigan, dismissively. But when he tried to stand back up, his cane slid across the damp earth and he fell forward. Kerrigan lunged toward Carmichael and caught him before he fell on his face. Carmichael was in distress. He was wheezing and gasping.

Kerrigan helped Carmichael to his feet. "I've got you." He could feel that Carmichael's legs were weak.

"I just need . . . I just need to sit a minute. Just a minute."

Kerrigan searched for something to sit Carmichael down on. He remembered the fallen tree—they hadn't traveled very far up the trail since they passed it. "I've got you, Monsignor."

Kerrigan carried Carmichael a few dozen yards until the fallen tree was in sight. It was the first time they'd backtracked all

255

day. He sat Carmichael down on the tree trunk and made sure he was steady enough. Carmichael was still breathing heavily.

"Are you alright?"

Carmichael waved his hand again. He couldn't speak. He was still catching his breath. He looked winded, even a little afraid.

Kerrigan took out his phone again. "I'm calling an ambulance." He dialed 911, but couldn't get a dial tone. "Are you in any pain? Is your chest bothering you?"

Carmichael shook his head.

Kerrigan paced the trail and waved his cellphone around. He still couldn't get a signal. "Son of a bitch! I'm gonna have to carry you out of here."

"Nathan, sit down."

Kerrigan looked at Carmichael, his cellphone still against his ear. Carmichael was patting the top of the tree trunk next to him. "Sit down."

"No. I'm getting you out of here."

"I'm fine."

"We've gone far enough, Monsignor. Too far."

Carmichael looked at Kerrigan, angrily. "Will you shut up and sit the hell down? Can't an old man take a moment to . . . to catch his breath for Christ's sake?"

Kerrigan stood there, speechless. It was the first time he'd ever heard the Monsignor take the Lord's name in vain.

"I'm fine. I promise. I'm an old man. Occasionally, I get winded. Doesn't mean I'm going to keel over and die. Now sit down."

In truth, Carmichael did look better. His breathing had stabilized and his color improved. Kerrigan approached the tree trunk and sat down hesitantly next to him. For a while both priests sat quietly, staring out into the trees.

Kerrigan reached back into his pocket for another cigarette. There were only a couple left. He lit the cigarette and took in a drag, but something felt different. He took another, but something was still off—the cigarette was making him dizzy, like he was inhaling smoke from a heavy, Cuban cigar. Kerrigan pulled the cigarette out of his mouth and examined it.

"What's the matter?" Carmichael asked.

"I don't know. It tastes funny."

"Let me try."

"What?"

"Give it here. Let me try it."

Kerrigan just looked at Carmichael. He was hesitant.

"Are you having trouble hearing?"

"No . . . it's just . . . I shouldn't."

"What do you mean, you shouldn't?"

"All it takes is one. You know that."

Carmichael scoffed, and waved that dismissive hand of his again. "It doesn't matter now, believe me. Give it here."

Kerrigan hesitated, but reluctantly passed the cigarette over. Carmichael took it eagerly and pulled in a long, deep drag.

"Easy!" Kerrigan exclaimed. But Carmichael kept pulling until he couldn't anymore, then breathed out a tremendous plume of smoke.

"Oh, how I've missed smoking," Carmichael said, smiling. He took in another drag.

"Doesn't it taste funny?"

"No. Tastes just fine to me. Sweet as raisins."

Kerrigan couldn't help but smile himself. Then something occurred to him. "Wait a second."

Carmichael looked at Kerrigan, still pulling on the cigarette. "What?"

"Why doesn't it matter?"

"Huh?"

"That's what you said."

"What did I say?"

"You know what you said."

"What? I'm an old man—what does it matter if I have a cigarette?"

Kerrigan leaned in closer to his old friend. "Monsignor?"

Carmichael turned away and shook his head. He was visibly frustrated. "Me and my big mouth. It's nothing of importance, Nathan. It holds no relevance as to why we're here. To this predicament you're facing."

"It's important to me. What is it? You're sick, aren't you?"

Carmichael looked at Kerrigan but turned away again. He scratched the back of his head, nervously. Kerrigan wasn't sure, but he thought he saw a tear run down the side of Carmichael's cheek.

"Ah, it's worse than that, I'm afraid. I'm out of time."

"What do you mean, out of time?"

"Out of time."

Kerrigan shifted in his seat. "No . . . it can't be."

Carmichael chuckled. "That's what I said when they first told me. I was feeling fine, Nathan, same as always. But saying it doesn't make it so, I'm afraid." Carmichael took another long drag from the cigarette. It was obvious he was enjoying it. "It happens to the best of us, you know."

Kerrigan shifted in his seat. As much as he didn't want to believe it, he'd known it all along. He'd known since he first saw Carmichael with the cane that morning. "Cancer?"

"What else?"

"Where?"

"Everywhere, just about. At least that's how it was by the time they found it. The doctors think it started in my prostate. But now it's in the bones. My hip. My liver."

Kerrigan bowed his head. "I don't know what to say except that I'm sorry. I'm so sorry."

"Don't be, Nathan. I've accepted it. Chosen it, as a matter of fact."

"What do you mean?"

Carmichael blew another pungent cloud of smoke. "They offered me that poison. Said I might have a shot at squeezing out a few more years."

"You told them no?"

"I told them no."

"Why?"

Carmichael finished the cigarette and put it out on the tree trunk. "Nathan, God has been good to me. He's given me many years of good health, time enough for me to accomplish everything I hoped to accomplish, and to witness the wonder and beauty of this marvelous world. To enjoy the gifts of love, friendship, wisdom, the opportunity to share them with others. To help others. Who am I to ask for more?"

Kerrigan was silent. His world was already coming apart by the seams, and this was just another crushing blow. Without Carmichael, he was alone in the world. "Are you afraid?"

"But of course. The fear of death—it's the most basic and powerful of our instincts. You know that. Impervious to reason . . . and to faith, I'm afraid, no matter how strong or steadfast it may be. There are some journeys we must make alone."

Kerrigan looked up. The sky above was cold and gray, the woods eerily quiet. So quiet he could hear himself breathing.

"Nathaniel."

"Yes?"

"What happened all those years ago in Vietnam, that's why you gave up medicine for the priesthood. Isn't it?"

Kerrigan opened his mouth to answer, but was overcome by the weight of the question. This was something he had never planned to discuss with another soul, not for as long as he lived. He only nodded. As he did, tears fell from his eyes, landing in the dirt below.

"Why?" Carmichael asked.

"I just knew. As soon as I left that hut, I knew. I couldn't do it. I couldn't treat another patient. I had betrayed my oaths before I even took them."

Kerrigan wept. It took him a while to notice Carmichael was weeping too.

"Why are you crying, Monsignor?"

"Because I had a hand in this."

"What? What are you talking about? You had nothing—"

"Do you remember when we first met all those years ago?"

"Of course. We met when I was trying to get into the seminary."

"Right. Do you remember how we met?"

Kerrigan had to think a minute. "I believe you were one of the priests I spoke to during the screening process. At least, that's how we first met. It wasn't until later that we—"

"Yes. Do you remember what I asked you when we spoke? The very first question I asked you?"

Kerrigan shrugged. "It was so many years ago, Monsignor."

"I remember."

"What did you ask?"

"I asked you why you were giving up your career as a doctor for the priesthood. I forget how I knew, maybe I read it in your file. Maybe somebody else told me. I don't remember. Anyway, I found it odd, of course. Troubling, actually. You'd already finished school, finished with high marks. You had just finished a tour in Vietnam as a combat medic, where surely you put those skills to use. You were a hero, received a medal."

"You knew that then?"

"I knew it then. And the only thing standing between you and becoming a doctor was a few years of residency. All those years of studying, and yet, you get back from the war and just give it all up for the priesthood. I didn't understand it. Not at all. And so I asked the question. Do you remember what you told me?"

Kerrigan remembered this time. "God was calling me."

"Right. God was calling you. That was it. A perfectly adequate response for some maybe, but you, a young, promising doctor?" Carmichael scoffed. "Didn't add up. Not at all. You see,

I couldn't imagine why God, in his infinite wisdom, would call a promising doctor to the priesthood. It seemed to me he'd given you those very special skills so you could use them. To help people. Like you'd planned. No, I suspected you were running from something. I even guessed something had happened to you during the war. And yet, I put you through anyway. Why did I do that? I don't know exactly. I remember I was so busy in those days, overwhelmed, the church was in dire need of priests. I suppose the truth is I didn't care enough."

"You think I shouldn't have become a priest? You think I wasted my life?"

Carmichael's eyes grew wide, alarmed. He grabbed Kerrigan's arms. "Don't you dare say that! Don't you dare think it! That's not what I'm saying, Nathaniel. I've seen you do more good as a priest than twenty other priests combined. What I'm saying is if I'd done my job, perhaps you might have faced this burden then, instead of carrying it all these years."

"There's nothing you could have done. I would have just—"

"It was my job, Nathan, my responsibility, to make sure you were seeking the priesthood for the right reasons, not as a means of paying restitution. Because that's what this was, isn't it?"

Kerrigan stood up and peered at the sky through the small spaces between the thousands of leaves above his head. "Not long after that night, I decided I was going to file a report. I didn't know how or who to file it with, but I wanted people to know what happened. I felt I owed her that. I even went as far as getting my hands on the paperwork. There was this space for me to write down what had happened. Just a couple of lines. I had the pen down on the paper, but I just couldn't do it. I couldn't write the words. I remember telling myself the report wouldn't mean a goddamned thing anyway, all those lieutenants and generals would just laugh in my face. And that was probably true. We were killing civilians in droves over there, a lot of times just for the fun of it. And they let it go like those peoples' lives didn't matter, wrote them off as the cost of doing business, I suppose. I never wrote the report. I was too ashamed. Afraid what people might think if they knew who I really was. So I made a deal with God."

"What were the terms?"

"That I would spend the rest of my life serving him." Kerrigan's voice wavered. Tears streamed down his cheeks. "That I would give up my life, everything, for the priesthood."

"And in return?"

"In return . . . in return, I would never have to talk about what happened in that hut ever again, for as long as I lived."

Carmichael was quiet. Kerrigan could see that he was deeply affected by everything they had just discussed.

"This has nothing to do with you, Monsignor."

"All these years. All these years I knew you were suffering, carrying something with you."

"How could you know?"

"Because no matter how tirelessly you worked to help others, it always struck me as though it was impossible for you to feel any sense of satisfaction for the selfless things you do. Instead you had to do more and more. Like you were paying off an unsettled debt. Restitution. I saw it, Nathan. Again and again, and I've done nothing."

"Monsignor, it wasn't your respons—"

"It's my biggest regret, Nathan!"

Kerrigan looked at Carmichael and then sat back down next to him. "The only person responsible is me. I killed her. Me and me alone."

"You didn't kill her. It was an accident. Sometimes accidents happen, and sometimes people get hurt. Sometimes they die."

"I left her there. I left her there for dead. I deserve this."

Carmichael grabbed Kerrigan's shoulders. "Nathan, look at me."

Kerrigan raised his chin and looked once more into Carmichael's green-blue eyes. His loving eyes.

"You are a good man. Do you understand?"

"I tried to do good with my life. I tried . . . ."

"You have. I've seen it. For forty years, with my own eyes. Do you understand me?"

Kerrigan nodded.

"Oh, Nathan. Seems we both have our regrets, don't we? But the past is the past. Nothing we can do with it. And so, the question is, what are we to do now? Hmm? Are you with me?"

Carmichael planted his cane into the dirt and stood back up.

"What are you doing?"

"I've caught my breath. And it's time to go."

"You need to go home and rest. You've done enough."

Carmichael ignored Kerrigan and took off down the trail. His pace was brisk, and there seemed to be a renewed spring in his step. "That's where I'm going! It's not far now."

Kerrigan shook his head. Despite his concern, he couldn't help but smile. Carmichael was as persistent as they came.

* * *

The trail curved around a large bend and charged through a grove of tall and imposing elm trees. Kerrigan had never seen elm trees so tall and wide.

"War does terrible things to people, doesn't it?" Carmichael asked.

"Yes. Yes, it does."

"I was lucky, Nathan. I never had to experience it. I don't think I could have done it."

"You did experience it. War touched your life, same as mine."

Carmichael shook his head. "I was never a participant."

"You were a victim."

"I understand now why you won't do the exorcism."

"How can I?"

"The girl. Do you care about her?"

Kerrigan thought for a while before he responded. He had never thought to ask himself that question. "I suppose I don't really know her, do I?"

"No, I suppose you don't."

"You wanna know something strange?"

"Sure."

"Mai Lan. I heard her speak, but I can't remember her voice. I remember all these other details, after all these years. Small details. The way the candlelight lit up her fair skin, the way her hair felt against mine. Her smell. But her voice, I've lost it. I can't hear it anymore. Now I know that's not uncommon. We hear the same thing from widows and widowers all the time."

Carmichael nodded. He knew exactly what Kerrigan was talking about.

"I've never heard Marianna's voice. Not once. Not even when I saw what I saw in her bedroom. And yet, somehow, I feel like I know it. Maybe I heard it in my dreams or made it up in my mind . . . I . . . I don't know. Yes, I care about her. I don't want her to die. Which is precisely why I cannot have any part in the exorcism, even if it's just to stand there next to the priest performing the ritual."

"You're worried the devil will use your past against you, compromise the whole exorcism. That Marianna Petrosian will be lost as a result."

"I can't let that happen."

"Yes, of course. But that's not all you're worried about, is it?"

Kerrigan stopped abruptly. Even as far as he'd come, the truth was still difficult. "No, it's not."

"You're still afraid what people will think if this demon exposes you?"

"Yes. But in truth, it's not just me I worry about."

"What else, then?"

Kerrigan hesitated. "Well, I don't know. What'll happen to the church if this comes out? Do we really need another scandal right now? Haven't we enough controversy to deal with?"

Carmichael shook his head. "Now you're jumping at shadows, kid." He tapped his index finger against Kerrigan's forehead. "That's what he wants, you know."

"How can I participate if it means putting her life at risk? How can I do that?"

"Your presence may put the girl at risk. There's no getting around that."

Kerrigan's brow wrinkled. "May?"

"It's one possibility. Maybe there's another."

Carmichael continued to walk the trail, more briskly than ever, it seemed. Kerrigan followed.

"What do you mean, another possibility?"

Carmichael took Kerrigan's arm as they walked together. "This dying business. As profoundly depressing as it is, I'll tell you what, it's given me a certain freedom of perspective. Suddenly the world and all the people in it look very different, like I've been given a new set of prescription glasses. I'd like to think that's clarity. Which is why I believe it is no coincidence we're talking to each other now, in this moment."

"You still think I should do it? After everything I've told you."

Carmichael shook his head. He stopped and looked directly into Kerrigan's eyes. "Nathan, all morning I've asked myself the same question you asked the boy when he first came to see you at Saint Michael's."

"What question?"

"What am I more afraid of? What might happen if you don't do the exorcism, or what might happen if you do?"

"Which is it?"

"You still don't see it, do you?"

Kerrigan shrugged. "No, I don't."

Carmichael took his arm again, and they continued to walk.

"Nathan, why do you think you experienced what you experienced in the confessional, in the girl's bedroom?"

"Those were warnings. Very clear ones."

"Ah, right, shots across the bow. But there's something I just can't wrap my head around. If this clever demon knows about your past, knows he might use it against you, that your very presence at the ritual might seal his victory, then why warn you? Why attempt to ward you off? Unless . . . unless he's the one who's afraid."

Kerrigan stopped and stared blindly into space. It took him a moment to process what Carmichael had told him. When he snapped out of it, he saw Carmichael was several yards ahead.

"Wait!" Kerrigan cried out. "Hold on."

Kerrigan sprinted until he caught up. "Wait! Why . . . why in the world would he be afraid?"

"What is this all about, Nathan? Hmm?"

"I'm not following."

Carmichael tugged on the crucifix hanging from his neck. "This. Why did the good Lord sacrifice his only son?"

"That our sins may be forgiven."

Carmichael nodded. "It's the key to everything, isn't it? Now I don't know, but I imagine a priest who's sinned, who's been forgiven, who's made himself right with God . . . he might be especially dangerous to one of Satan's minions. Might he not?"

"How can I be forgiven?"

Carmichael chuckled. "Have you forgotten everything? You do it the same way as everyone else, Nathaniel. You just ask."

"But I can't ask her. I can't ask her mother and her father or her brothers and sisters. How can they forgive me if they don't even know who I am?"

"That didn't stop me, did it?"

Kerrigan said nothing. He didn't know what to say.

"You really don't think it was a coincidence the boy found you, all that way from home, that you were the only one who could see what he saw, when even his mother couldn't?"

"I don't know, Monsignor. I really don't."

"Although I hate to give him credit, what I'm suggesting, Nathan, is that maybe Bishop Gailey is right. Maybe there is a reason God brought you and this girl together. After all, she isn't the only one who needs saving, is she?"

The two priests came upon another fork in the trail and paused in front of it. The left fork continued to carve through elm trees. The right fork carved through bramble.

"What if you're wrong?" Kerrigan asked.

"Ah, well, I can't help you there, Nathan. Only God knows all the answers. This is a path you have to walk alone."

Carmichael suddenly wheeled around like he'd been startled by a loud noise. Kerrigan had heard nothing. Carmichael was staring down the right fork, seemingly looking or listening for something. He stood there for several moments.

"What is it?" Kerrigan asked.

Carmichael turned around. "Nothing. It's time for me to go. I'm going to take this exit." He nodded toward the right fork.

"What?"

"I've got to go, Nathan."

Kerrigan stared at Carmichael blankly. "Go where?"

Carmichael looked down at his watch, then back at Kerrigan. "Home."

"Okay, I'll walk you back."

Carmicahel shook his head incessantly. "No."

"Monsignor, I'm not leaving you."

"Nathan, stop."

"No, Monsignor. There's no way I'm leaving you. You were just attacked by a dog—"

"Stop it, Nathan."

"You just collapsed from exhaustion. No. Absolutely not. I'm not doing—"

Carmichael suddenly slammed his cane into the ground, startling Kerrigan. "Enough! Enough."

"I don't understand," Kerrigan said.

Carmichael approached Kerrigan and put a hand on his shoulder. "I'll be fine, Nathan. I promise."

Kerrigan said nothing.

"Come on," Carmichael said. "You keep going. I imagine you've got some thinking to do."

Kerrigan looked down the left fork. "How will I know where to go?"

"You'll find your way. Besides, you've got GPS on that phone of yours, don't you?"

Kerrigan smiled, then looked up at the trees. He thought he heard birds again. "If I decide not to do it?"

"We'll cross that bridge when we get to it. If you decide not to do it."

"Thank you, Monsignor. For everything."

"Thank you, Nathaniel. For everything."

Carmichael winked at Kerrigan and took the right fork. Kerrigan watched him walk away. After several yards, Carmichael turned around.

"And Nathan, for what it's worth, whatever you decide, I do think it's time you start facing demons."

Kerrigan watched until Carmichael disappeared around a bend. As soon as Carmichael was out of sight, he felt immensely alone. He turned toward the left fork and took a deep breath.

The sky grew even darker, as if another layer of clouds had rolled in on top of the ones already there. Thunder rumbled, and a light shower began to fall. Kerrigan did what Carmichael had encouraged him to do all day—place one foot in front of the other and keep going.

As he walked, the black birds suddenly began to scream raucously from the trees. Dogs growled and howled menacingly in the distance. Wind buffeted Kerrigan from all directions. Thick pockets of bramble with large, sharp thorns choked the edges of the trail. With each step, the rain came down harder. But he kept going, one step at a time. One foot in front of another.

Kerrigan struggled forward, head down, pushing against the rain and wind. His heart pounded in his chest. His stomach churned. He raised his head and saw a sliver of orange light. The spaces between the trees became wider. The rain and wind began to ease. Instead of the deafening roar of the snarling animals, Kerrigan heard children giggling. As he finally emerged from the trail, he was blinded momentarily by fiery streaks of sunlight piercing through the dissipating clouds. Astonished, he realized he was right back where he'd started. The pond was just ahead, surrounded by children steering their remote control sailboats. The birds, nestled in the trees, suddenly croaked and took to the sky, flying toward the sun.

Kerrigan felt his cell phone buzz in his pocket. He saw there were seven voice messages waiting from him, all from the rectory at Saint Michael's. Rather than listen to them, he called the rectory directly. After a few rings, one of his altar servers picked up the phone.

"Yeah, it's Father K. Is someone trying to reach me? I have seven messages on my phone. Is everything alright?"

"Yes, hold on, Father K. Father A has been trying to reach you."

"Is he there?"

"Yes, I'll put you through."

"Thanks."

Music played through the phone. Not long after, Father Anderson, one of Kerrigan's colleagues, picked up.

"Nathan?"

"Yeah, what's going on?"

"I've been trying to reach you all day."

"I saw the messages. I was in the woods and didn't have service. What's up?"

"I got a call from Saint Paul's. It was Father Pfeiffer. He had some bad news, Nathan."

"What is it?"

"Monsignor Carmichael passed away early this morning."

"Wait, what?"

"I said Monsignor Carmichael passed away early this morning. I'm sor—"

"That's imposs—but I was just with—"

"I'm sorry, Nathan. They said it was cancer. Spread all through his body. I didn't even know he was ill. Sounds like he kept it to himself. I hate to give you news like this over the phone, but Father Pfeiffer said something about the two of you meeting this morning? I didn't know anything about it, so—"

Kerrigan let the hand holding his cellphone fall to his side. He turned and looked back at the trail in wonderment and then up into the sky. The birds were still flying into the sun.

"Nathan, are you there?"

Kerrigan raised the phone back to his ear. "It . . . it can't be."

"I'm afraid it is. I didn't know if you might be looking for him, so I reached out. I'm sorry, Nathan. I know you were very close."

"But I was just . . . ."

"Anyway, they said they'll keep us posted with the arrangements. I'll talk to Maryanne about sending some flowers."

"Yeah . . . yeah, sure." Kerrigan's voice was distant, flat. "Listen, I've got to go. I need a minute. I'll be at the rectory later."

"Okay, Nathan. Just call if you need anything."

Kerrigan hung up the phone and put it back in his pocket. He stopped near the pond and watched the children playing. A brother and sister, laughing as they chased each other, caught his attention. Behind them, their parents were glued to the screens on their smartphones, oblivious to their joyful children. The bright sunlight sparkled over the ripples in the greenish water. Ducks bobbed peacefully on the surface. It was beautiful.

Unconsciously, Kerrigan reached into his pocket for another cigarette. He was almost out. He put the cigarette in his mouth. As he reached for his matches, the cigarette slipped out of his mouth and fell to the ground at the edge of the pond. Kerrigan knelt down to retrieve it, but a duckling popped out of the water and snatched the cigarette away, retreating further into the pond.

Kerrigan couldn't help but react with a grin that widened into a full-blown smile.

"You mind if I bum one of those, Father?" a strange voice called out to Kerrigan. He turned to his right and found a stranger standing next to him. He handed the entire pack to the man. "Here, take the rest."

"You sure?"

"Yeah," Kerrigan said. He was still smiling. "I don't think I need them anymore."

The man smiled back. "Thanks, Father."

Kerrigan left the pond and headed for his Impala. As he approached, he noticed wet leaves had fallen onto the windshield and began to peel them off. His cell phone buzzed in his pocket. He picked up.

"We have an exorcist," the voice on the other phone said.

Kerrigan looked over his shoulder and back at the trees, one last time. "I'm on my way."

THE END.

ACKNOWLEDGEMENTS

I may have written Walking Among the Trees, but there are many others without whom this book would never have come into existence. First, I must extend my immeasurable gratitude to the late Father Arthur C. Anderson. Our long and engrossing conversations about the nature of good and evil directly inspired this novel, and some of the chilling tales he shared with me formed the basis of the more unnerving scenes in the story. I will always cherish our philosophical discussions, the laughs, and the mentorship.

I want to acknowledge my parents, Margaret and Corrado Oliva, to whom I've dedicated this book. Every opportunity I've had in this life is a result of their sacrifices. I owe them everything.

Next, my wife Amy, who's supported me for as long as I've been chasing this wild dream of mine. Writing Walking Among the Trees as a busy attorney, at the dawn of our children's lives, meant sacrificing a good deal of the little time we've had for each other. It took almost four years from start to finish, and Amy never once complained. I hope she is proud.

I want to thank my sister-in-law Stacey Fowler (my very first beta reader), as well as my brother Matt Oliva and dear friend

James Niesuchouski (my second and third beta readers). Their feedback on the very first draft was invaluable and helped me mold Walking Among the Trees into what it is today.

I want to reserve a very special thanks for my publisher, Sage's Tower, and in particular, Amy Reeves and Nicole Taylor. Their faith in this novel was evident from the start, and it has meant the world to me. That, in itself, has been a dream come true.

Last, but certainty not least, I'd like to extend a heartfelt thanks to one of my editors (the other wished to remain anonymous), Lori Brandt. It didn't take long for me to see that I was in very good hands with Lori—she always understood exactly what I was trying to say and helped me say it better. The difference is truly night and day. I really hope I can work with her on the next one.

ABOUT THE AUTHOR

Frank Michael Oliva is a practicing attorney and law professor from Long Island, New York. As a teenager, he worked as a receptionist at the rectory of his local parish and developed a close relationship with one of the priests, a former English teacher. Their philosophical conversations about the nature of good and evil left a lasting impression on Frank and inspired him to write his first novel, *Walking Among the Trees*, nearly two decades later. When he isn't busy working or writing, Frank can be found spending time with his wife and twin children, reading, or playing video games.

CPSIA information can be obtained
at www.ICGtesting.com
Printed in the USA
LVHW111325100821
694760LV00001B/11